Beechen, Adam
Justice League Unlimited
World's Greatest Heroes

JUSTICE LEAGUE UNLIMITED

WORLD'S GREATEST HEROES

Written by:
Adam Beechen

Illustrated by:
Carlo Barberi
Ethen Beavers
Walden Wong

Colored by:
Heroic Age

Lettered by:
Phil Balsman
Pat Brosseau
Nick J. Napolitano

Superman created by Jerry Siegel and Joe Shuster
Batman created by Bob Kane
Wonder Woman created by William Moulton Marston

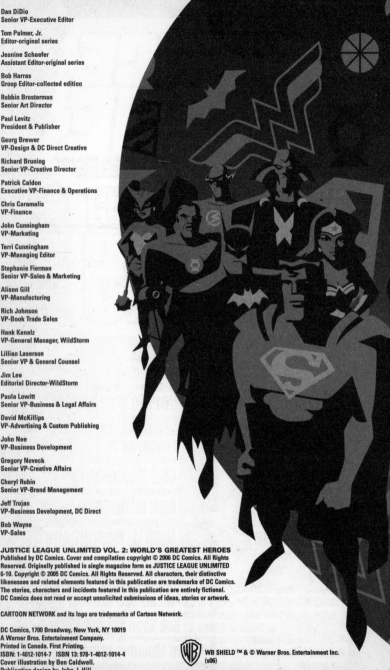

Dan DiDio
Senior VP-Executive Editor

Tom Palmer, Jr.
Editor-original series

Jeanine Schaefer
Assistant Editor-original series

Bob Harras
Group Editor-collected edition

Robbin Brosterman
Senior Art Director

Paul Levitz
President & Publisher

Georg Brewer
VP-Design & DC Direct Creative

Richard Bruning
Senior VP-Creative Director

Patrick Caldon
Executive VP-Finance & Operations

Chris Caramalis
VP-Finance

John Cunningham
VP-Marketing

Terri Cunningham
VP-Managing Editor

Stephanie Fierman
Senior VP-Sales & Marketing

Alison Gill
VP-Manufacturing

Rich Johnson
VP-Book Trade Sales

Hank Kanalz
VP-General Manager, WildStorm

Lillian Laserson
Senior VP & General Counsel

Jim Lee
Editorial Director-WildStorm

Paula Lowitt
Senior VP-Business & Legal Affairs

David McKillips
VP-Advertising & Custom Publishing

John Nee
VP-Business Development

Gregory Noveck
Senior VP-Creative Affairs

Cheryl Rubin
Senior VP-Brand Management

Jeff Trojan
VP-Business Development, DC Direct

Bob Wayne
VP-Sales

JUSTICE LEAGUE UNLIMITED VOL. 2: WORLD'S GREATEST HEROES

DC Comics, 1700 Broadway, New York, NY 10019
A Warner Bros. Entertainment Company.
Printed in Canada. First Printing.
ISBN: 1-4012-1014-7 ISBN 13: 978-1-4012-1014-4
Cover illustration by Ben Caldwell.
Publication design by John J. Hill.

WB SHIELD ™ & © Warner Bros. Entertainment Inc.
(s06)

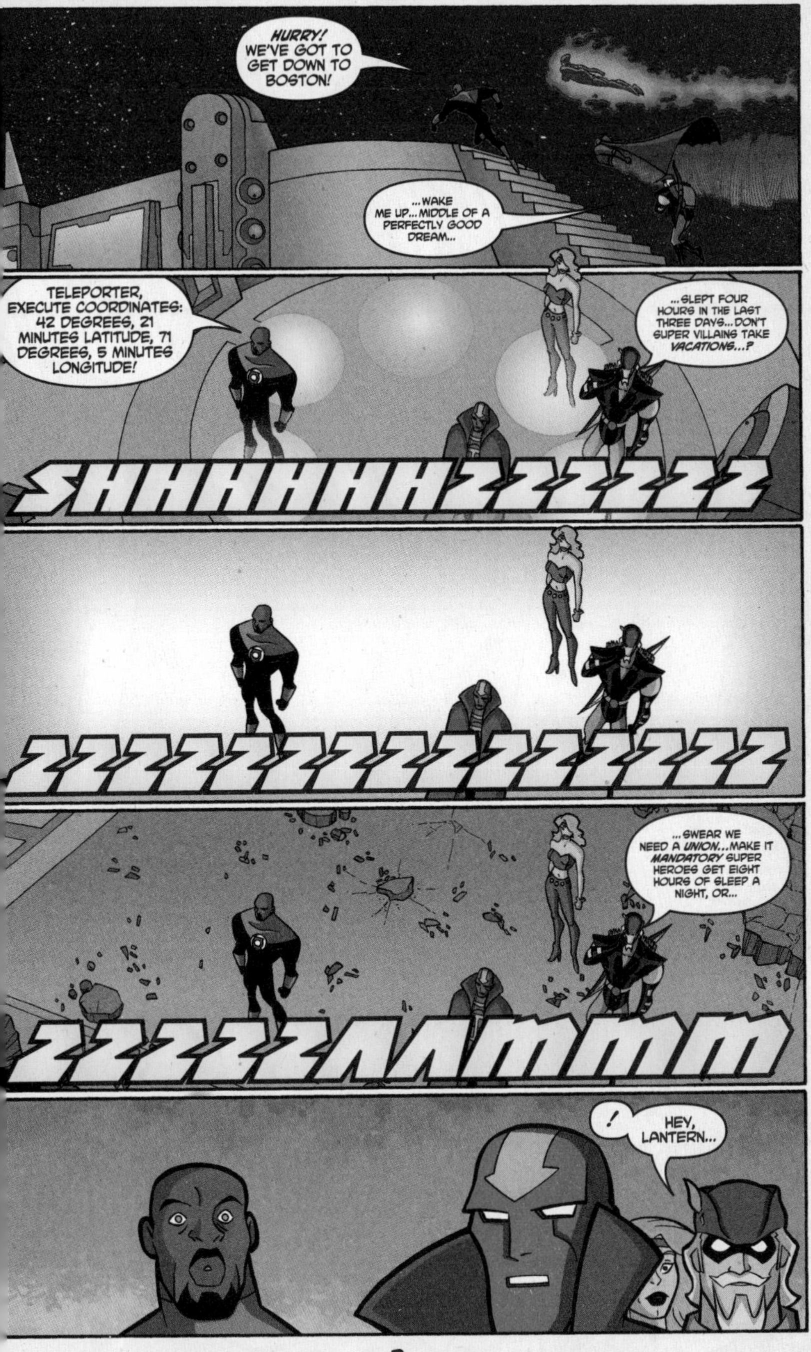
HURRY! WE'VE GOT TO GET DOWN TO BOSTON!
...WAKE ME UP...MIDDLE OF A PERFECTLY GOOD DREAM...
TELEPORTER, EXECUTE COORDINATES: 42 DEGREES, 21 MINUTES LATITUDE, 71 DEGREES, 5 MINUTES LONGITUDE!
...SLEPT FOUR HOURS IN THE LAST THREE DAYS...DON'T SUPER VILLAINS TAKE VACATIONS...?
SHHHHHHZZZZZZ
ZZZZZZZZZZZZZZZ
...SWEAR WE NEED A UNION...MAKE IT MANDATORY SUPER HEROES GET EIGHT HOURS OF SLEEP A NIGHT, OR...
ZZZZZAAMMMM
!
HEY, LANTERN...

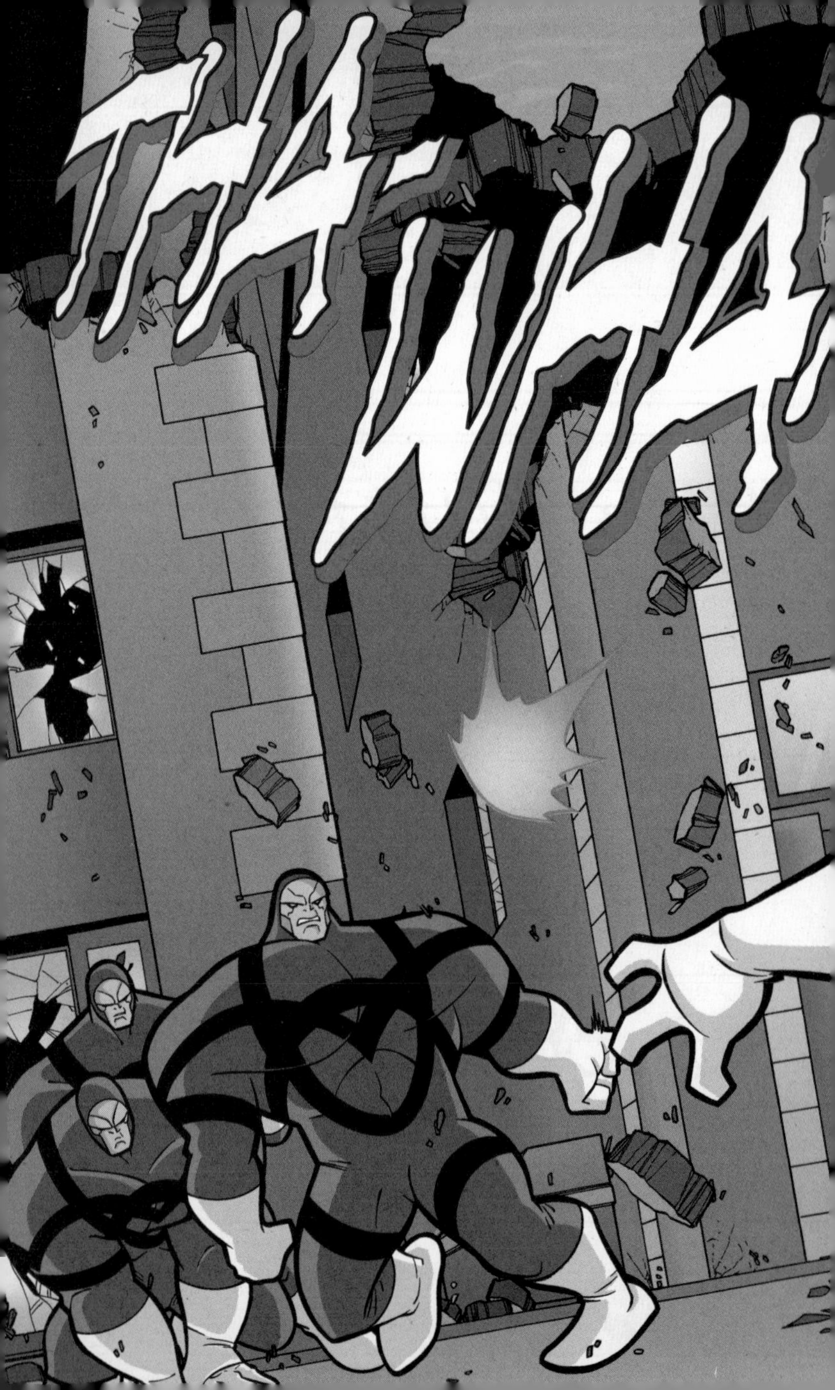
THWA

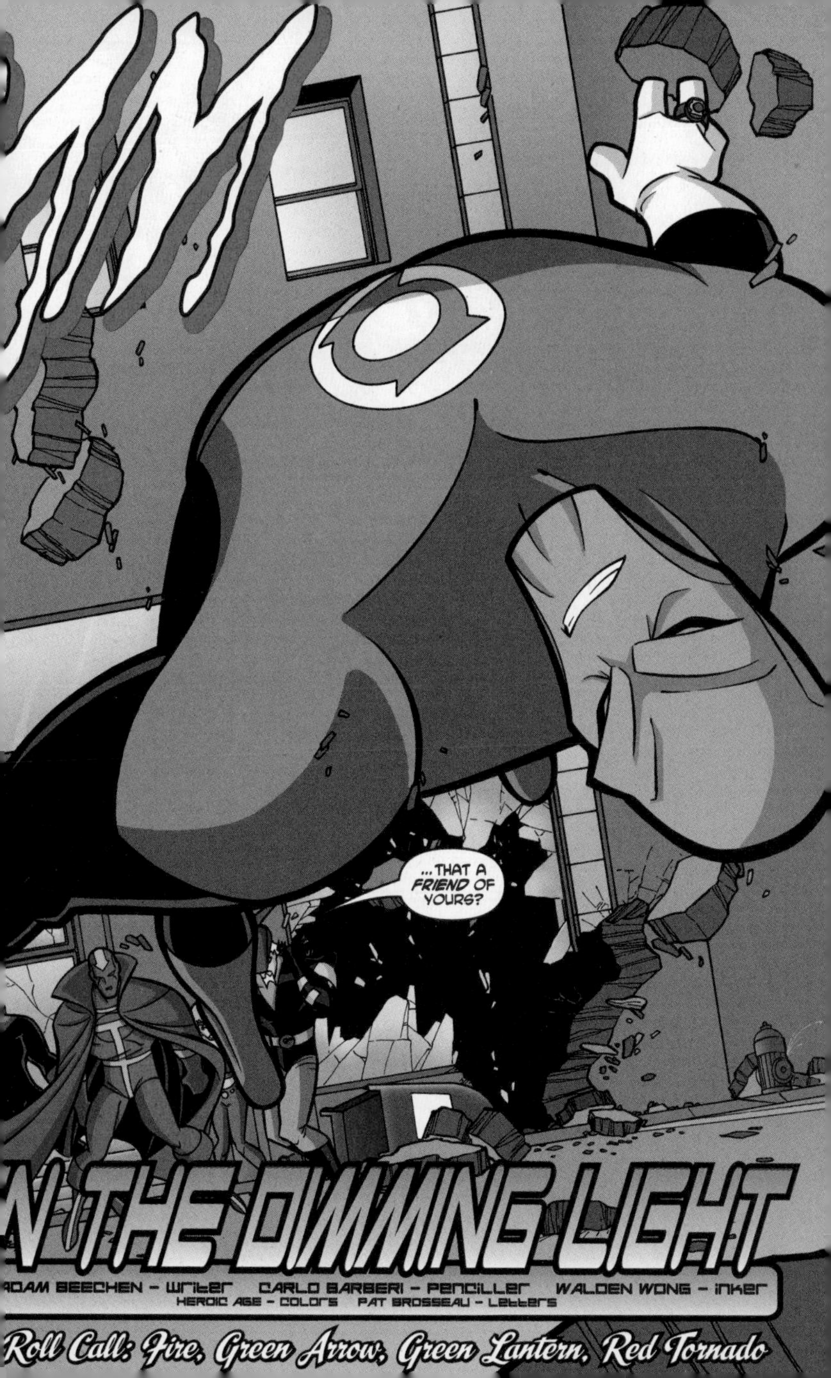
...THAT A *FRIEND* OF YOURS?
N THE DIMMING LIGHT
ADAM BEECHEN – WRITER CARLO BARBERI – PENCILLER WALDEN WONG – INKER
HEROIC AGE – COLORS PAT BROSSEAU – LETTERS
Roll Call: Fire, Green Arrow, Green Lantern, Red Tornado

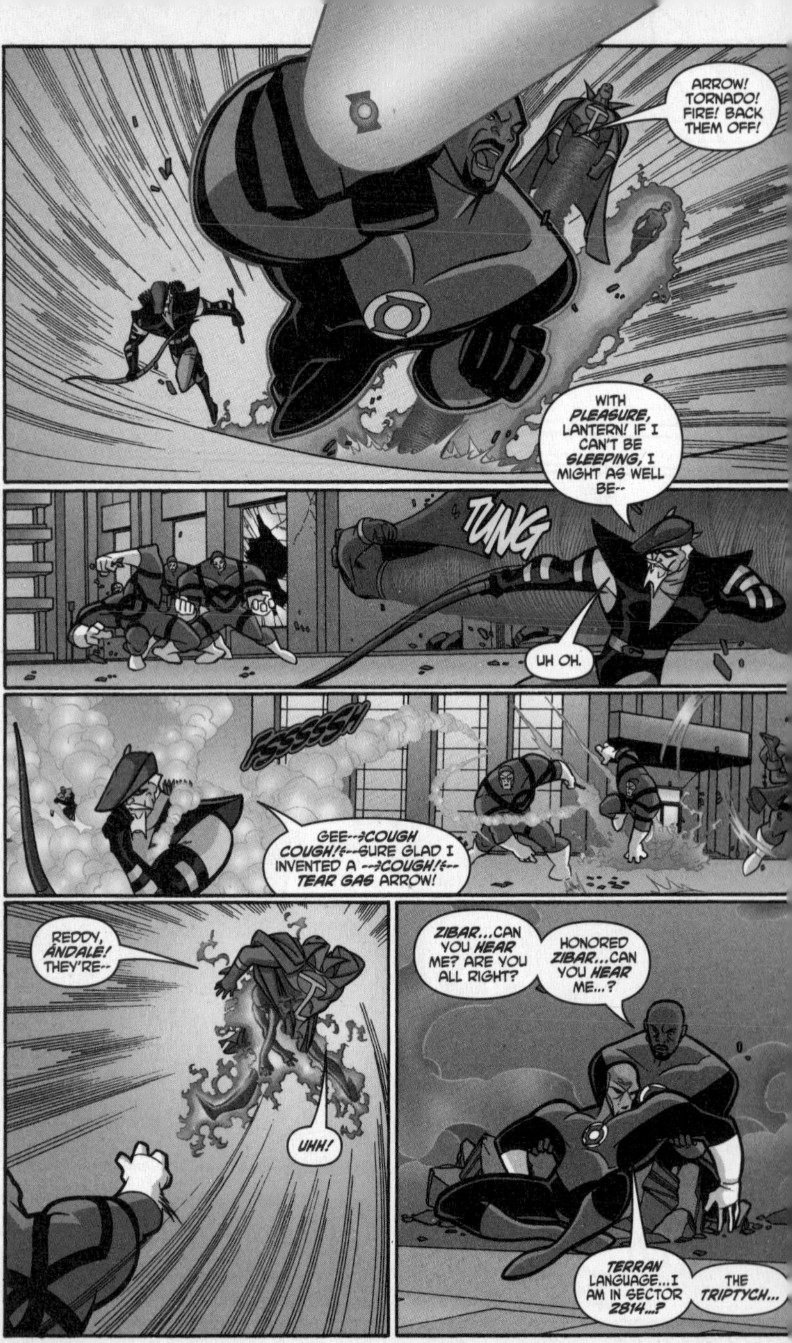
ARROW! TORNADO! FIRE! BACK THEM OFF!
WITH PLEASURE, LANTERN! IF I CAN'T BE SLEEPING, I MIGHT AS WELL BE--
TUNG
UH OH.
FSSSSSH
GEE--COUGH COUGH!--SURE GLAD I INVENTED A --COUGH!-- TEAR GAS ARROW!
REDDY, ÁNDALE! THEY'RE--
UHH!
ZIBAR...CAN YOU HEAR ME? ARE YOU ALL RIGHT?
HONORED ZIBAR...CAN YOU HEAR ME...?
TERRAN LANGUAGE...I AM IN SECTOR 2814...?
THE TRIPTYCH...

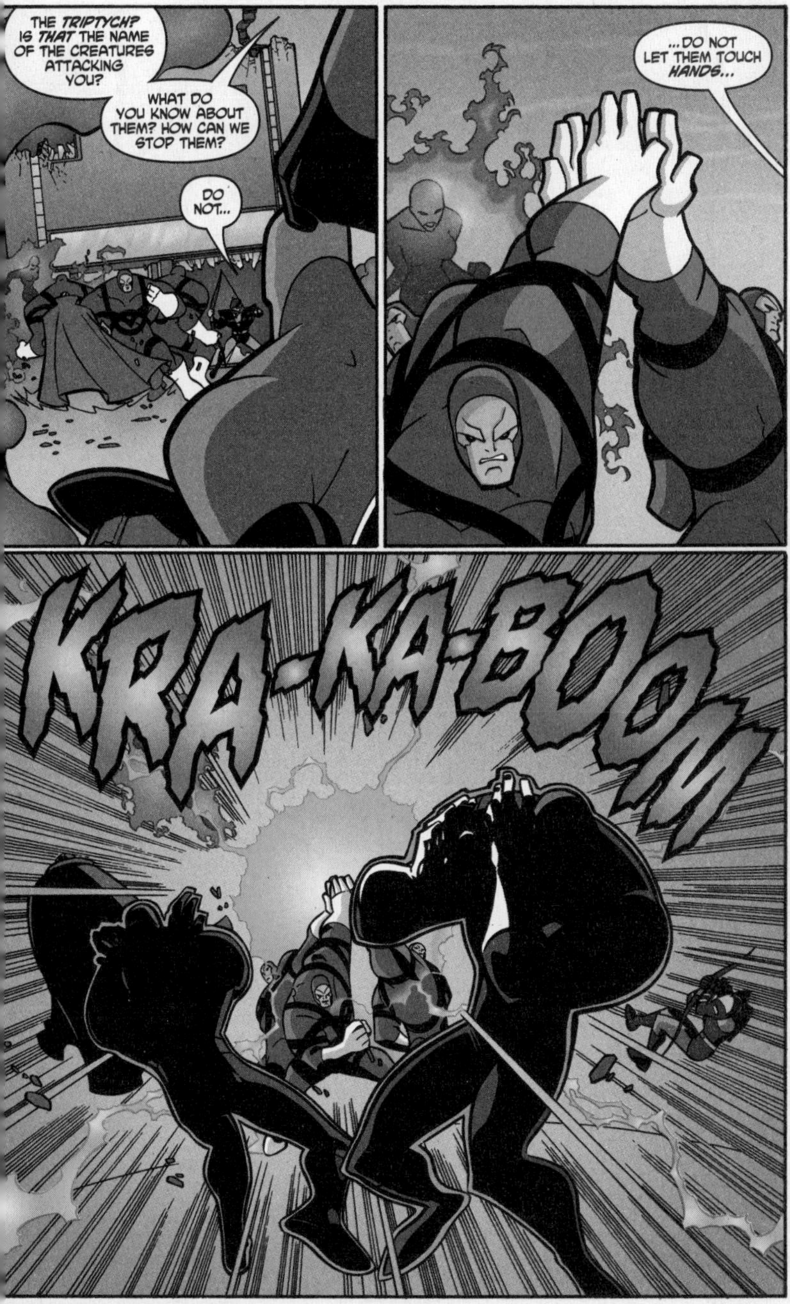
THE TRIPTYCH? IS THAT THE NAME OF THE CREATURES ATTACKING YOU?
WHAT DO YOU KNOW ABOUT THEM? HOW CAN WE STOP THEM?
DO NOT...
...DO NOT LET THEM TOUCH HANDS...
KRA-KA-BOOM

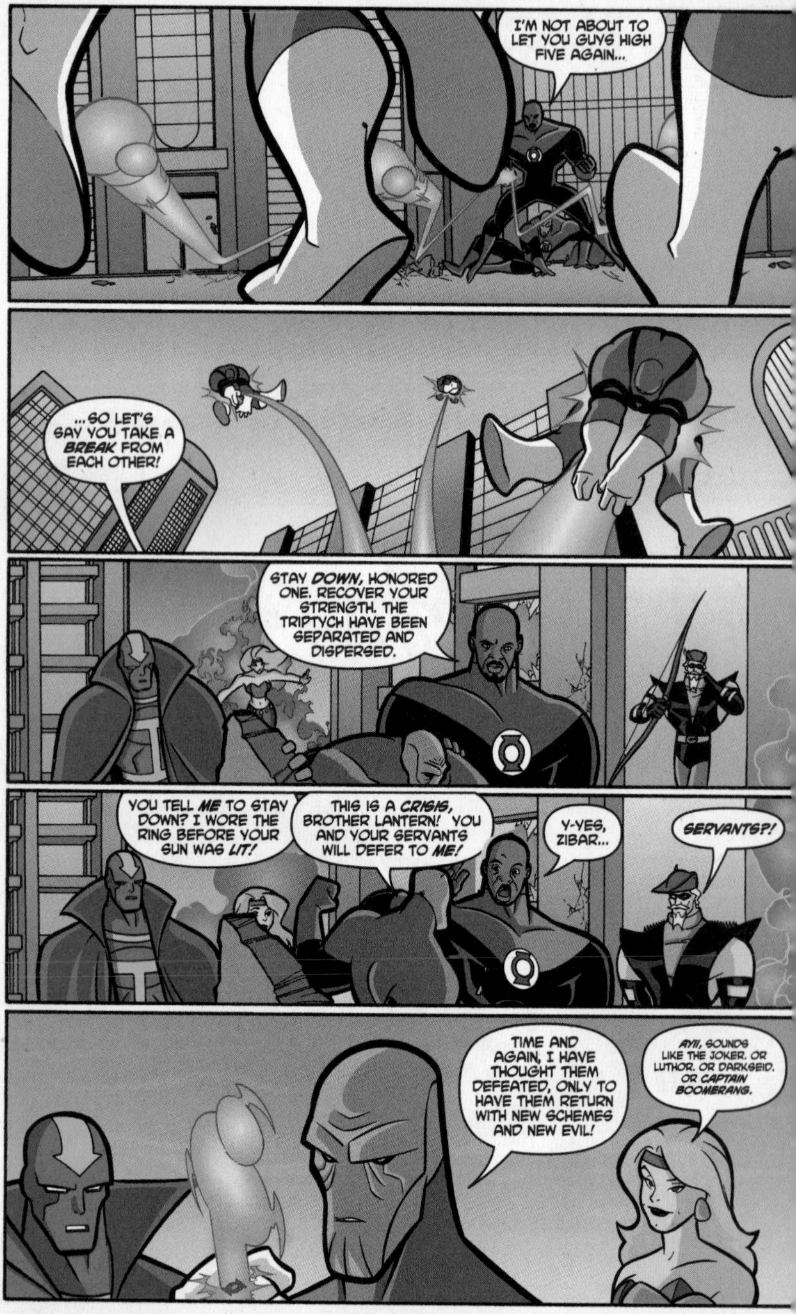
I'M NOT ABOUT TO LET YOU GUYS HIGH FIVE AGAIN...
...SO LET'S SAY YOU TAKE A BREAK FROM EACH OTHER!
STAY DOWN, HONORED ONE. RECOVER YOUR STRENGTH. THE TRIPTYCH HAVE BEEN SEPARATED AND DISPERSED.
YOU TELL ME TO STAY DOWN? I WORE THE RING BEFORE YOUR SUN WAS LIT!
THIS IS A CRISIS, BROTHER LANTERN! YOU AND YOUR SERVANTS WILL DEFER TO ME!
Y-YES, ZIBAR...
SERVANTS?!
TIME AND AGAIN, I HAVE THOUGHT THEM DEFEATED, ONLY TO HAVE THEM RETURN WITH NEW SCHEMES AND NEW EVIL!
AYII, SOUNDS LIKE THE JOKER. OR LUTHOR. OR DARKSEID. OR CAPTAIN BOOMERANG.

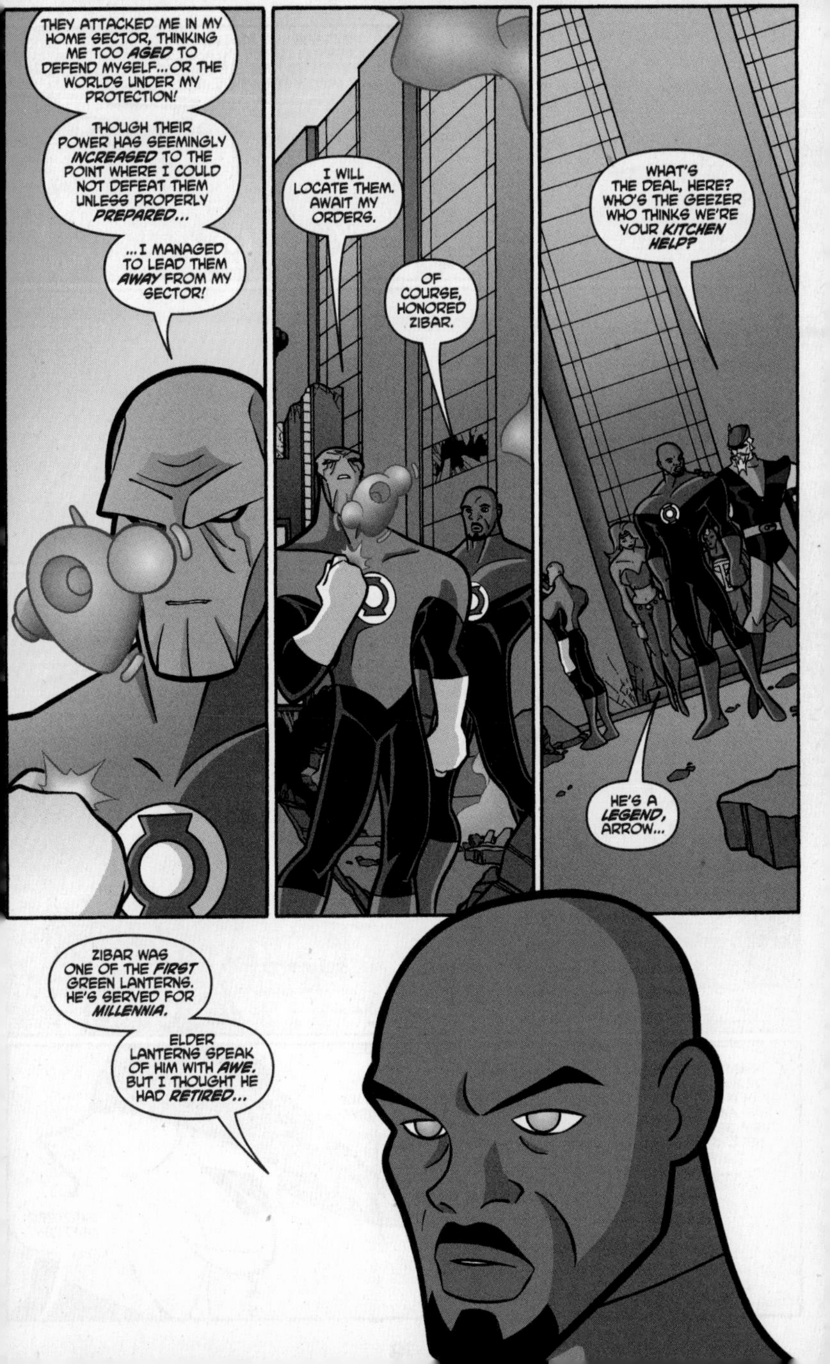
THEY ATTACKED ME IN MY HOME SECTOR, THINKING ME TOO AGED TO DEFEND MYSELF...OR THE WORLDS UNDER MY PROTECTION!
THOUGH THEIR POWER HAS SEEMINGLY INCREASED TO THE POINT WHERE I COULD NOT DEFEAT THEM UNLESS PROPERLY PREPARED...
...I MANAGED TO LEAD THEM AWAY FROM MY SECTOR!
I WILL LOCATE THEM. AWAIT MY ORDERS.
OF COURSE, HONORED ZIBAR.
WHAT'S THE DEAL, HERE? WHO'S THE GEEZER WHO THINKS WE'RE YOUR KITCHEN HELP?
HE'S A LEGEND, ARROW...
ZIBAR WAS ONE OF THE FIRST GREEN LANTERNS. HE'S SERVED FOR MILLENNIA.
ELDER LANTERNS SPEAK OF HIM WITH AWE. BUT I THOUGHT HE HAD RETIRED...

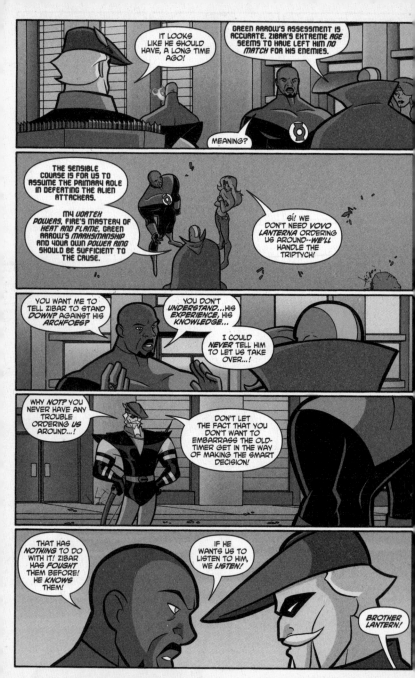

IT LOOKS LIKE HE SHOULD HAVE, A LONG TIME AGO!

GREEN ARROW'S ASSESSMENT IS ACCURATE. ZIBAR'S EXTREME *AGE* SEEMS TO HAVE LEFT HIM *NO MATCH* FOR HIS ENEMIES.

MEANING?

THE SENSIBLE COURSE IS FOR US TO ASSUME THE PRIMARY ROLE IN DEFEATING THE ALIEN ATTACKERS.

MY *VORTEX* POWERS, FIRE'S MASTERY OF *HEAT AND FLAME*, GREEN ARROW'S *MARKSMANSHIP* AND YOUR OWN *POWER RING* SHOULD BE SUFFICIENT TO THE CAUSE.

SÍ! WE DON'T NEED *VOVO LANTERNA* ORDERING US AROUND--*WE'LL* HANDLE THE TRIPTYCH!

YOU WANT ME TO TELL ZIBAR TO STAND *DOWN?* AGAINST HIS *ARCHFOES?*

YOU DON'T *UNDERSTAND...* HIS *EXPERIENCE*, HIS *KNOWLEDGE...*

I COULD *NEVER* TELL HIM TO LET US TAKE OVER...!

WHY *NOT?* YOU NEVER HAVE ANY TROUBLE ORDERING *US* AROUND...!

DON'T LET THE FACT THAT YOU DON'T WANT TO EMBARRASS THE OLD-TIMER GET IN THE WAY OF MAKING THE SMART DECISION!

THAT HAS *NOTHING* TO DO WITH IT! ZIBAR HAS *FOUGHT* THEM BEFORE! HE *KNOWS* THEM!

IF HE WANTS US TO LISTEN TO HIM, WE *LISTEN!*

BROTHER LANTERN!

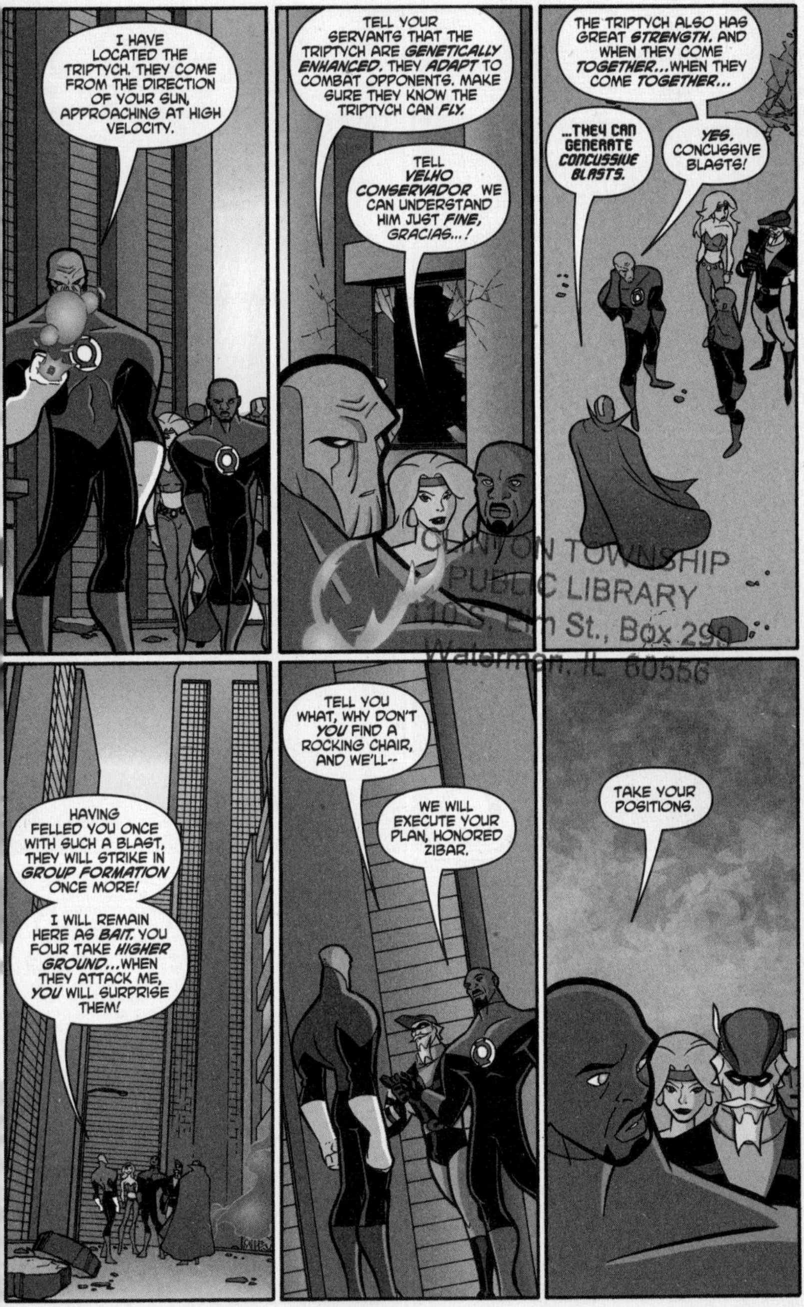
I HAVE LOCATED THE TRIPTYCH. THEY COME FROM THE DIRECTION OF YOUR SUN, APPROACHING AT HIGH VELOCITY.
TELL YOUR SERVANTS THAT THE TRIPTYCH ARE GENETICALLY ENHANCED. THEY ADAPT TO COMBAT OPPONENTS. MAKE SURE THEY KNOW THE TRIPTYCH CAN FLY.
TELL VELHO CONSERVADOR WE CAN UNDERSTAND HIM JUST FINE, GRACIAS...!
THE TRIPTYCH ALSO HAS GREAT STRENGTH. AND WHEN THEY COME TOGETHER...WHEN THEY COME TOGETHER...
...THEY CAN GENERATE CONCUSSIVE BLASTS.
YES. CONCUSSIVE BLASTS!
HAVING FELLED YOU ONCE WITH SUCH A BLAST, THEY WILL STRIKE IN GROUP FORMATION ONCE MORE!
I WILL REMAIN HERE AS BAIT. YOU FOUR TAKE HIGHER GROUND...WHEN THEY ATTACK ME, YOU WILL SURPRISE THEM!
TELL YOU WHAT, WHY DON'T YOU FIND A ROCKING CHAIR, AND WE'LL--
WE WILL EXECUTE YOUR PLAN, HONORED ZIBAR.
TAKE YOUR POSITIONS.

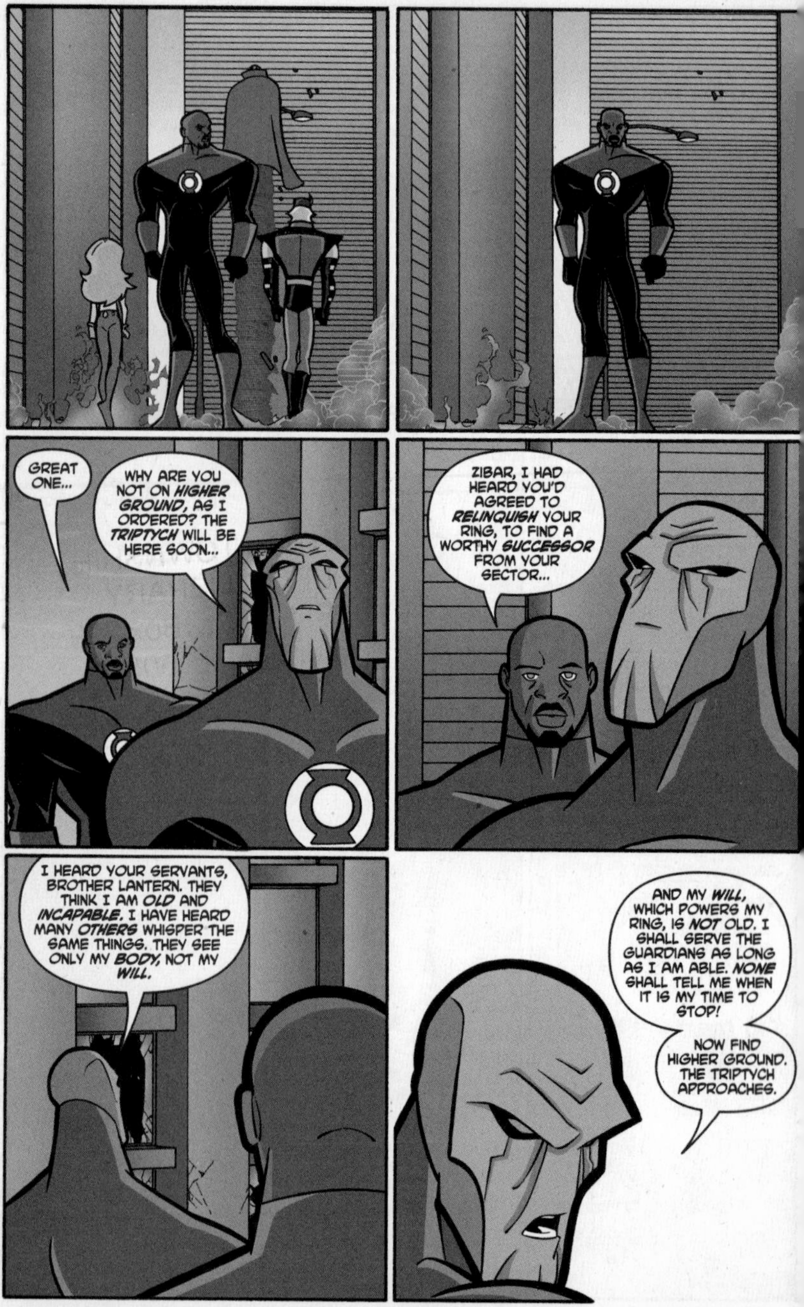
GREAT ONE...
WHY ARE YOU NOT ON HIGHER GROUND, AS I ORDERED? THE TRIPTYCH WILL BE HERE SOON...
ZIBAR, I HAD HEARD YOU'D AGREED TO RELINQUISH YOUR RING, TO FIND A WORTHY SUCCESSOR FROM YOUR SECTOR...
I HEARD YOUR SERVANTS, BROTHER LANTERN. THEY THINK I AM OLD AND INCAPABLE. I HAVE HEARD MANY OTHERS WHISPER THE SAME THINGS. THEY SEE ONLY MY BODY, NOT MY WILL.
AND MY WILL, WHICH POWERS MY RING, IS NOT OLD. I SHALL SERVE THE GUARDIANS AS LONG AS I AM ABLE. NONE SHALL TELL ME WHEN IT IS MY TIME TO STOP!
NOW FIND HIGHER GROUND. THE TRIPTYCH APPROACHES.

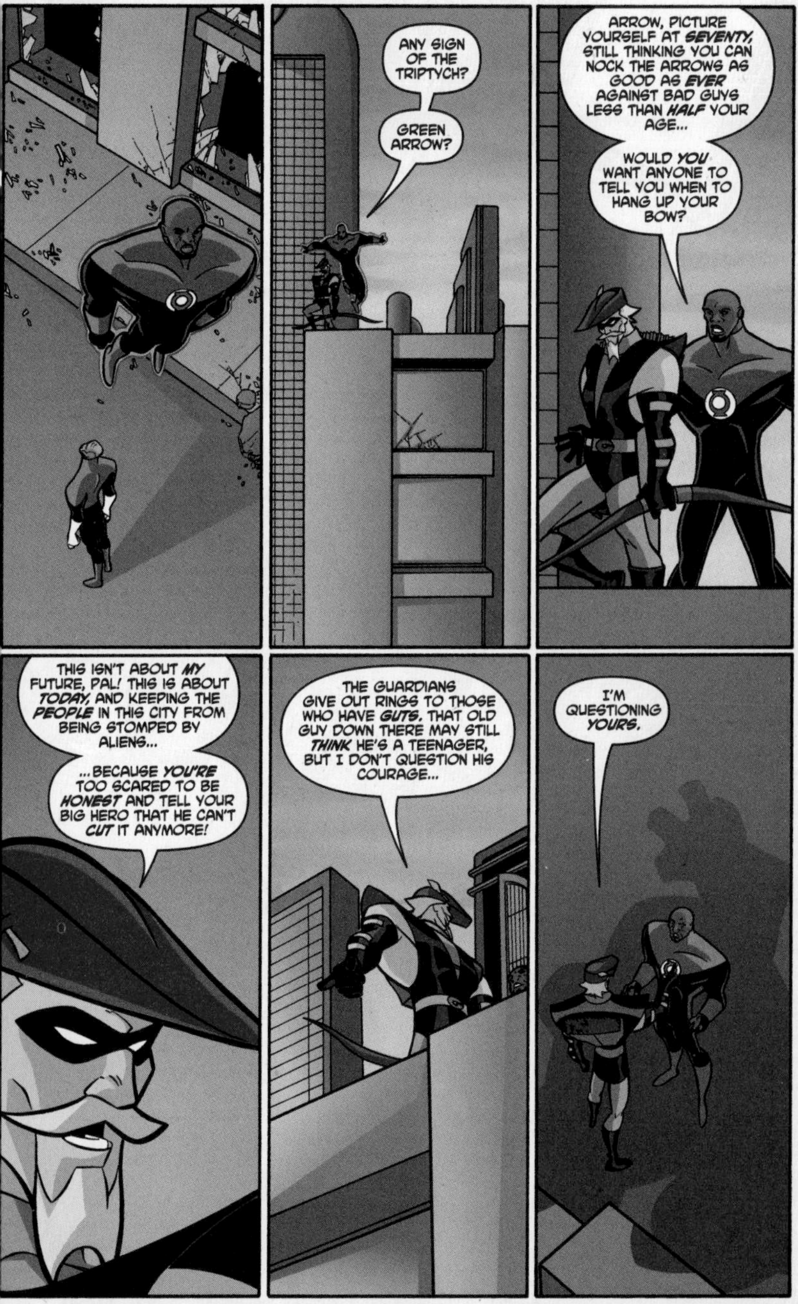
ANY SIGN OF THE TRIPTYCH?
GREEN ARROW?
ARROW, PICTURE YOURSELF AT SEVENTY, STILL THINKING YOU CAN NOCK THE ARROWS AS GOOD AS EVER AGAINST BAD GUYS LESS THAN HALF YOUR AGE...
WOULD YOU WANT ANYONE TO TELL YOU WHEN TO HANG UP YOUR BOW?
THIS ISN'T ABOUT MY FUTURE, PAL! THIS IS ABOUT TODAY, AND KEEPING THE PEOPLE IN THIS CITY FROM BEING STOMPED BY ALIENS...
...BECAUSE YOU'RE TOO SCARED TO BE HONEST AND TELL YOUR BIG HERO THAT HE CAN'T CUT IT ANYMORE!
THE GUARDIANS GIVE OUT RINGS TO THOSE WHO HAVE GUTS. THAT OLD GUY DOWN THERE MAY STILL THINK HE'S A TEENAGER, BUT I DON'T QUESTION HIS COURAGE...
I'M QUESTIONING YOURS.

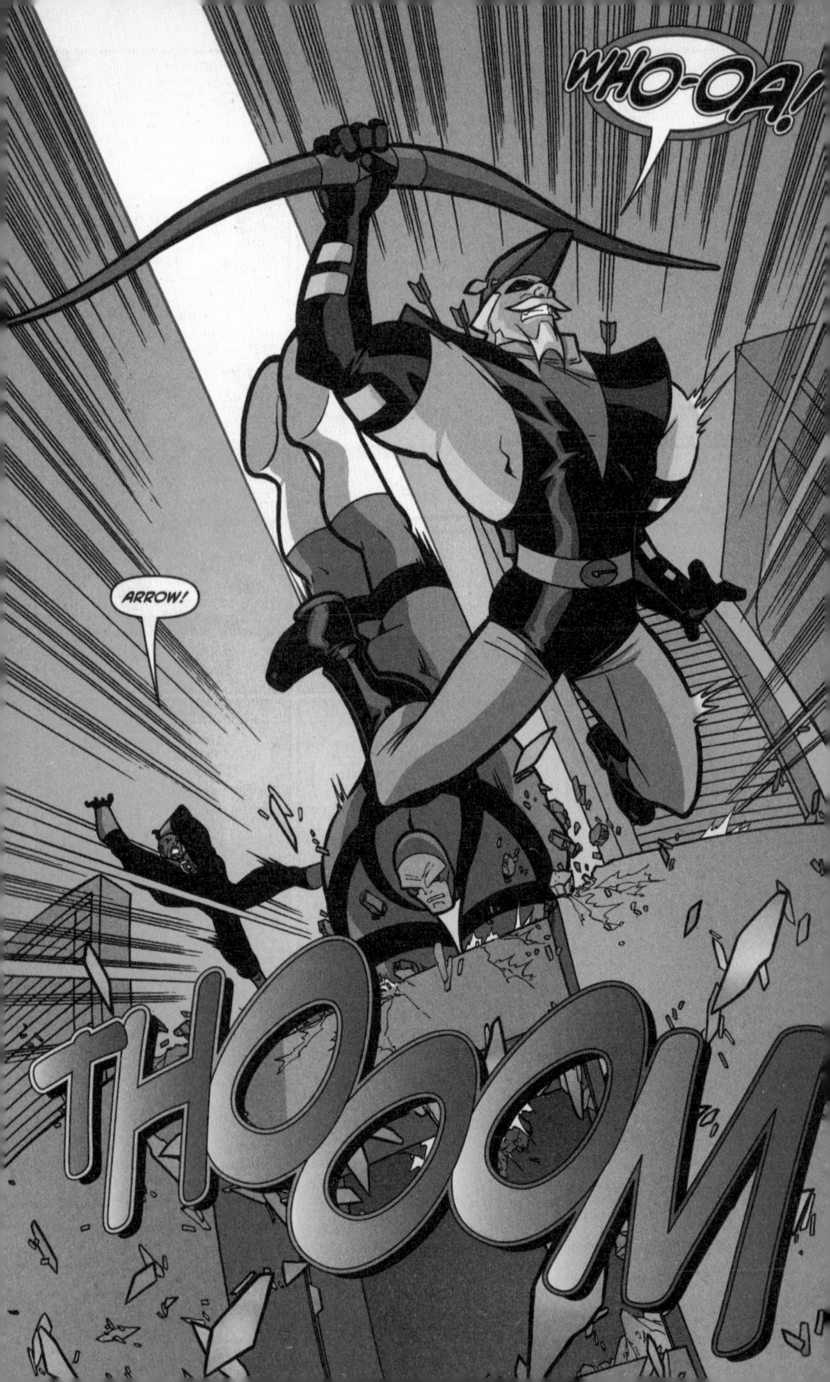
WHO-OA!
ARROW!
THOOOM!

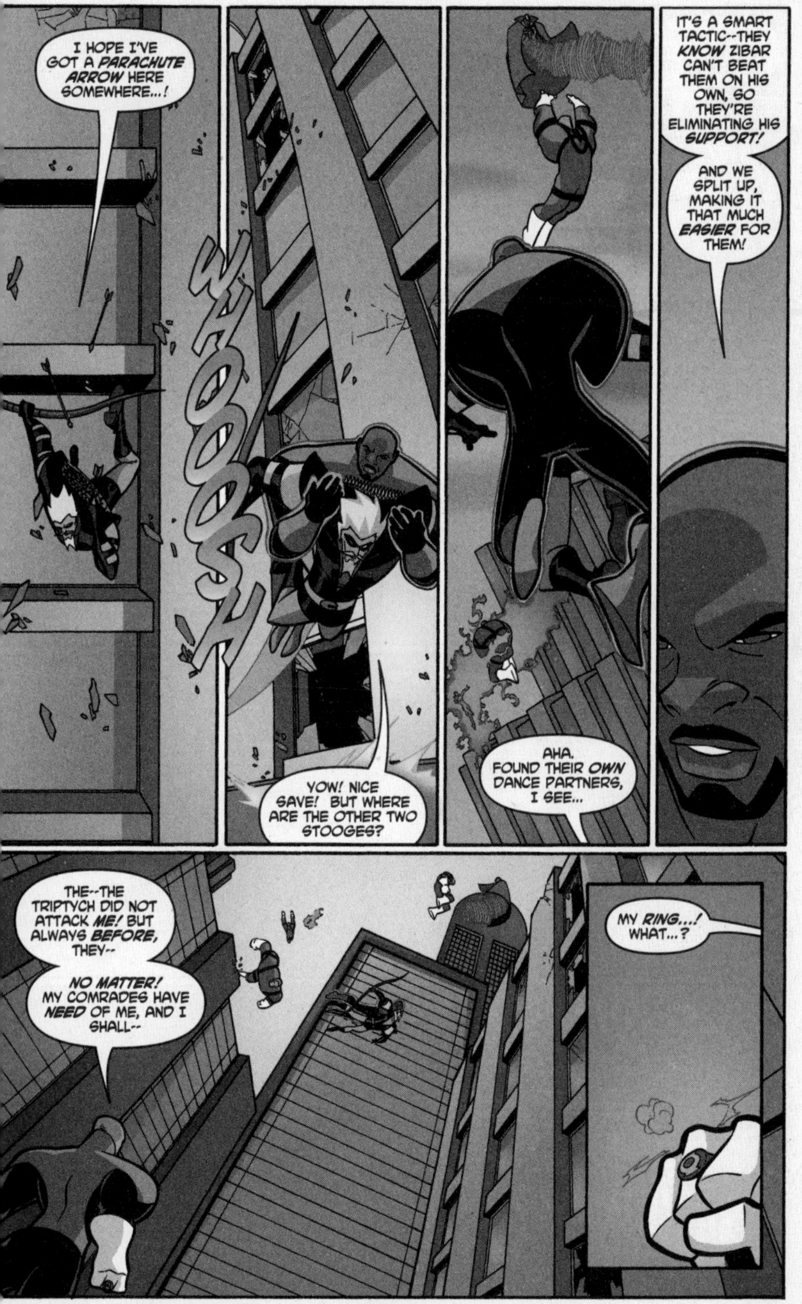
I HOPE I'VE GOT A *PARACHUTE ARROW* HERE SOMEWHERE...!
WHOOOOSH
YOW! NICE SAVE! BUT WHERE ARE THE OTHER TWO STOOGES?
AHA. FOUND THEIR *OWN* DANCE PARTNERS, I SEE...
IT'S A SMART TACTIC--THEY *KNOW* ZIBAR CAN'T BEAT THEM ON HIS OWN, SO THEY'RE ELIMINATING HIS *SUPPORT!*
AND WE SPLIT UP, MAKING IT THAT MUCH *EASIER* FOR THEM!
THE--THE TRIPTYCH DID NOT ATTACK *ME!* BUT ALWAYS *BEFORE,* THEY--
NO MATTER! MY COMRADES HAVE *NEED* OF ME, AND I SHALL--
MY *RING...!* WHAT...?

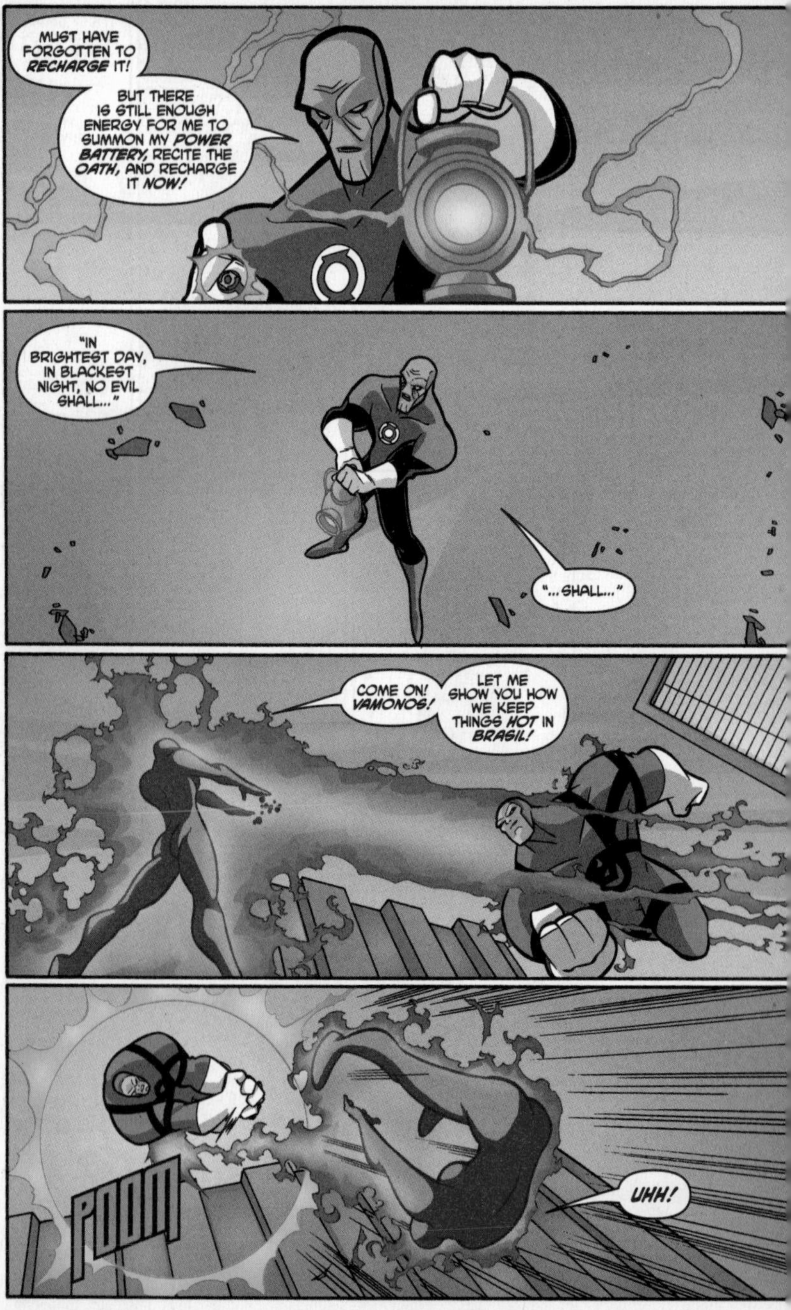

MUST HAVE FORGOTTEN TO *RECHARGE* IT!
BUT THERE IS STILL ENOUGH ENERGY FOR ME TO SUMMON MY *POWER BATTERY,* RECITE THE *OATH,* AND RECHARGE IT *NOW!*
"IN BRIGHTEST DAY, IN BLACKEST NIGHT, NO EVIL SHALL..."
"...SHALL..."
COME ON! *VAMONOS!*
LET ME SHOW YOU HOW WE KEEP THINGS *HOT* IN *BRASIL!*
POOM
UHH!

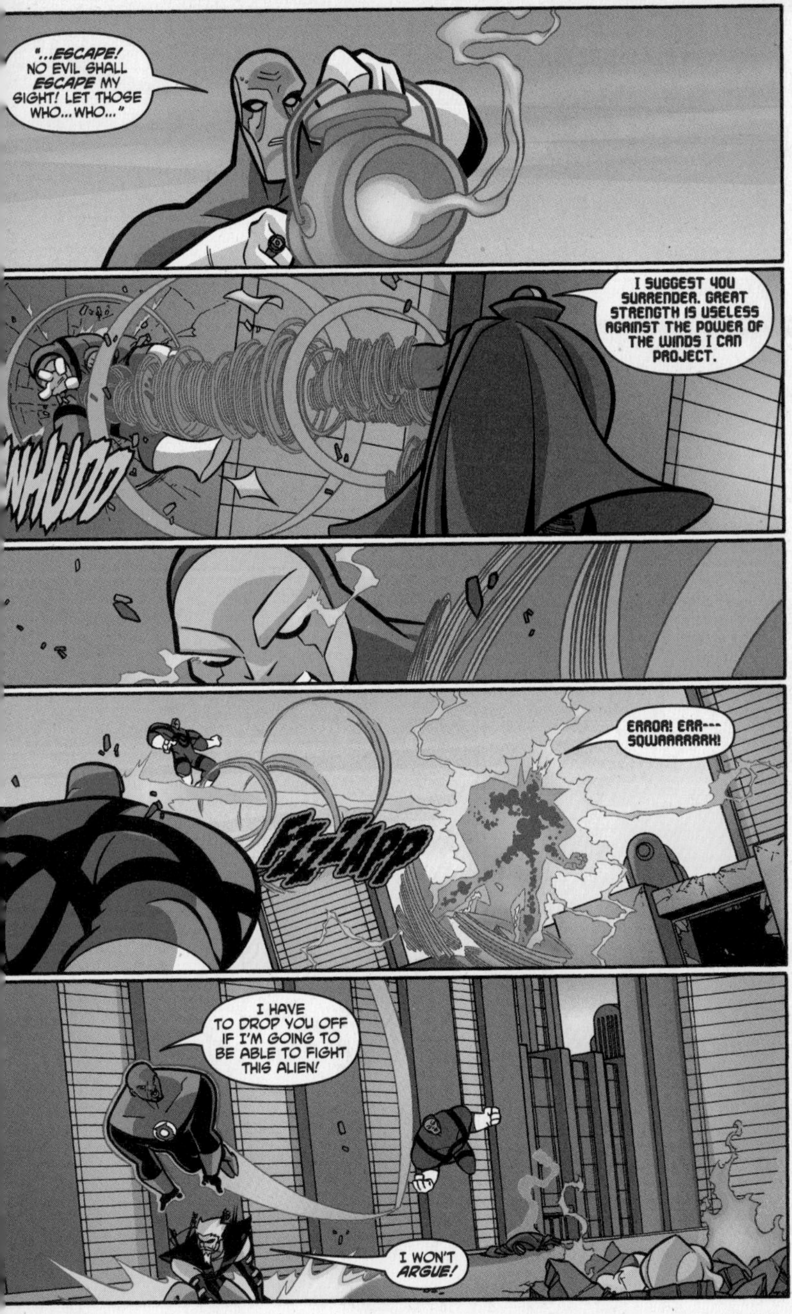
"...ESCAPE! NO EVIL SHALL ESCAPE MY SIGHT! LET THOSE WHO...WHO..."
I SUGGEST YOU SURRENDER. GREAT STRENGTH IS USELESS AGAINST THE POWER OF THE WINDS I CAN PROJECT.
WHOOO
ERROR! ERR--- SQWAARRRRK!
FZZZAPP
I HAVE TO DROP YOU OFF IF I'M GOING TO BE ABLE TO FIGHT THIS ALIEN!
I WON'T ARGUE!

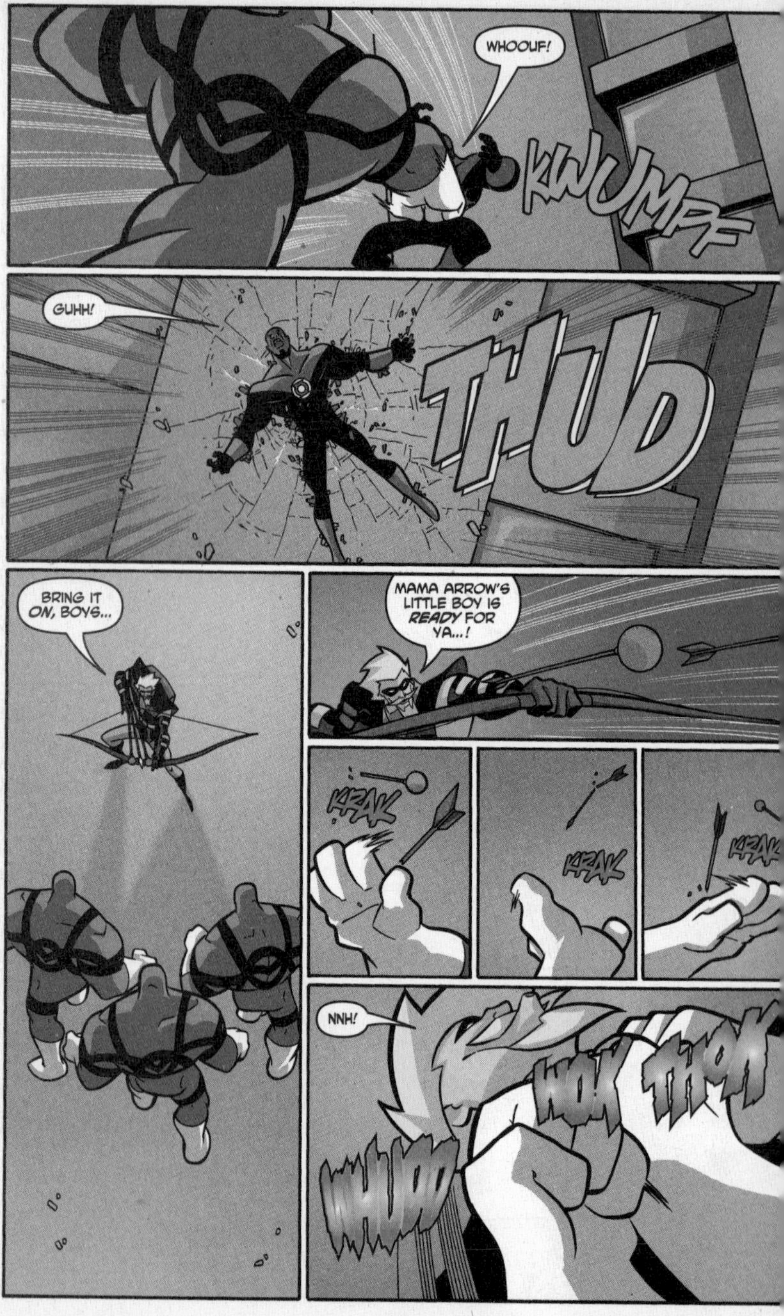

WHOOUF!
KWUMPF
GUHH!
THUD
BRING IT ON, BOYS...
MAMA ARROW'S LITTLE BOY IS *READY* FOR YA...!
KRAK
KRAK
KRAK
NNH!
WHOK
THOK
WHUDD

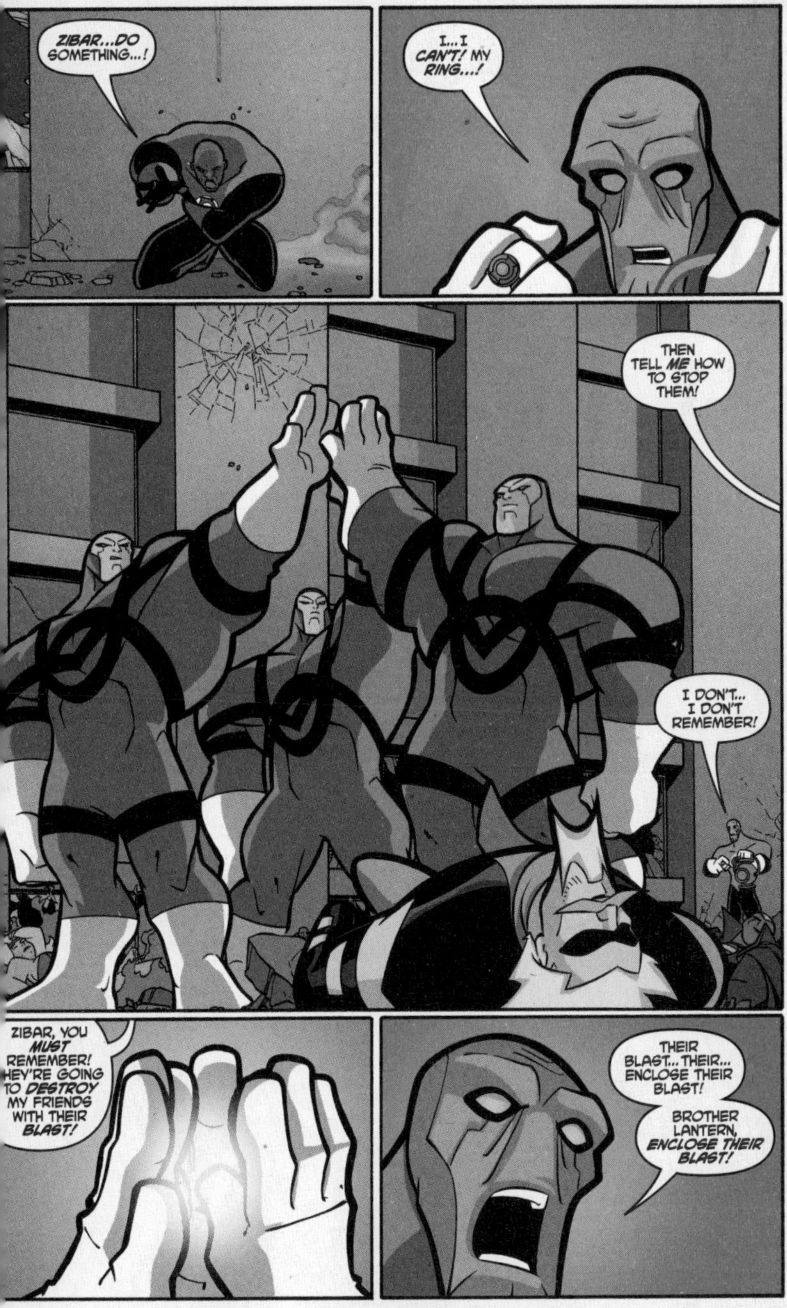
ZIBAR...DO SOMETHING...!
I...I *CAN'T!* MY *RING...!*
THEN TELL *ME* HOW TO STOP THEM!
I DON'T... I DON'T REMEMBER!
ZIBAR, YOU *MUST* REMEMBER! HEY'RE GOING TO *DESTROY* MY FRIENDS WITH THEIR *BLAST!*
THEIR BLAST... THEIR... ENCLOSE THEIR BLAST!
BROTHER LANTERN, *ENCLOSE THEIR BLAST!*

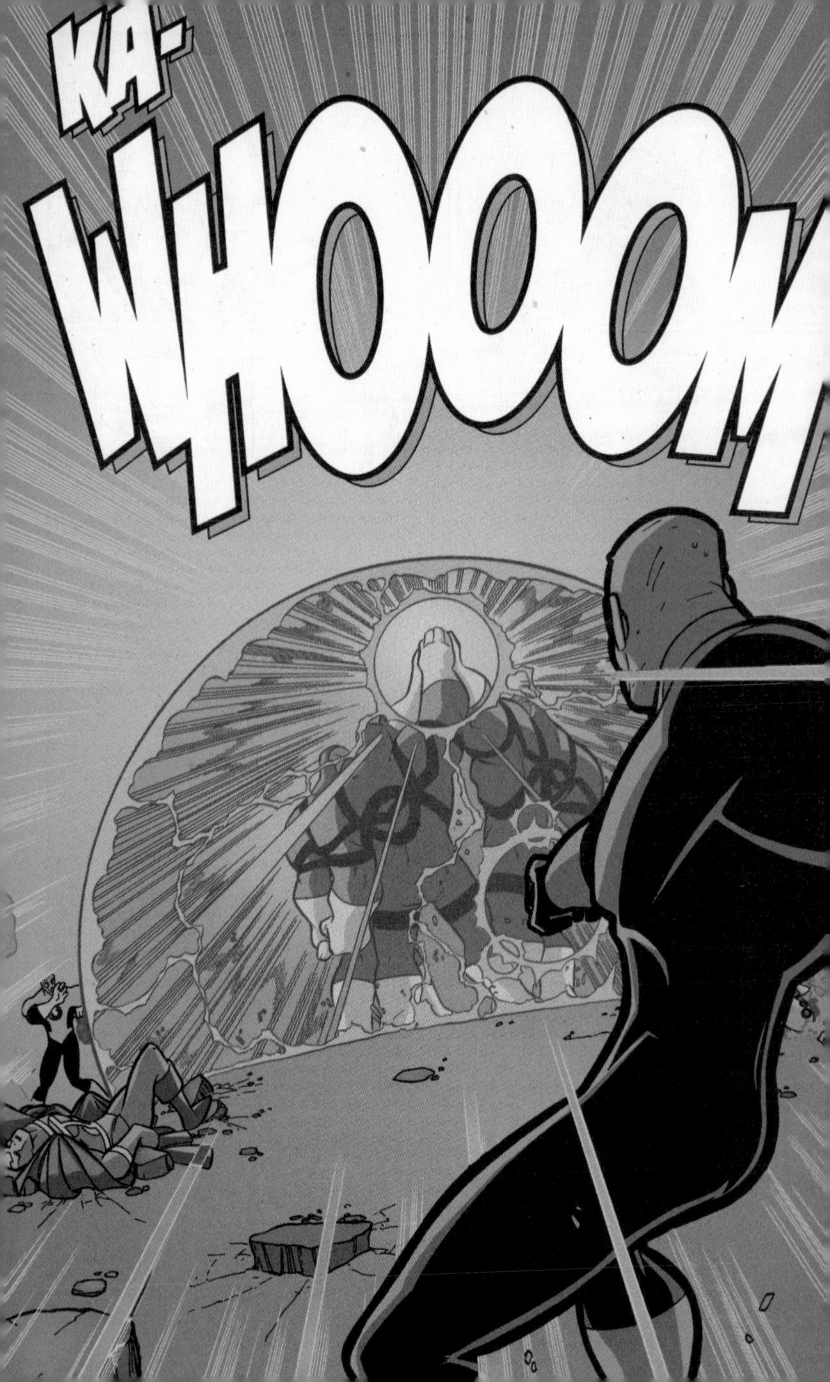
KA-WHOOOM

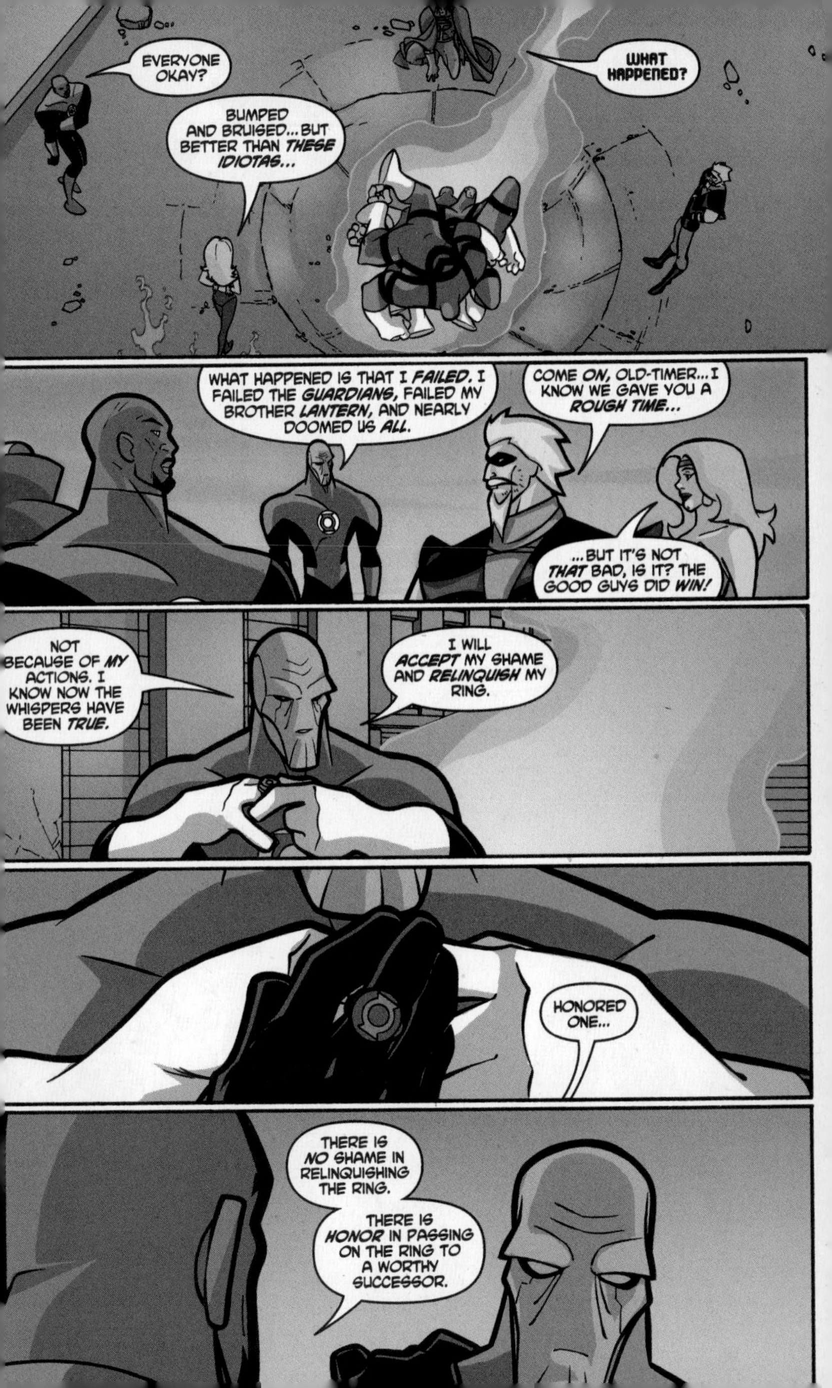
EVERYONE OKAY?
WHAT HAPPENED?
BUMPED AND BRUISED... BUT BETTER THAN THESE IDIOTAS...
WHAT HAPPENED IS THAT I FAILED. I FAILED THE GUARDIANS, FAILED MY BROTHER LANTERN, AND NEARLY DOOMED US ALL.
COME ON, OLD-TIMER... I KNOW WE GAVE YOU A ROUGH TIME...
...BUT IT'S NOT THAT BAD, IS IT? THE GOOD GUYS DID WIN!
NOT BECAUSE OF MY ACTIONS. I KNOW NOW THE WHISPERS HAVE BEEN TRUE.
I WILL ACCEPT MY SHAME AND RELINQUISH MY RING.
HONORED ONE...
THERE IS NO SHAME IN RELINQUISHING THE RING.
THERE IS HONOR IN PASSING ON THE RING TO A WORTHY SUCCESSOR.

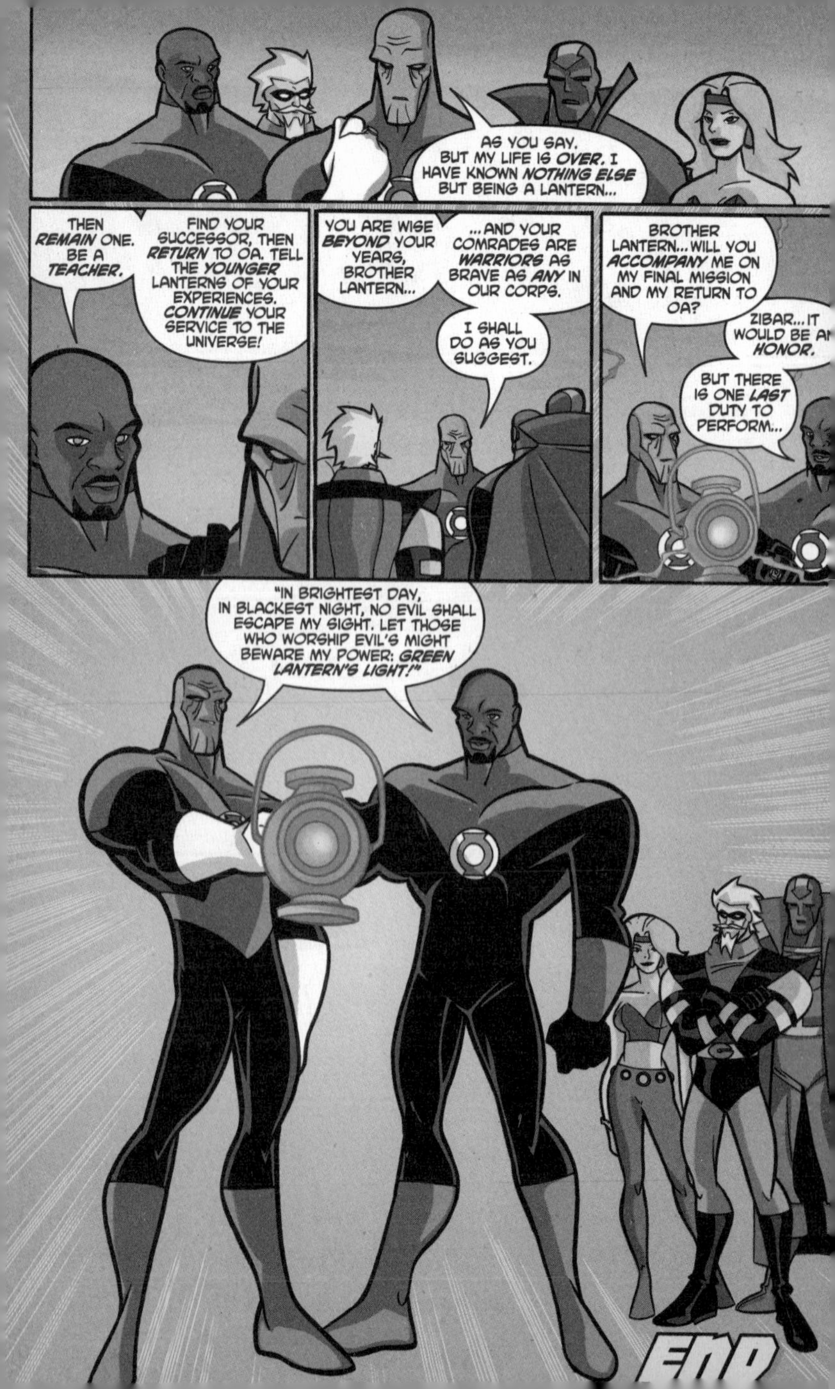
AS YOU SAY. BUT MY LIFE IS OVER. I HAVE KNOWN NOTHING ELSE BUT BEING A LANTERN...
THEN REMAIN ONE. BE A TEACHER.
FIND YOUR SUCCESSOR, THEN RETURN TO OA. TELL THE YOUNGER LANTERNS OF YOUR EXPERIENCES. CONTINUE YOUR SERVICE TO THE UNIVERSE!
YOU ARE WISE BEYOND YOUR YEARS, BROTHER LANTERN...
...AND YOUR COMRADES ARE WARRIORS AS BRAVE AS ANY IN OUR CORPS.
I SHALL DO AS YOU SUGGEST.
BROTHER LANTERN... WILL YOU ACCOMPANY ME ON MY FINAL MISSION AND MY RETURN TO OA?
ZIBAR... IT WOULD BE AN HONOR.
BUT THERE IS ONE LAST DUTY TO PERFORM...
"IN BRIGHTEST DAY, IN BLACKEST NIGHT, NO EVIL SHALL ESCAPE MY SIGHT. LET THOSE WHO WORSHIP EVIL'S MIGHT BEWARE MY POWER: GREEN LANTERN'S LIGHT!"
END

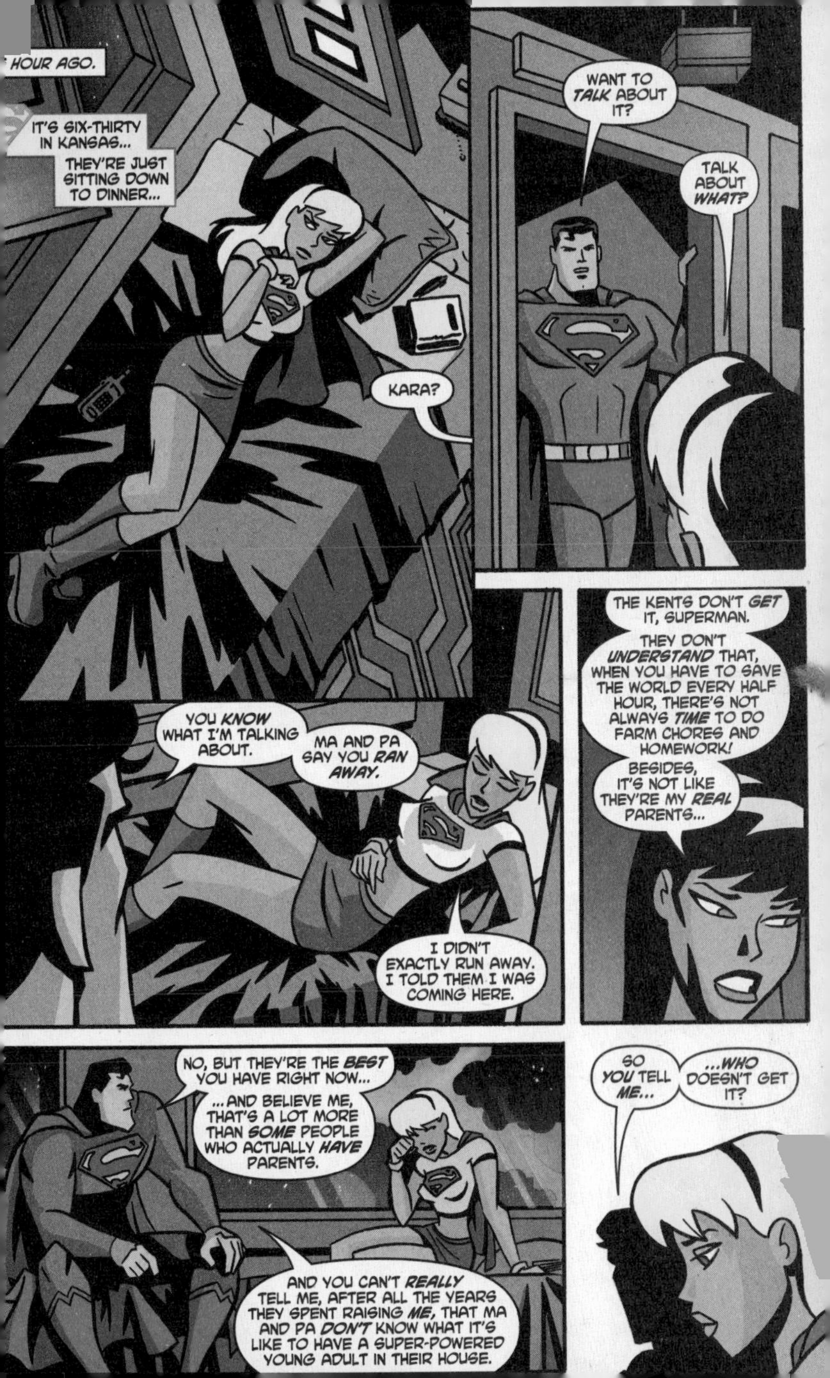
HOUR AGO.
IT'S SIX-THIRTY IN KANSAS...
THEY'RE JUST SITTING DOWN TO DINNER...
KARA?
WANT TO TALK ABOUT IT?
TALK ABOUT WHAT?
YOU KNOW WHAT I'M TALKING ABOUT.
MA AND PA SAY YOU RAN AWAY.
I DIDN'T EXACTLY RUN AWAY. I TOLD THEM I WAS COMING HERE.
THE KENTS DON'T GET IT, SUPERMAN.
THEY DON'T UNDERSTAND THAT, WHEN YOU HAVE TO SAVE THE WORLD EVERY HALF HOUR, THERE'S NOT ALWAYS TIME TO DO FARM CHORES AND HOMEWORK!
BESIDES, IT'S NOT LIKE THEY'RE MY REAL PARENTS...
NO, BUT THEY'RE THE BEST YOU HAVE RIGHT NOW...
...AND BELIEVE ME, THAT'S A LOT MORE THAN SOME PEOPLE WHO ACTUALLY HAVE PARENTS.
AND YOU CAN'T REALLY TELL ME, AFTER ALL THE YEARS THEY SPENT RAISING ME, THAT MA AND PA DON'T KNOW WHAT IT'S LIKE TO HAVE A SUPER-POWERED YOUNG ADULT IN THEIR HOUSE.
SO YOU TELL ME...
...WHO DOESN'T GET IT?

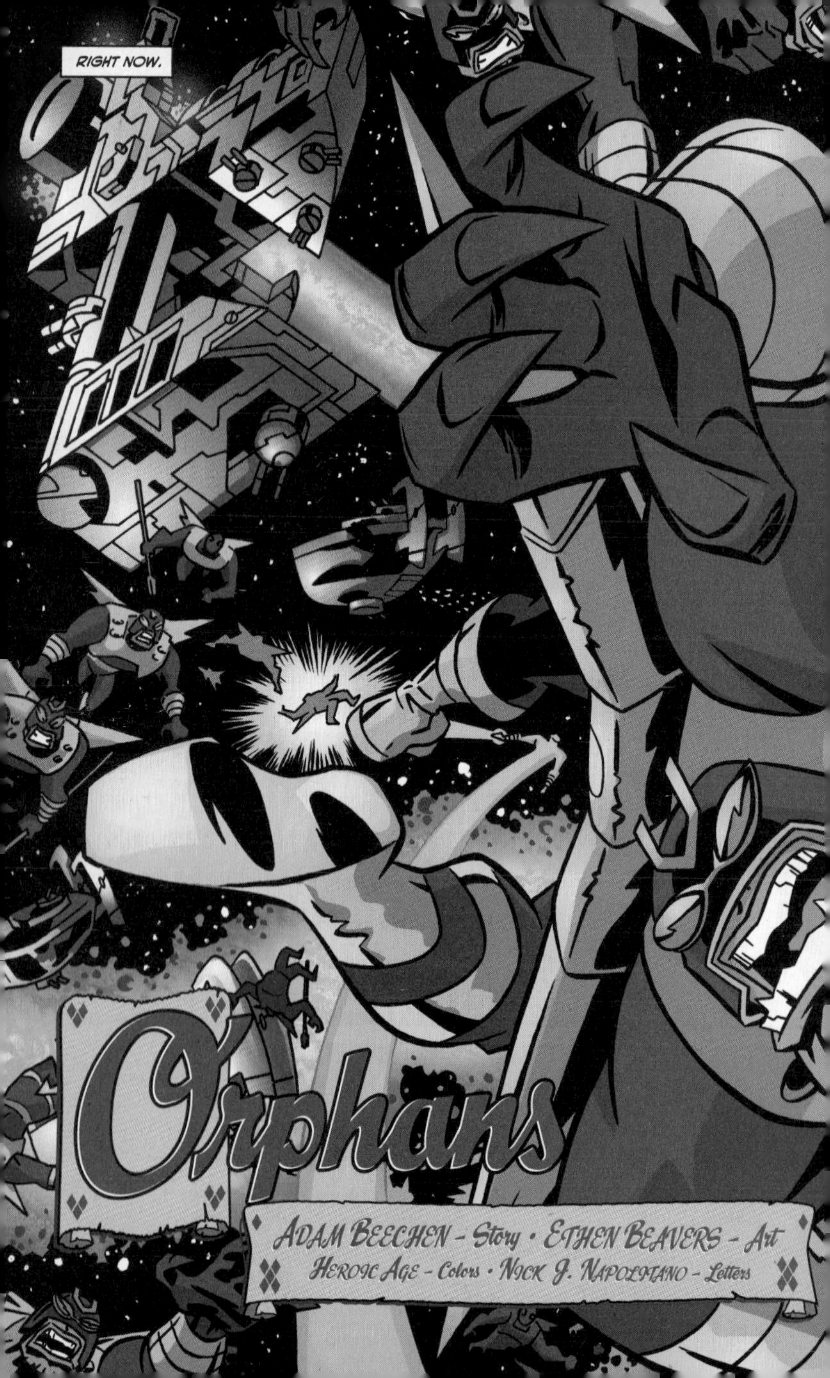

RIGHT NOW.
Orphans
ADAM BEECHEN - Story • ETHEN BEAVERS - Art
HEROIC AGE - Colors • NICK J. NAPOLITANO - Letters

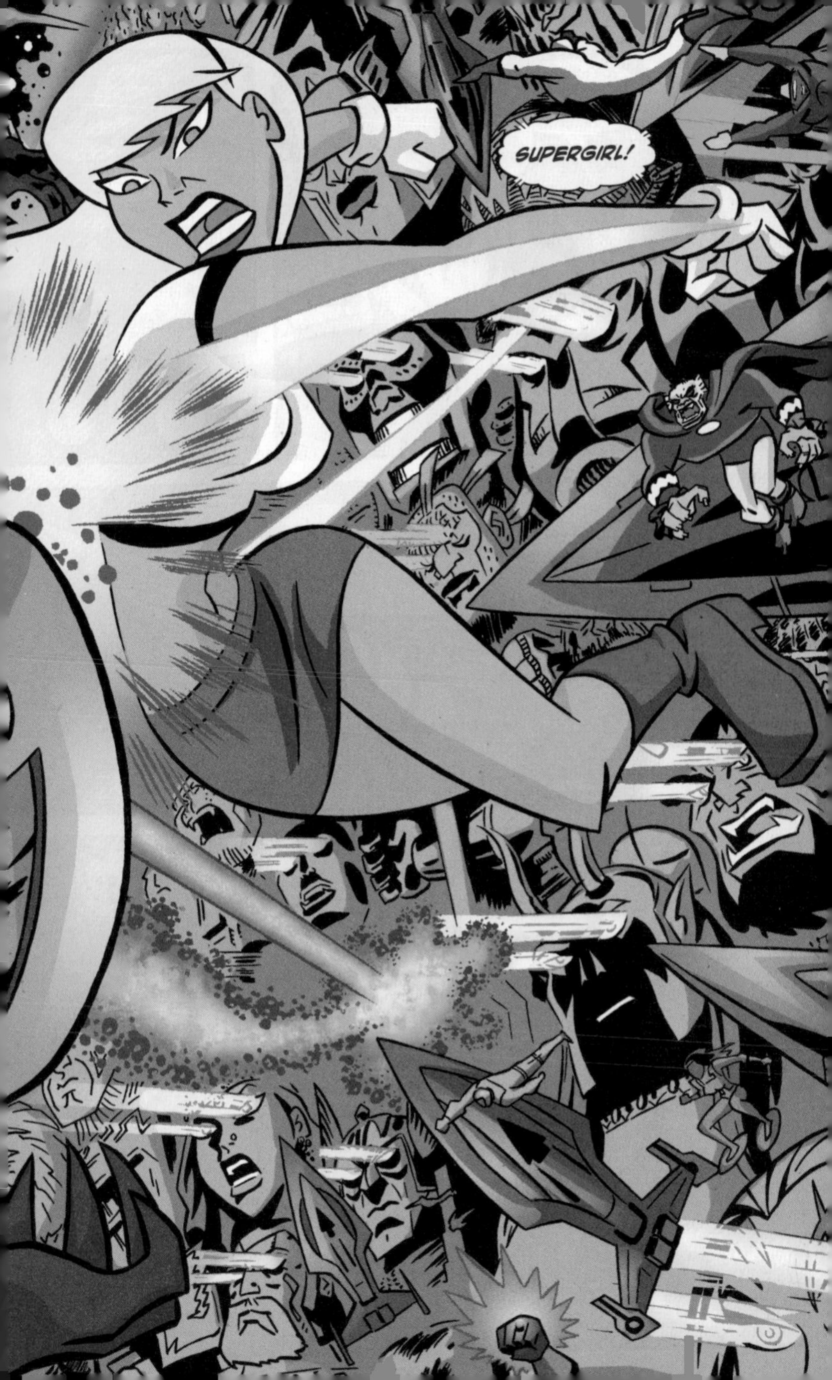
SUPERGIRL!

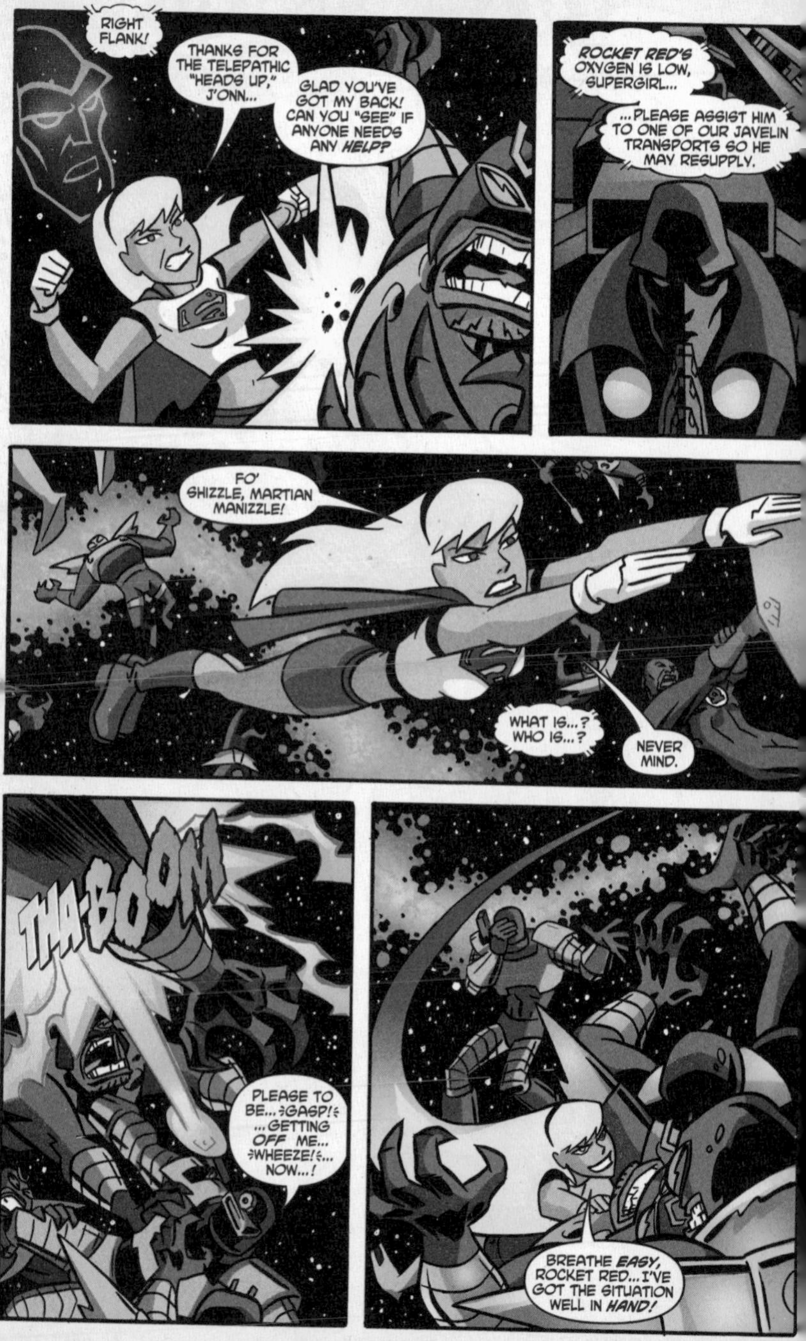
RIGHT FLANK!
THANKS FOR THE TELEPATHIC "HEADS UP," J'ONN...
GLAD YOU'VE GOT MY BACK! CAN YOU "SEE" IF ANYONE NEEDS ANY *HELP?*
ROCKET RED'S OXYGEN IS LOW, SUPERGIRL...
...PLEASE ASSIST HIM TO ONE OF OUR JAVELIN TRANSPORTS SO HE MAY RESUPPLY.
FO' SHIZZLE, MARTIAN MANIZZLE!
WHAT IS...? WHO IS...?
NEVER MIND.
THA-BOOM
PLEASE TO BE... GASP! ...GETTING *OFF* ME... WHEEZE!... NOW...!
BREATHE *EASY,* ROCKET RED... I'VE GOT THE SITUATION WELL IN *HAND!*

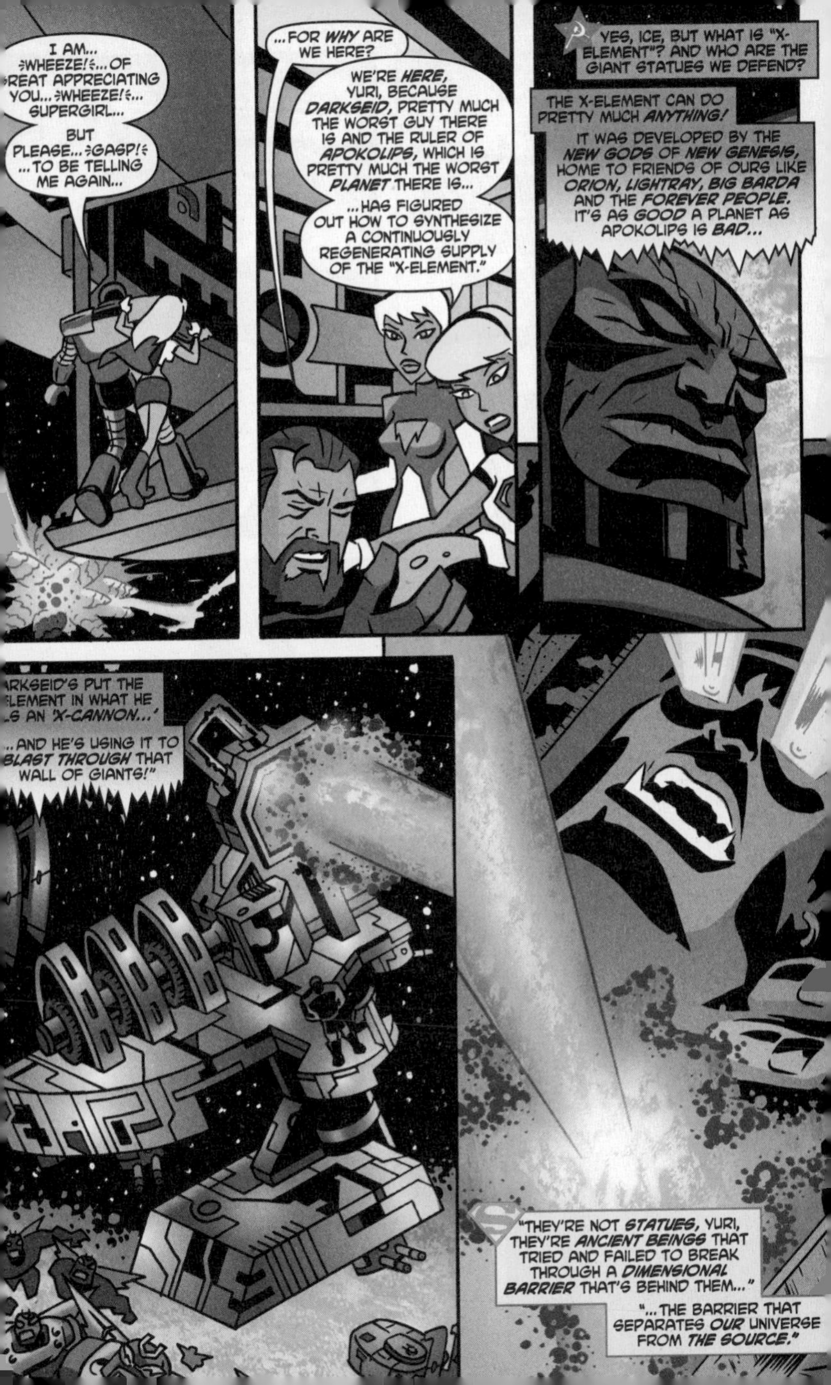

I AM... WHEEZE!...OF REAT APPRECIATING YOU... WHEEZE!... SUPERGIRL...
BUT PLEASE... GASP! ...TO BE TELLING ME AGAIN...
...FOR WHY ARE WE HERE?
WE'RE HERE, YURI, BECAUSE DARKSEID, PRETTY MUCH THE WORST GUY THERE IS AND THE RULER OF APOKOLIPS, WHICH IS PRETTY MUCH THE WORST PLANET THERE IS...
...HAS FIGURED OUT HOW TO SYNTHESIZE A CONTINUOUSLY REGENERATING SUPPLY OF THE "X-ELEMENT."
YES, ICE, BUT WHAT IS "X-ELEMENT"? AND WHO ARE THE GIANT STATUES WE DEFEND?
THE X-ELEMENT CAN DO PRETTY MUCH ANYTHING!
IT WAS DEVELOPED BY THE NEW GODS OF NEW GENESIS, HOME TO FRIENDS OF OURS LIKE ORION, LIGHTRAY, BIG BARDA AND THE FOREVER PEOPLE. IT'S AS GOOD A PLANET AS APOKOLIPS IS BAD...
ARKSEID'S PUT THE ELEMENT IN WHAT HE S AN 'X-CANNON...'
...AND HE'S USING IT TO BLAST THROUGH THAT WALL OF GIANTS!"
"THEY'RE NOT STATUES, YURI, THEY'RE ANCIENT BEINGS THAT TRIED AND FAILED TO BREAK THROUGH A DIMENSIONAL BARRIER THAT'S BEHIND THEM..."
"...THE BARRIER THAT SEPARATES OUR UNIVERSE FROM THE SOURCE."

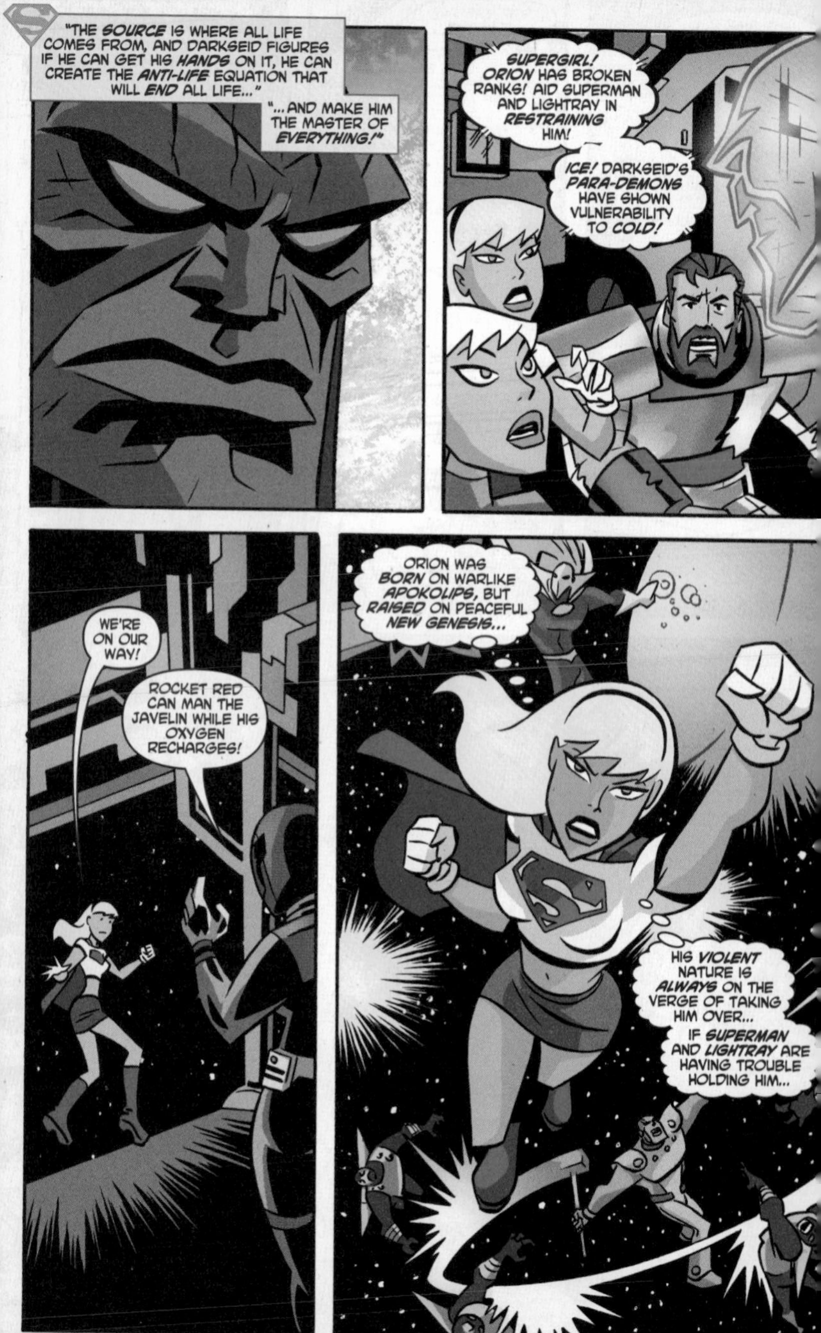
"THE SOURCE IS WHERE ALL LIFE COMES FROM, AND DARKSEID FIGURES IF HE CAN GET HIS HANDS ON IT, HE CAN CREATE THE ANTI-LIFE EQUATION THAT WILL END ALL LIFE..."
"...AND MAKE HIM THE MASTER OF EVERYTHING!"
SUPERGIRL! ORION HAS BROKEN RANKS! AID SUPERMAN AND LIGHTRAY IN RESTRAINING HIM!
ICE! DARKSEID'S PARA-DEMONS HAVE SHOWN VULNERABILITY TO COLD!
WE'RE ON OUR WAY!
ROCKET RED CAN MAN THE JAVELIN WHILE HIS OXYGEN RECHARGES!
ORION WAS BORN ON WARLIKE APOKOLIPS, BUT RAISED ON PEACEFUL NEW GENESIS...
HIS VIOLENT NATURE IS ALWAYS ON THE VERGE OF TAKING HIM OVER...
IF SUPERMAN AND LIGHTRAY ARE HAVING TROUBLE HOLDING HIM...

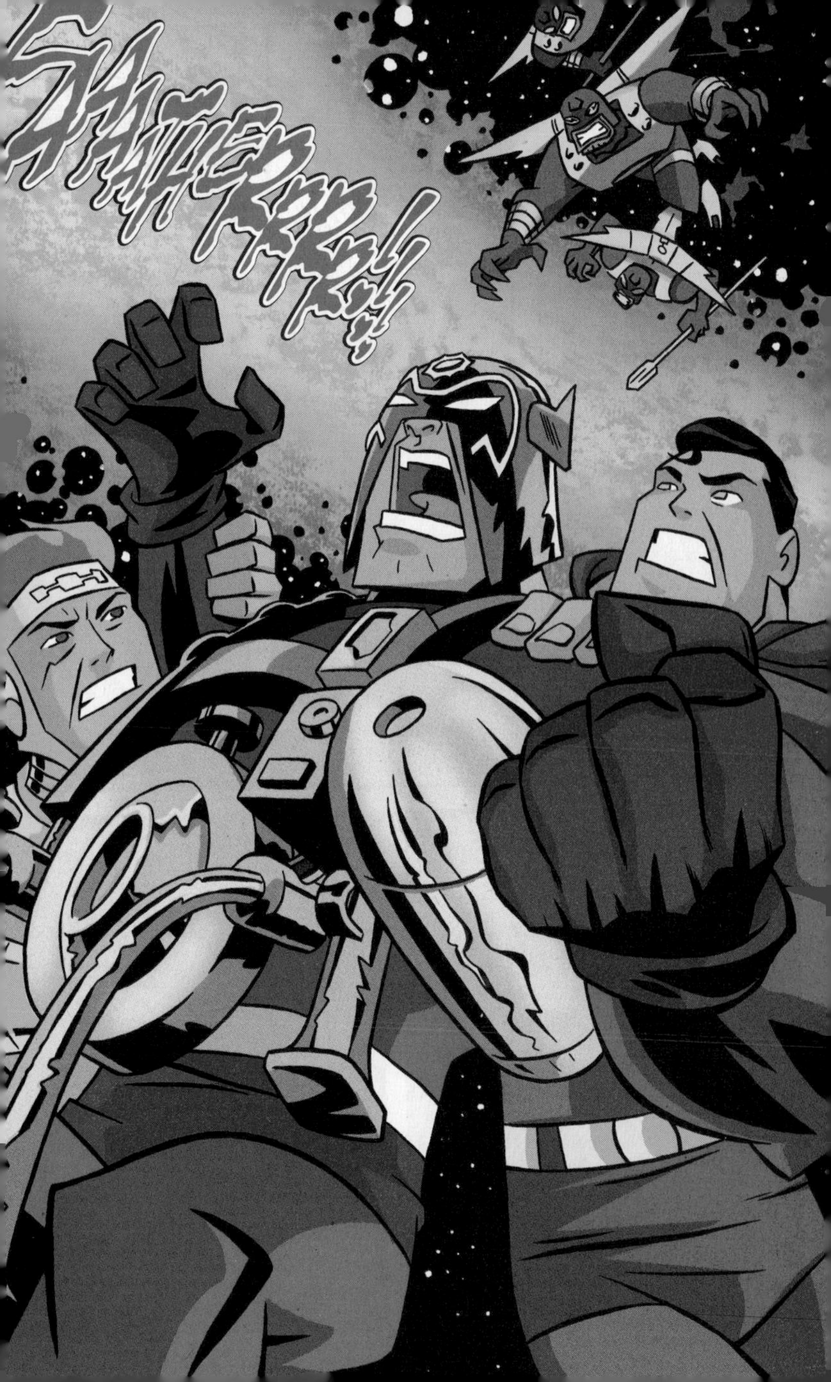
GAAAHHRRR!!

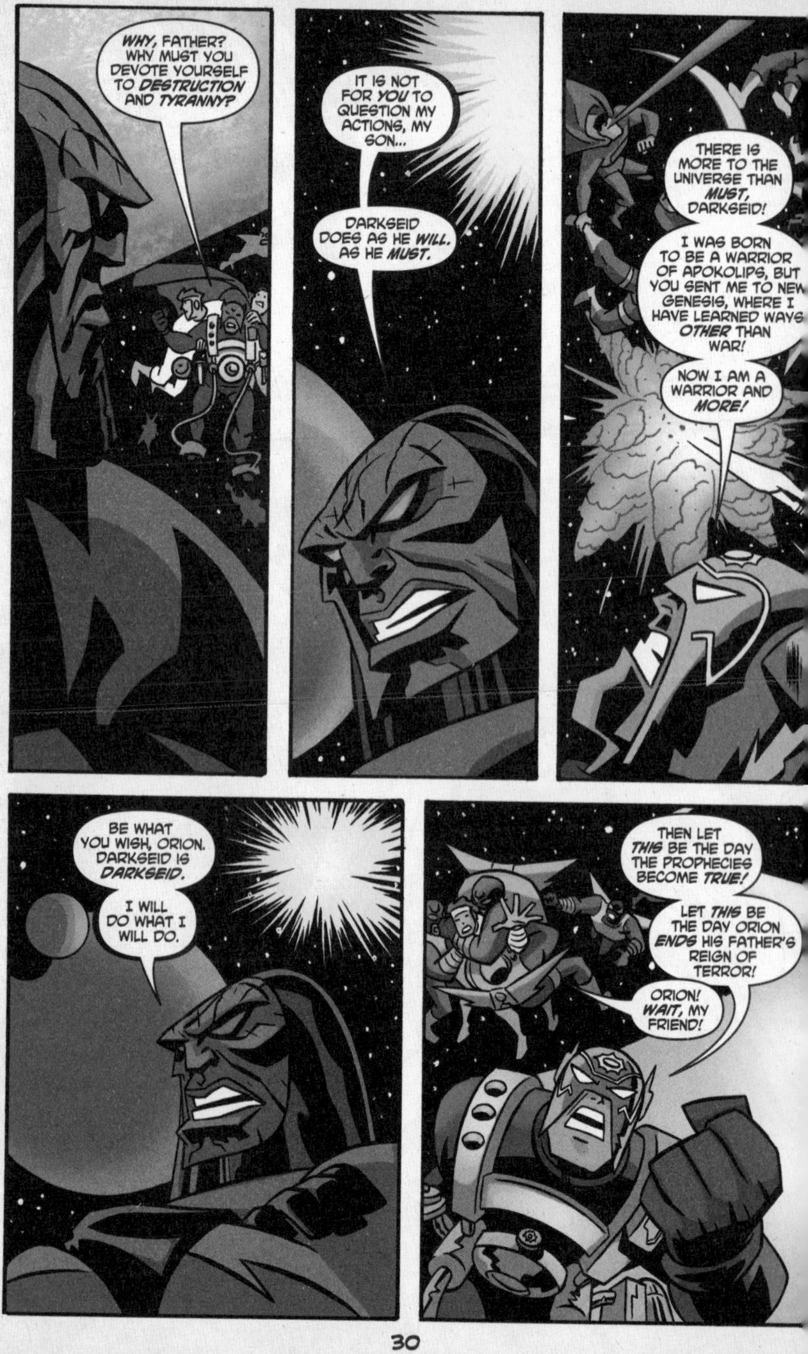

WHY, FATHER? WHY MUST YOU DEVOTE YOURSELF TO DESTRUCTION AND TYRANNY?
IT IS NOT FOR YOU TO QUESTION MY ACTIONS, MY SON...
DARKSEID DOES AS HE WILL. AS HE MUST.
THERE IS MORE TO THE UNIVERSE THAN MUST, DARKSEID!
I WAS BORN TO BE A WARRIOR OF APOKOLIPS, BUT YOU SENT ME TO NEW GENESIS, WHERE I HAVE LEARNED WAYS OTHER THAN WAR!
NOW I AM A WARRIOR AND MORE!
BE WHAT YOU WISH, ORION. DARKSEID IS DARKSEID.
I WILL DO WHAT I WILL DO.
THEN LET THIS BE THE DAY THE PROPHECIES BECOME TRUE!
LET THIS BE THE DAY ORION ENDS HIS FATHER'S REIGN OF TERROR!
ORION! WAIT, MY FRIEND!

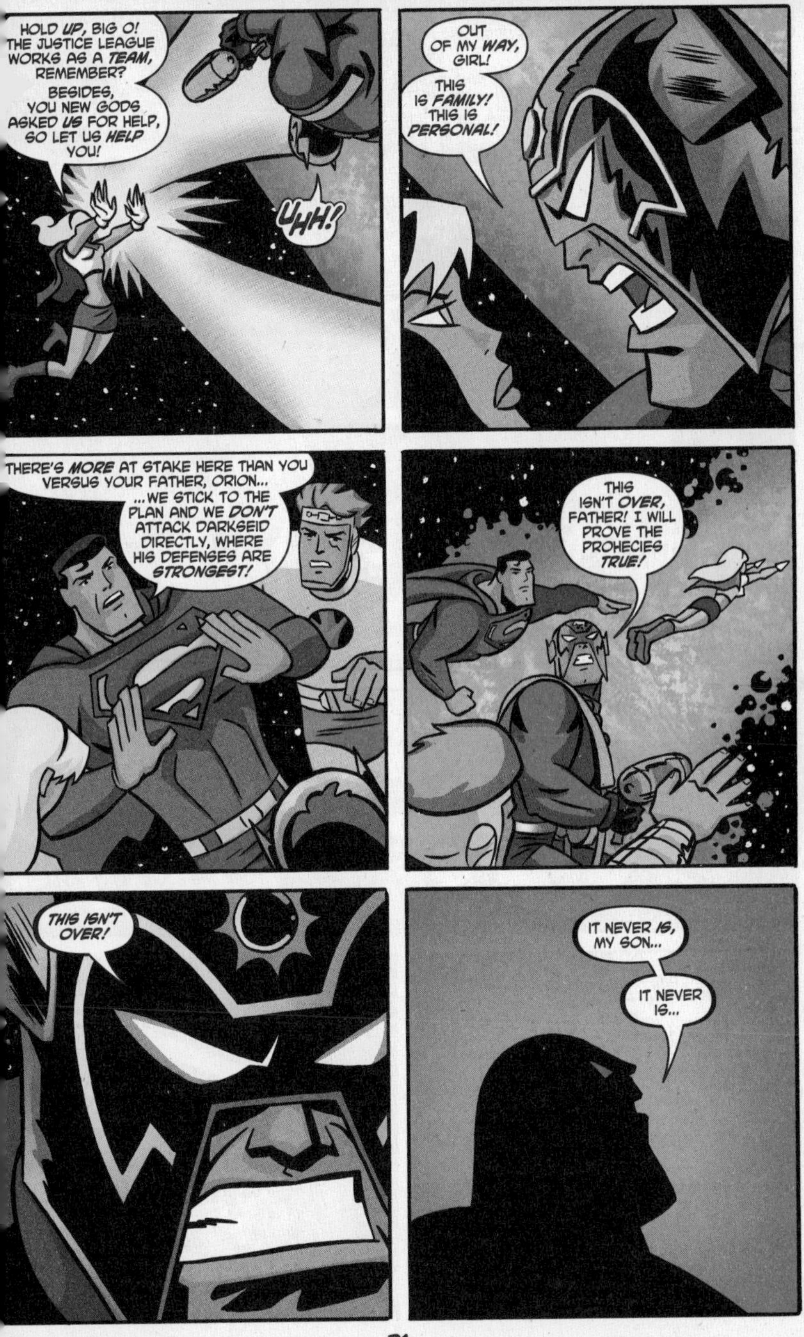
HOLD UP, BIG O! THE JUSTICE LEAGUE WORKS AS A TEAM, REMEMBER?
BESIDES, YOU NEW GODS ASKED US FOR HELP, SO LET US HELP YOU!
UHH!
OUT OF MY WAY, GIRL!
THIS IS FAMILY! THIS IS PERSONAL!
THERE'S MORE AT STAKE HERE THAN YOU VERSUS YOUR FATHER, ORION...
...WE STICK TO THE PLAN AND WE DON'T ATTACK DARKSEID DIRECTLY, WHERE HIS DEFENSES ARE STRONGEST!
THIS ISN'T OVER, FATHER! I WILL PROVE THE PROHECIES TRUE!
THIS ISN'T OVER!
IT NEVER IS, MY SON...
IT NEVER IS...

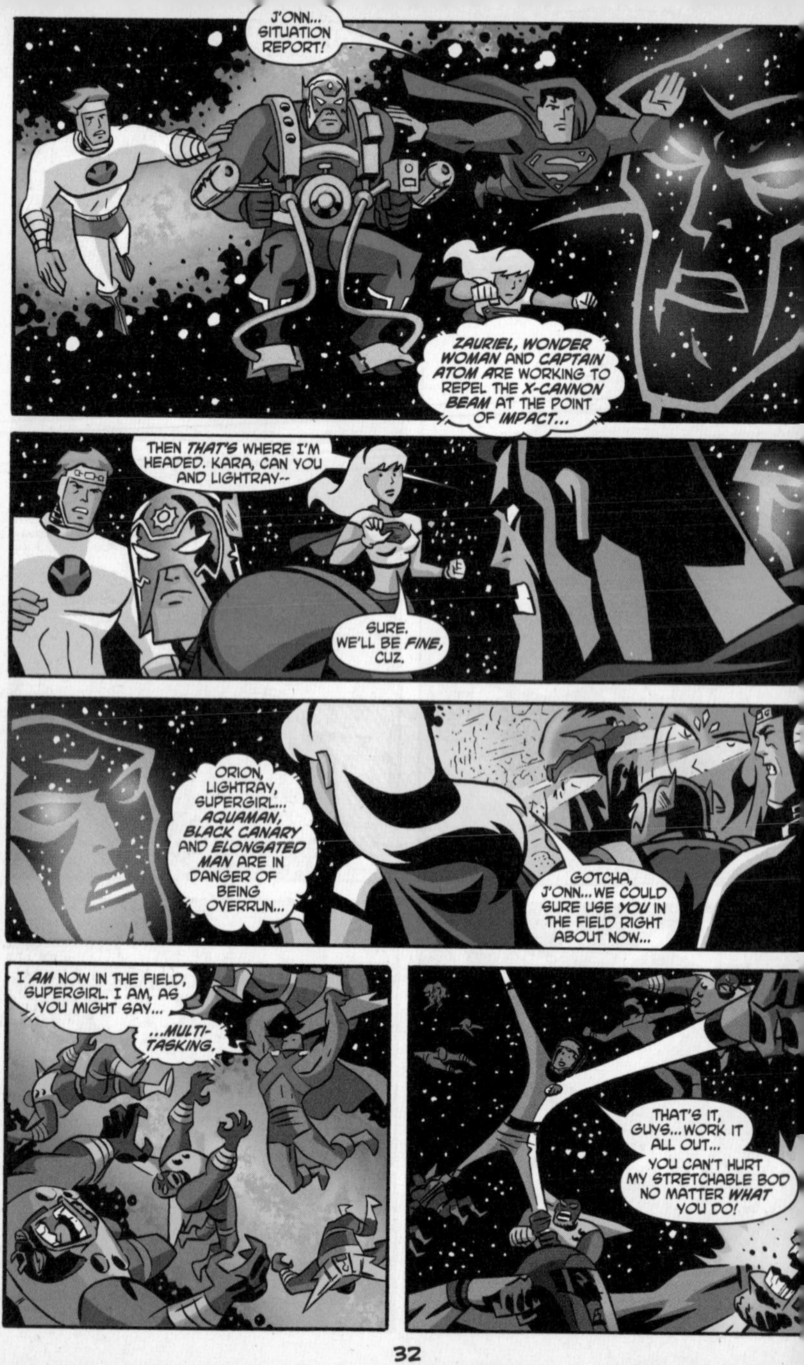
J'ONN... SITUATION REPORT!
ZAURIEL, WONDER WOMAN AND CAPTAIN ATOM ARE WORKING TO REPEL THE X-CANNON BEAM AT THE POINT OF IMPACT...
THEN THAT'S WHERE I'M HEADED. KARA, CAN YOU AND LIGHTRAY--
SURE. WE'LL BE FINE, CUZ.
ORION, LIGHTRAY, SUPERGIRL... AQUAMAN, BLACK CANARY AND ELONGATED MAN ARE IN DANGER OF BEING OVERRUN...
GOTCHA, J'ONN...WE COULD SURE USE YOU IN THE FIELD RIGHT ABOUT NOW...
I AM NOW IN THE FIELD, SUPERGIRL. I AM, AS YOU MIGHT SAY...
...MULTI-TASKING.
THAT'S IT, GUYS...WORK IT ALL OUT...
YOU CAN'T HURT MY STRETCHABLE BOD NO MATTER WHAT YOU DO!

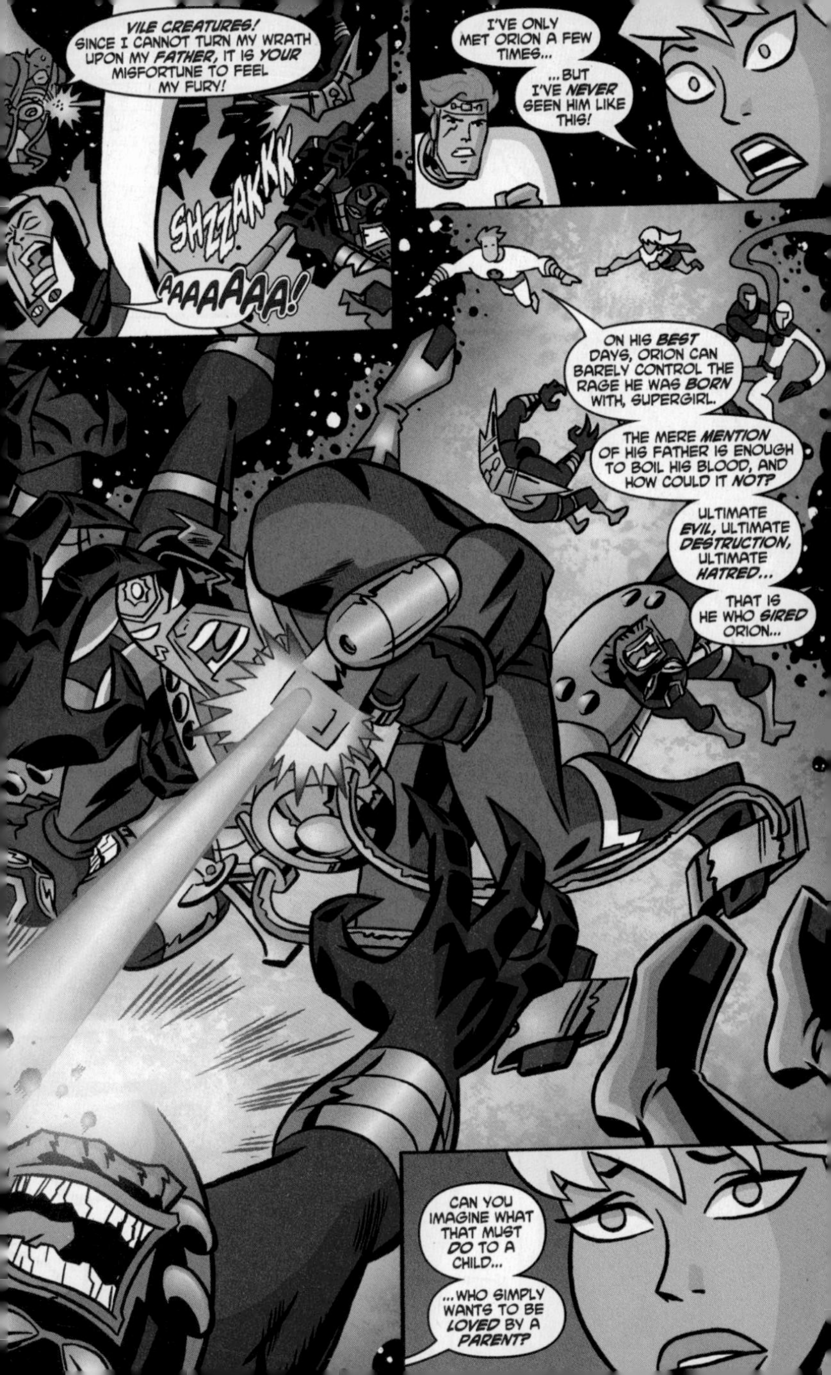
VILE CREATURES! SINCE I CANNOT TURN MY WRATH UPON MY FATHER, IT IS YOUR MISFORTUNE TO FEEL MY FURY!
SHZZAKKK
AAAAAAA!
I'VE ONLY MET ORION A FEW TIMES...
...BUT I'VE NEVER SEEN HIM LIKE THIS!
ON HIS BEST DAYS, ORION CAN BARELY CONTROL THE RAGE HE WAS BORN WITH, SUPERGIRL.
THE MERE MENTION OF HIS FATHER IS ENOUGH TO BOIL HIS BLOOD, AND HOW COULD IT NOT?
ULTIMATE EVIL, ULTIMATE DESTRUCTION, ULTIMATE HATRED...
THAT IS HE WHO SIRED ORION...
CAN YOU IMAGINE WHAT THAT MUST DO TO A CHILD...
...WHO SIMPLY WANTS TO BE LOVED BY A PARENT?

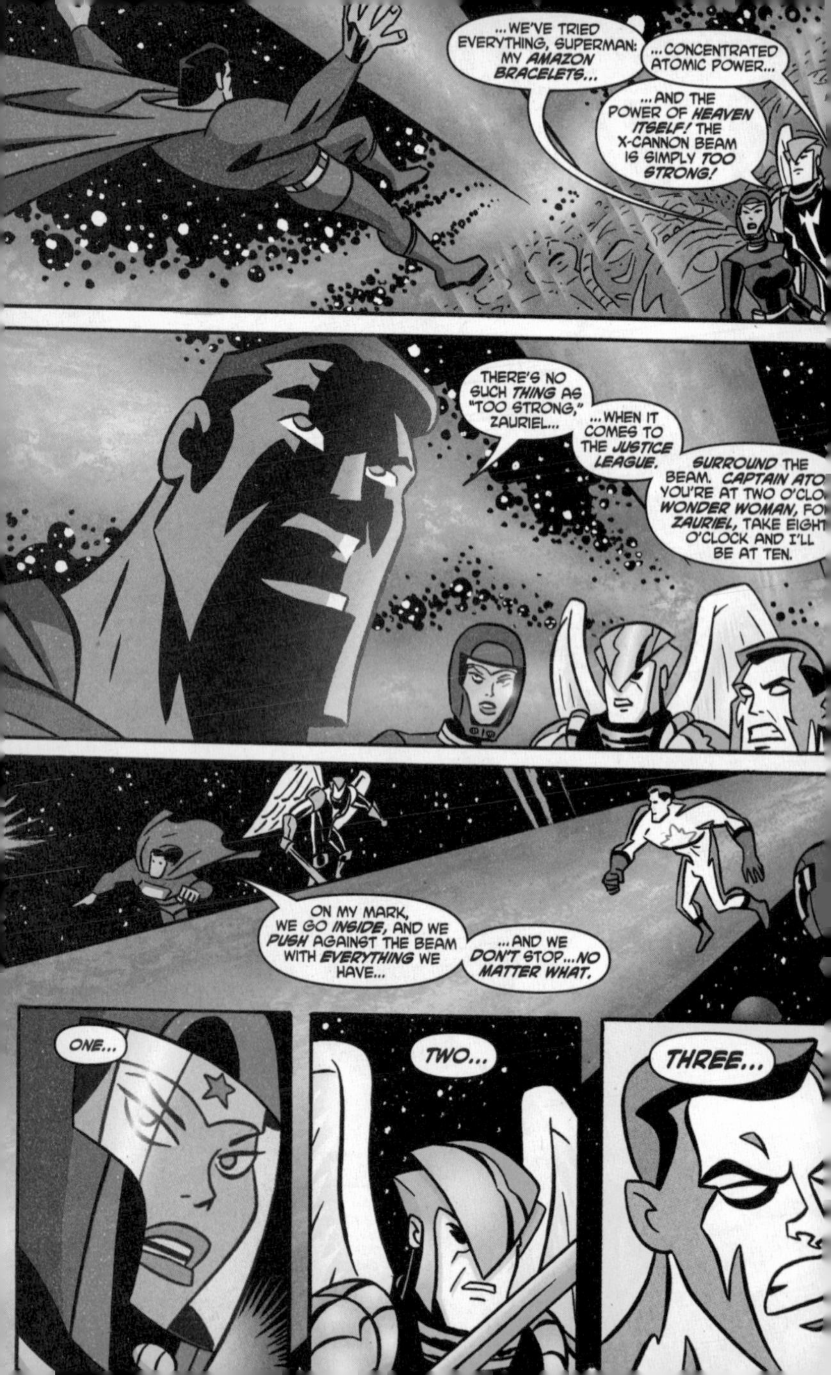
...WE'VE TRIED EVERYTHING, SUPERMAN: MY AMAZON BRACELETS...
...CONCENTRATED ATOMIC POWER...
...AND THE POWER OF HEAVEN ITSELF! THE X-CANNON BEAM IS SIMPLY TOO STRONG!
THERE'S NO SUCH THING AS "TOO STRONG," ZAURIEL...
...WHEN IT COMES TO THE JUSTICE LEAGUE.
SURROUND THE BEAM. CAPTAIN ATO YOU'RE AT TWO O'CLO WONDER WOMAN, FO ZAURIEL, TAKE EIGHT O'CLOCK AND I'LL BE AT TEN.
ON MY MARK, WE GO INSIDE, AND WE PUSH AGAINST THE BEAM WITH EVERYTHING WE HAVE...
...AND WE DON'T STOP...NO MATTER WHAT.
ONE...
TWO...
THREE...

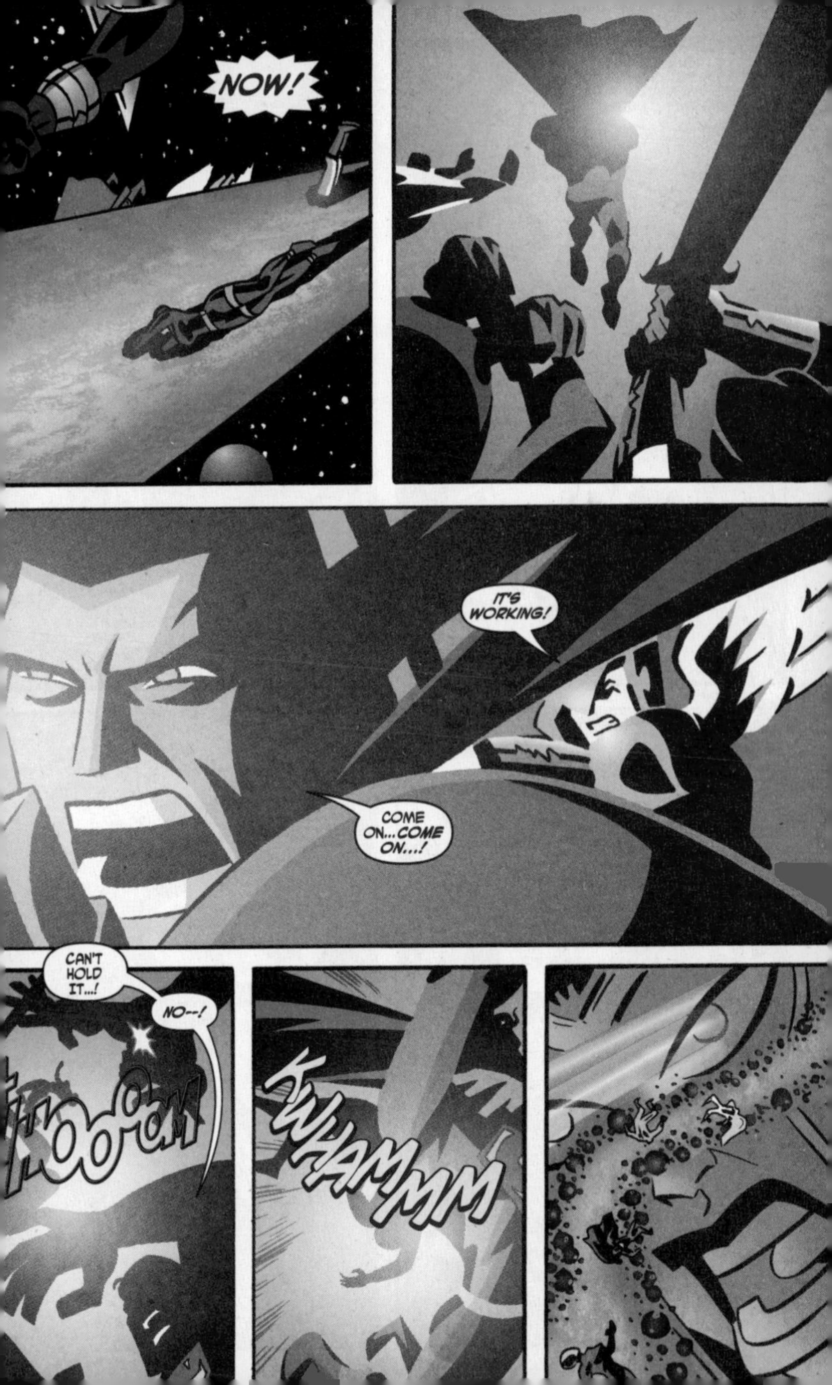
NOW!
IT'S WORKING!
COME ON...COME ON...!
CAN'T HOLD IT...!
NO--!
THOOOOM
KWHAMMMM

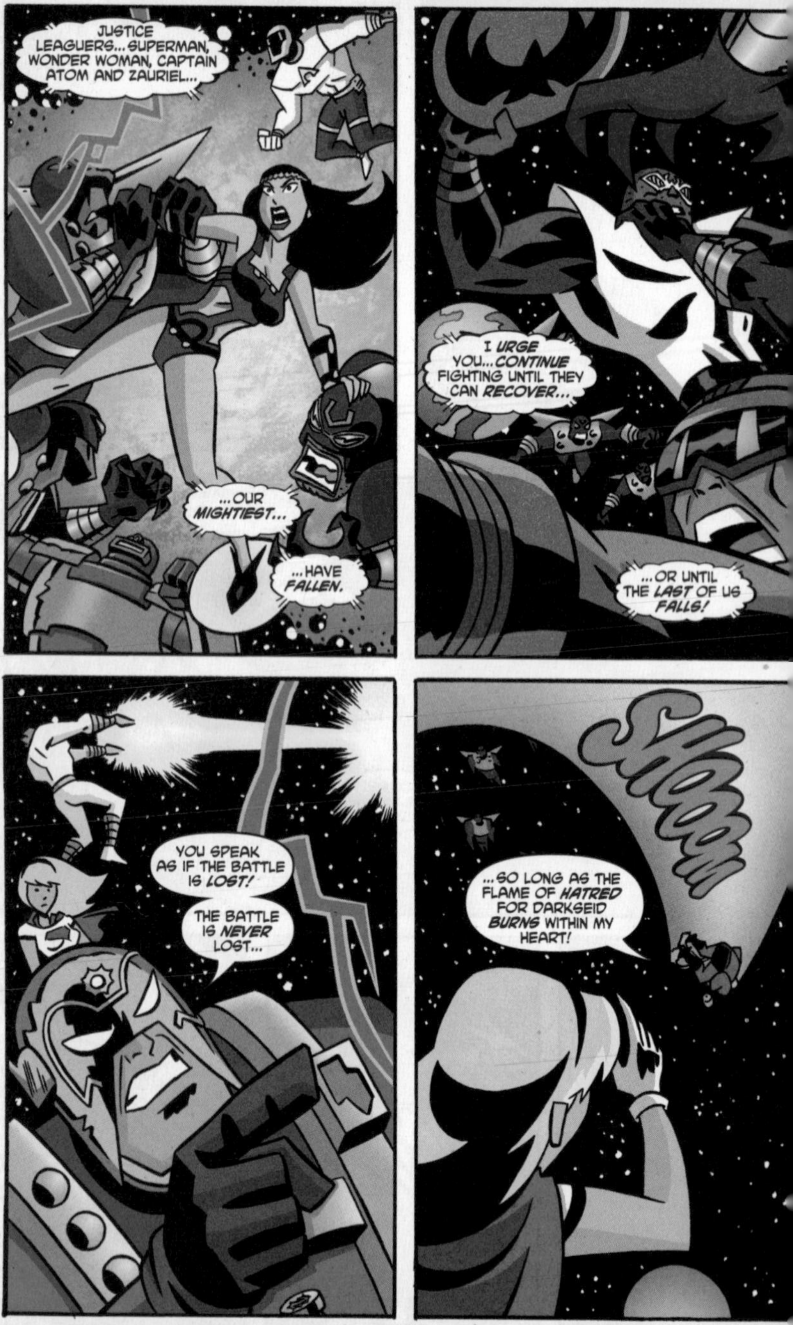
JUSTICE LEAGUERS... SUPERMAN, WONDER WOMAN, CAPTAIN ATOM AND ZAURIEL...
...OUR MIGHTIEST...
...HAVE FALLEN.
I URGE YOU... CONTINUE FIGHTING UNTIL THEY CAN RECOVER...
...OR UNTIL THE LAST OF US FALLS!
YOU SPEAK AS IF THE BATTLE IS LOST!
THE BATTLE IS NEVER LOST...
...SO LONG AS THE FLAME OF HATRED FOR DARKSEID BURNS WITHIN MY HEART!
SHOOM

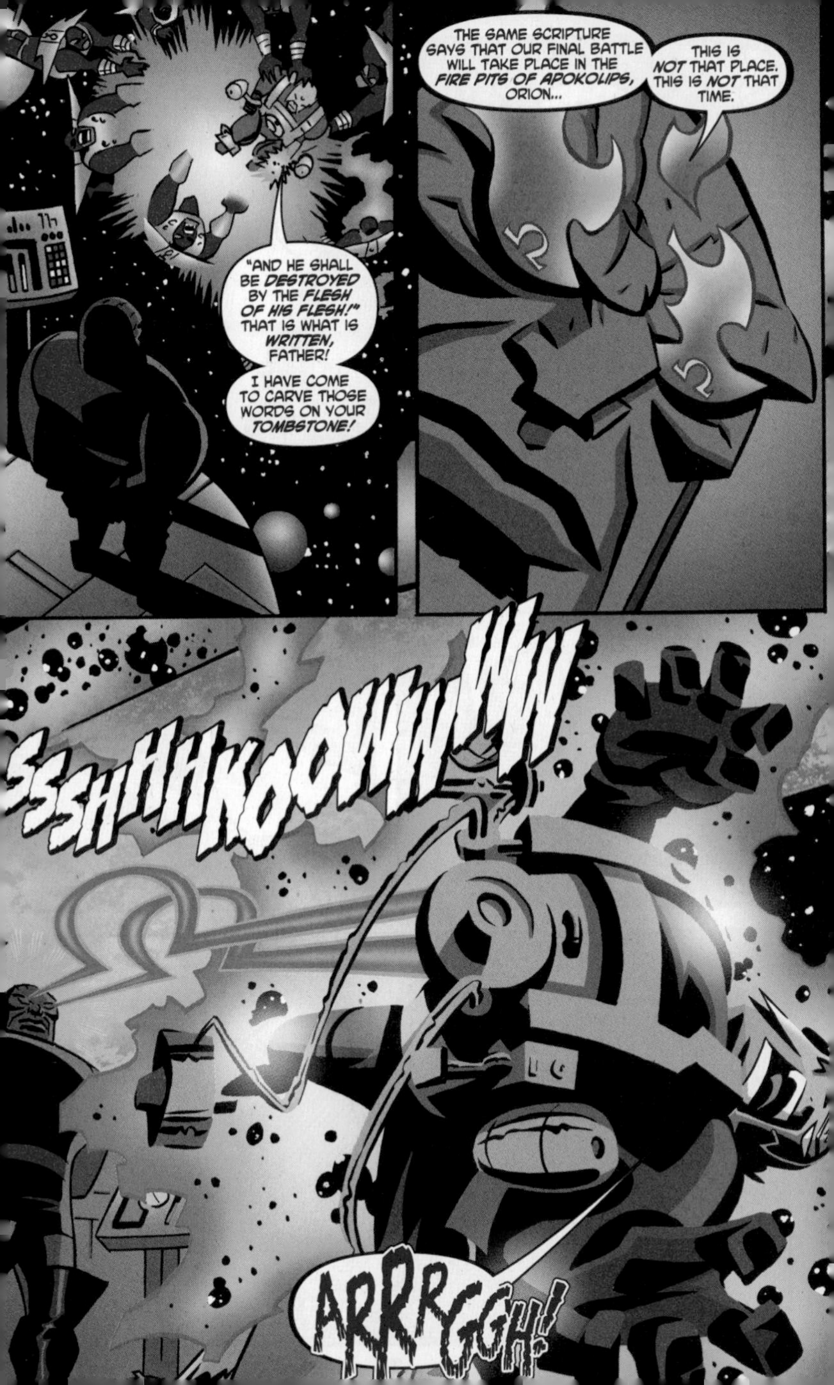

"AND HE SHALL BE *DESTROYED* BY THE *FLESH OF HIS FLESH!*" THAT IS WHAT IS *WRITTEN,* FATHER!
I HAVE COME TO CARVE THOSE WORDS ON YOUR *TOMBSTONE!*
THE SAME SCRIPTURE SAYS THAT OUR FINAL BATTLE WILL TAKE PLACE IN THE *FIRE PITS OF APOKOLIPS,* ORION...
THIS IS *NOT* THAT PLACE. THIS IS *NOT* THAT TIME.
SSSHHHKOOWWWWW
ARRRGGH!

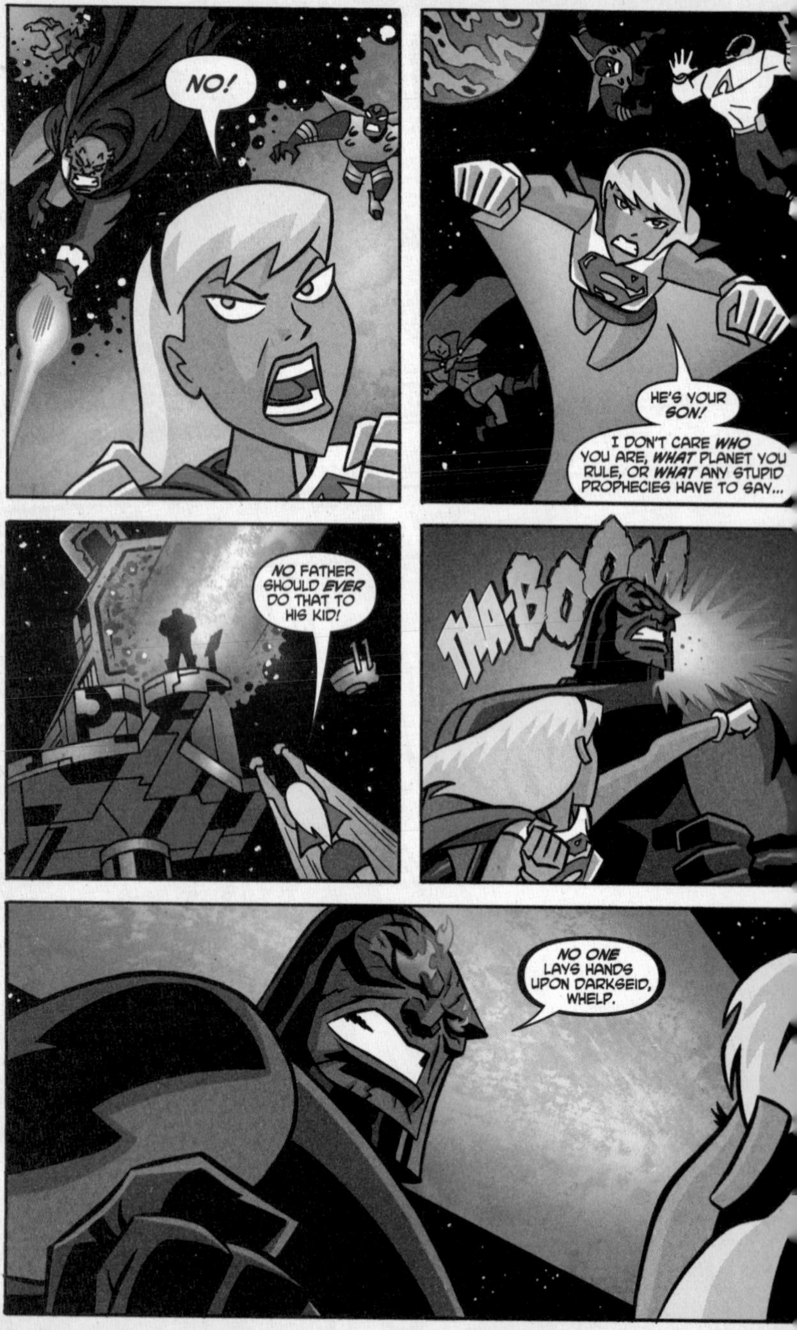

NO!
HE'S YOUR SON!
I DON'T CARE WHO YOU ARE, WHAT PLANET YOU RULE, OR WHAT ANY STUPID PROPHECIES HAVE TO SAY...
NO FATHER SHOULD EVER DO THAT TO HIS KID!
THA-BOOM
NO ONE LAYS HANDS UPON DARKSEID, WHELP.

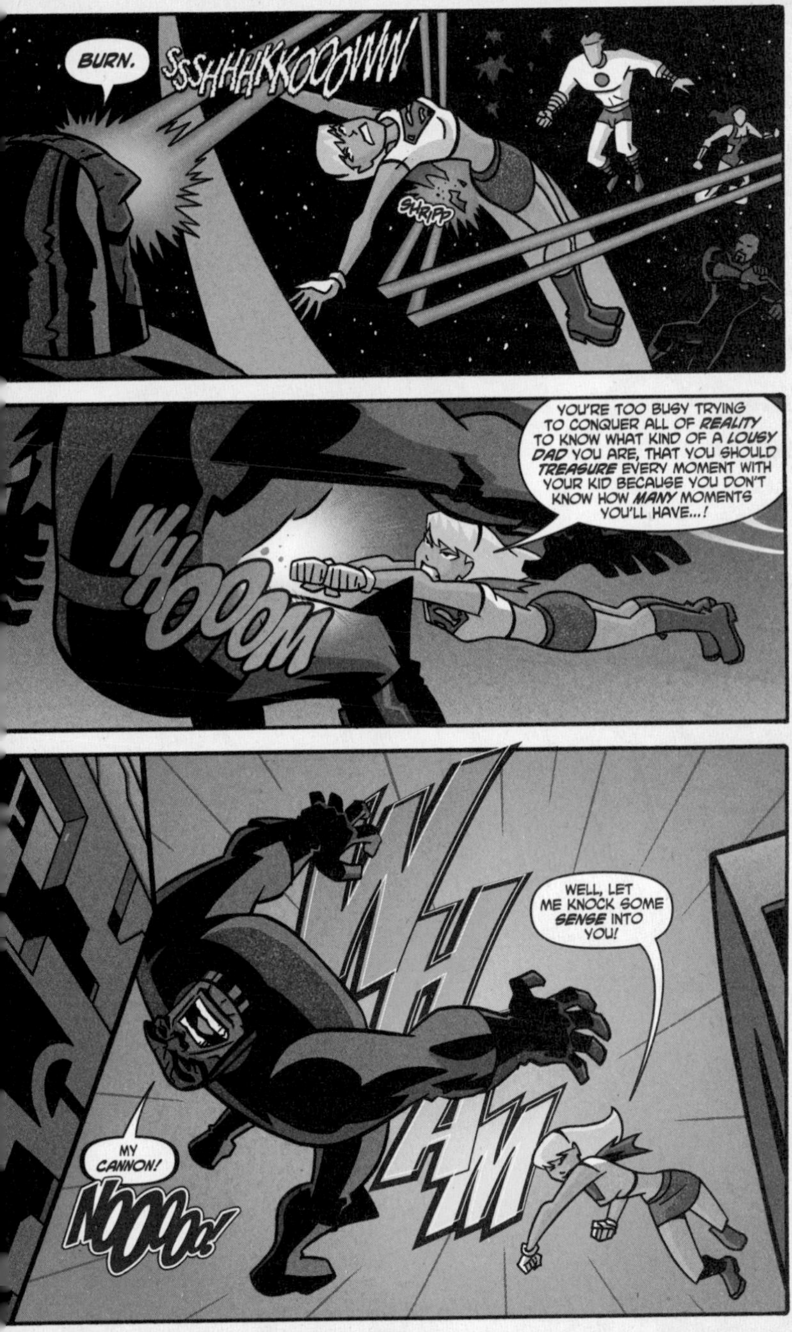
BURN.
SSSHHHKKOOOWW
SHRIPP
YOU'RE TOO BUSY TRYING TO CONQUER ALL OF *REALITY* TO KNOW WHAT KIND OF A *LOUSY DAD* YOU ARE, THAT YOU SHOULD *TREASURE* EVERY MOMENT WITH YOUR KID BECAUSE YOU DON'T KNOW HOW *MANY* MOMENTS YOU'LL HAVE...!
WHOOOM
WELL, LET ME KNOCK SOME *SENSE* INTO YOU!
MY *CANNON!*
NOOOOO!

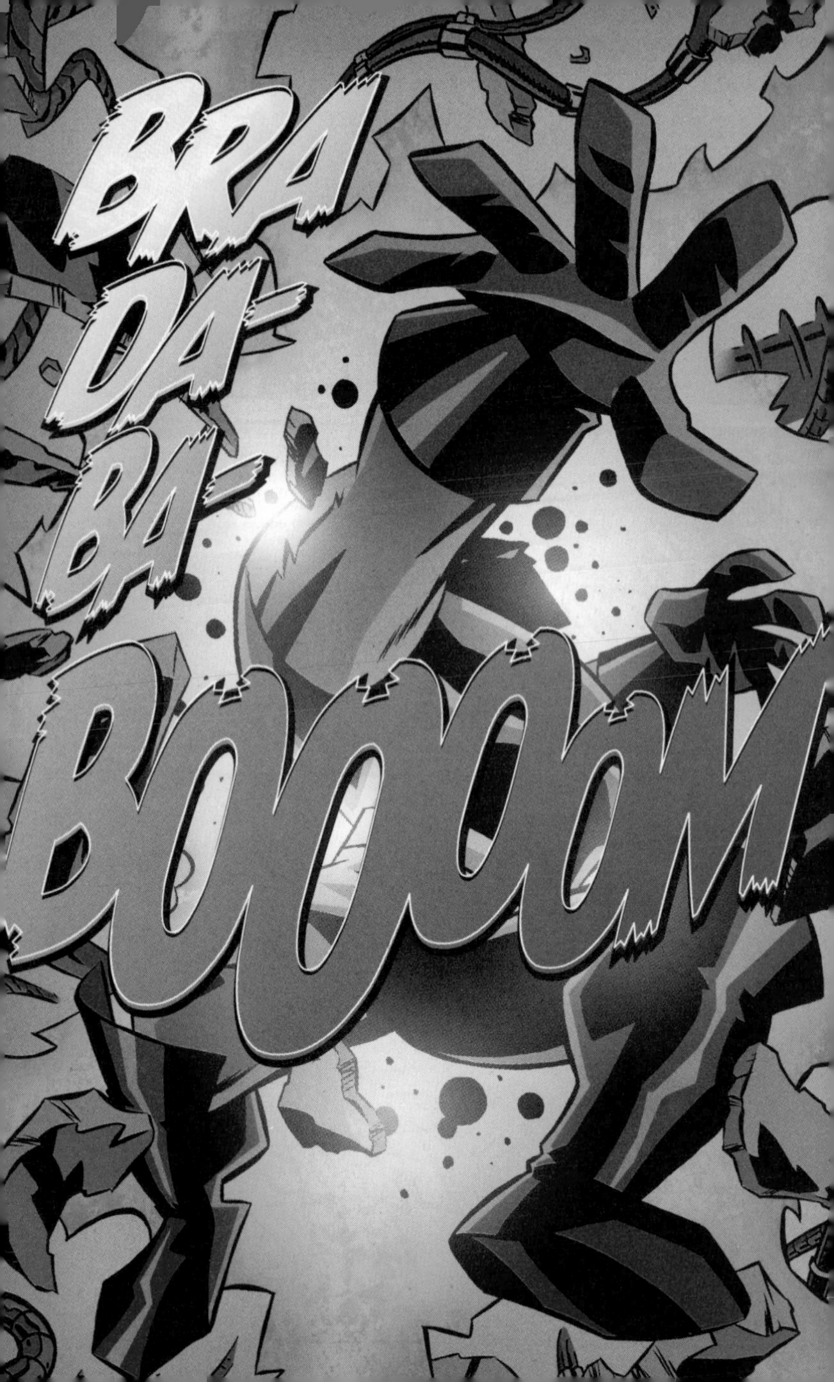
BRA
DA-
BA-
BOOOOM

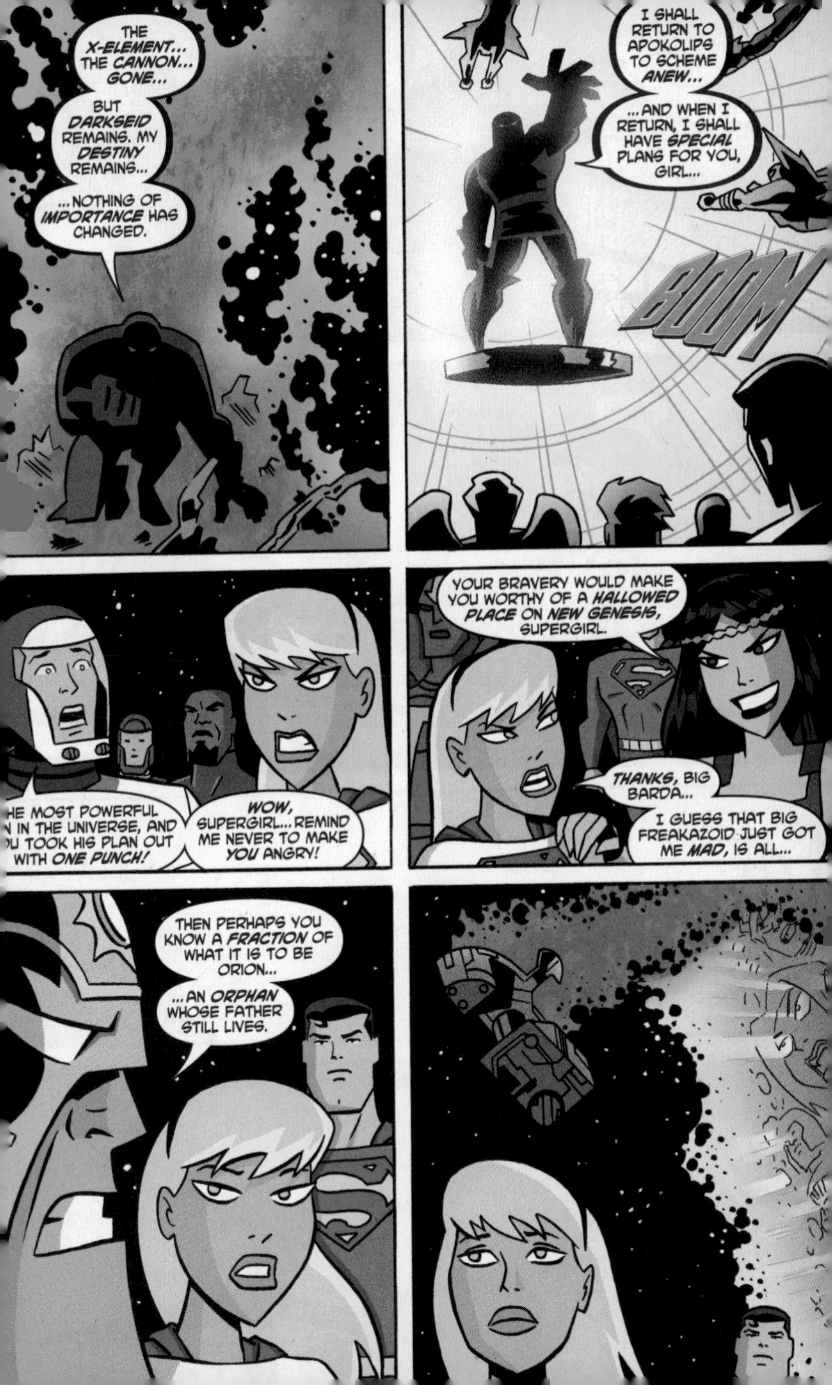
THE X-ELEMENT... THE CANNON... GONE...
BUT DARKSEID REMAINS. MY DESTINY REMAINS...
...NOTHING OF IMPORTANCE HAS CHANGED.
I SHALL RETURN TO APOKOLIPS TO SCHEME ANEW...
...AND WHEN I RETURN, I SHALL HAVE SPECIAL PLANS FOR YOU, GIRL...
BOOM
HE MOST POWERFUL N IN THE UNIVERSE, AND U TOOK HIS PLAN OUT WITH ONE PUNCH!
WOW, SUPERGIRL... REMIND ME NEVER TO MAKE YOU ANGRY!
YOUR BRAVERY WOULD MAKE YOU WORTHY OF A HALLOWED PLACE ON NEW GENESIS, SUPERGIRL.
THANKS, BIG BARDA...
I GUESS THAT BIG FREAKAZOID JUST GOT ME MAD, IS ALL...
THEN PERHAPS YOU KNOW A FRACTION OF WHAT IT IS TO BE ORION...
...AN ORPHAN WHOSE FATHER STILL LIVES.

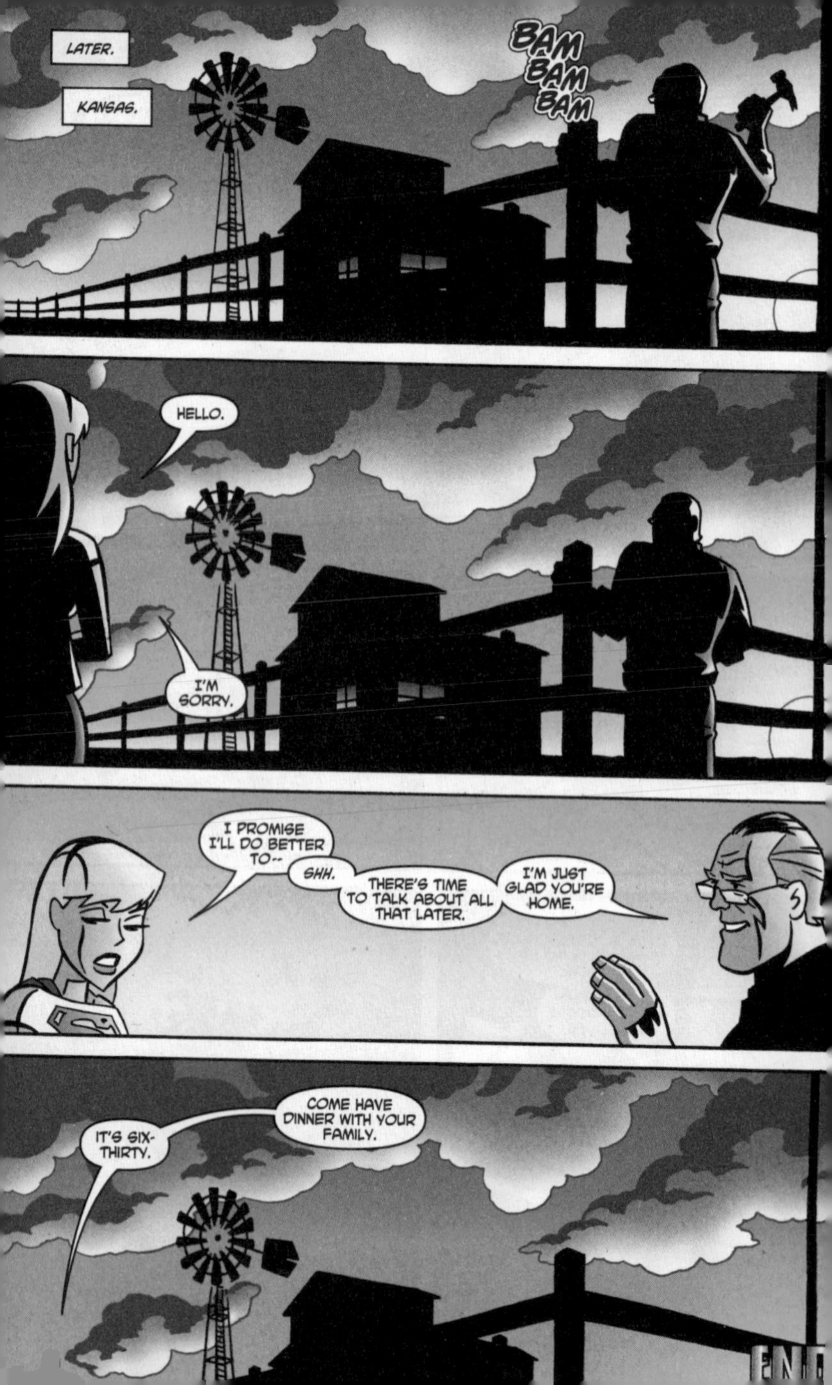
LATER.
KANSAS.
BAM BAM BAM
HELLO.
I'M SORRY.
I PROMISE I'LL DO BETTER TO--
SHH.
THERE'S TIME TO TALK ABOUT ALL THAT LATER.
I'M JUST GLAD YOU'RE HOME.
IT'S SIX-THIRTY.
COME HAVE DINNER WITH YOUR FAMILY.
END

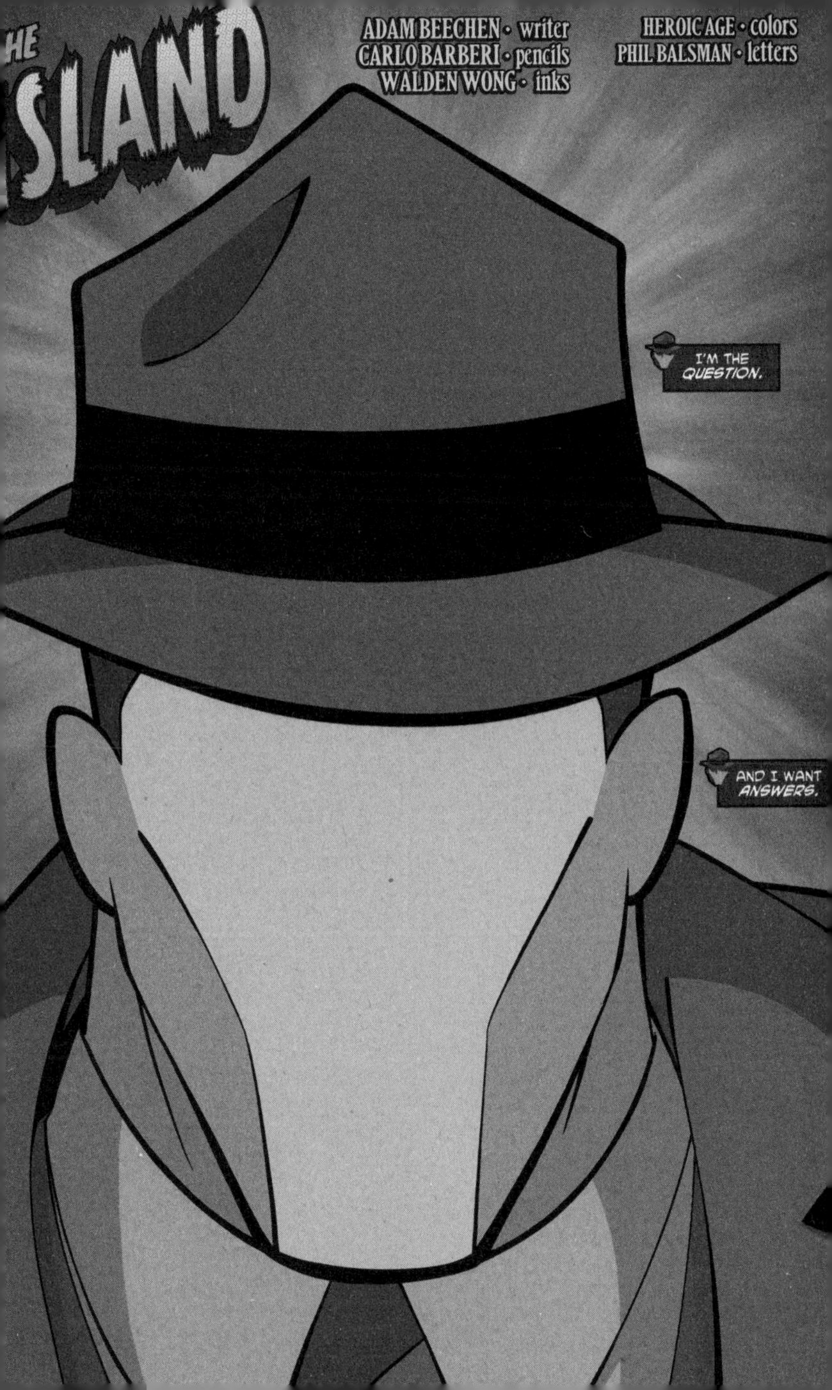
THE ISLAND
ADAM BEECHEN • writer
CARLO BARBERI • pencils
WALDEN WONG • inks
HEROIC AGE • colors
PHIL BALSMAN • letters
I'M THE QUESTION.
AND I WANT ANSWERS.

NORMALLY, I WORK *ALONE*, AND THAT'S THE WAY I *LIKE* IT. I WON'T *RELY* ON ANYONE, AND I DON'T *TRUST* ANYONE.

BUT WHEN THE *JUSTICE LEAGUE* ASKED ME TO JOIN THEIR RANKS, I *HAD* TO SAY YES...

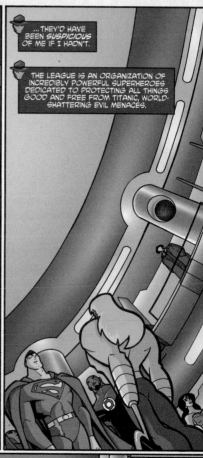

... THEY'D HAVE BEEN *SUSPICIOUS* OF ME IF I HADN'T.

THE LEAGUE IS AN ORGANIZATION OF INCREDIBLY POWERFUL SUPERHEROES DEDICATED TO PROTECTING ALL THINGS GOOD AND FREE FROM TITANIC, WORLD-SHATTERING EVIL MENACES.

THEY'RE *VERY GOOD* AT DEFEATING THE *BIG, OBVIOUS* THREATS...

... BUT SOMETIMES, THE *LITTLE DETAILS* CAN SLIP THROUGH THE CRACKS.

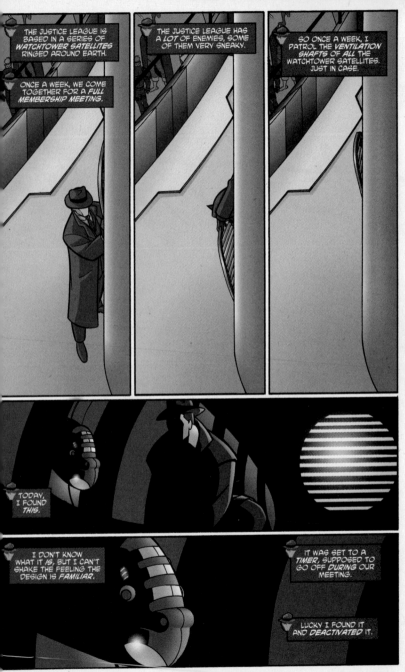

THE JUSTICE LEAGUE IS BASED IN A SERIES OF *WATCHTOWER SATELLITES* RINGED AROUND EARTH.

ONCE A WEEK, WE COME TOGETHER FOR A *FULL MEMBERSHIP MEETING.*

THE JUSTICE LEAGUE HAS A *LOT* OF ENEMIES, SOME OF THEM VERY SNEAKY.

SO ONCE A WEEK, I PATROL THE *VENTILATION SHAFTS* OF ALL THE WATCHTOWER SATELLITES. JUST IN CASE.

TODAY, I FOUND *THIS.*

I DON'T KNOW WHAT IT *IS,* BUT I CAN'T SHAKE THE FEELING THE DESIGN IS *FAMILIAR.*

IT WAS SET TO A *TIMER,* SUPPOSED TO GO OFF *DURING* OUR MEETING.

LUCKY I FOUND IT AND *DEACTIVATED* IT.

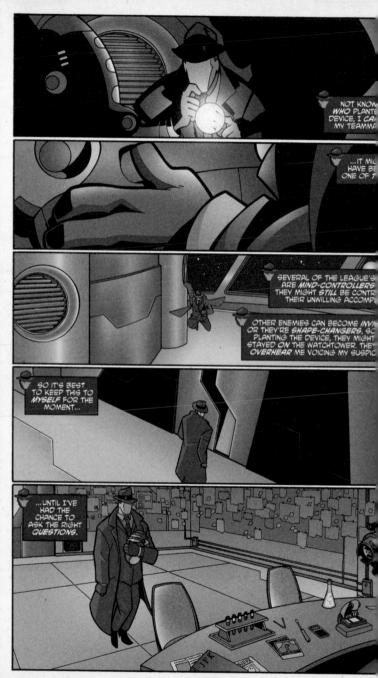

NOT KNOW
WHO PLANTE
DEVICE, I CA
MY TEAMMA

...IT MIG
HAVE BE
ONE OF T

SEVERAL OF THE LEAGUE'S
ARE *MIND-CONTROLLERS*
THEY MIGHT *STILL* BE CONTR
THEIR UNWILLING ACCOMPL

OTHER ENEMIES CAN BECOME *INVI*
OR THEY'RE *SHAPE-CHANGERS*, SO
PLANTING THE DEVICE, THEY MIGHT
STAYED *ON* THE WATCHTOWER. THEY
OVERHEAR ME VOICING MY SUSPIC

SO IT'S BEST
TO KEEP THIS TO
MYSELF FOR THE
MOMENT...

...UNTIL I'VE
HAD THE
CHANCE TO
ASK THE RIGHT
QUESTIONS.

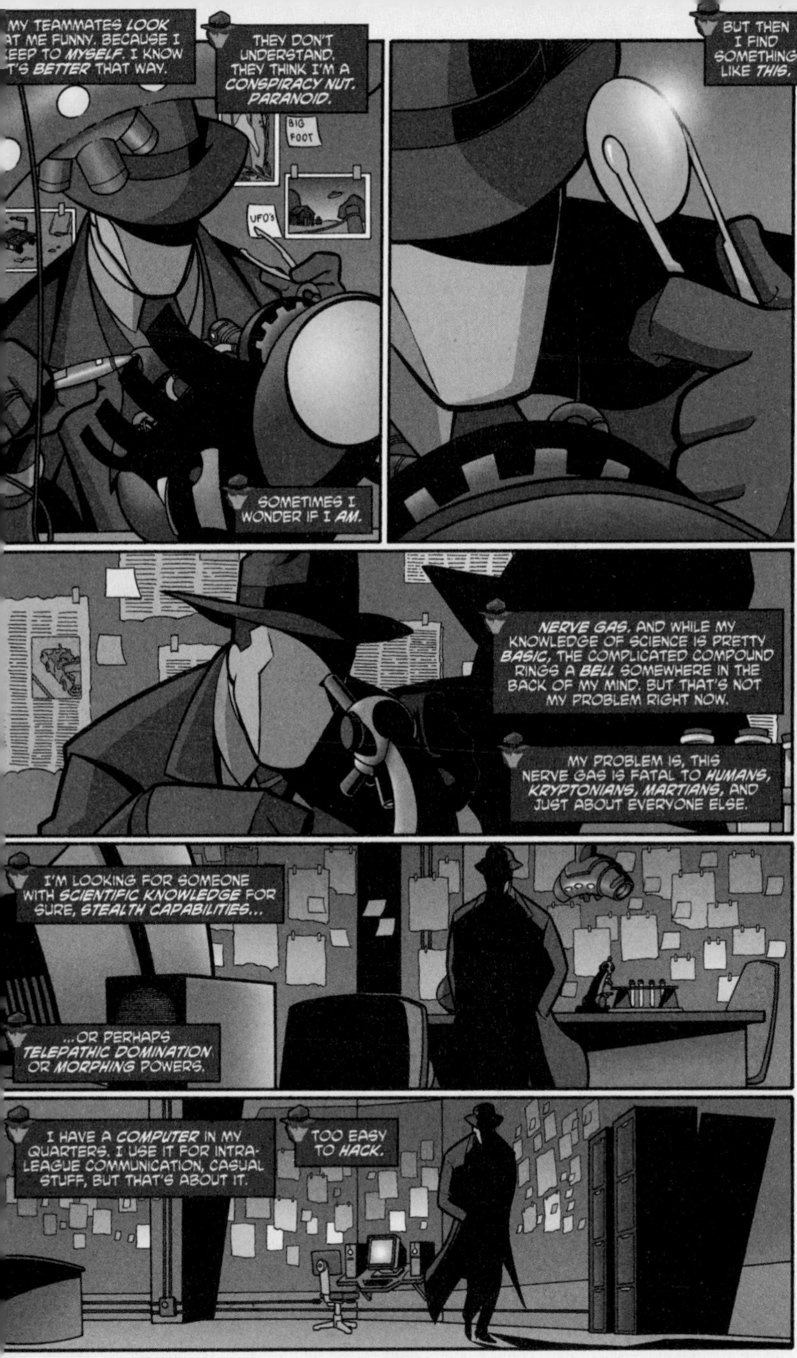
MY TEAMMATES LOOK AT ME FUNNY. BECAUSE I KEEP TO MYSELF. I KNOW IT'S BETTER THAT WAY.
THEY DON'T UNDERSTAND. THEY THINK I'M A CONSPIRACY NUT. PARANOID.
BIG FOOT
UFO's
SOMETIMES I WONDER IF I AM.
BUT THEN I FIND SOMETHING LIKE THIS.
NERVE GAS. AND WHILE MY KNOWLEDGE OF SCIENCE IS PRETTY BASIC, THE COMPLICATED COMPOUND RINGS A BELL SOMEWHERE IN THE BACK OF MY MIND. BUT THAT'S NOT MY PROBLEM RIGHT NOW.
MY PROBLEM IS, THIS NERVE GAS IS FATAL TO HUMANS, KRYPTONIANS, MARTIANS, AND JUST ABOUT EVERYONE ELSE.
I'M LOOKING FOR SOMEONE WITH SCIENTIFIC KNOWLEDGE FOR SURE, STEALTH CAPABILITIES...
...OR PERHAPS TELEPATHIC DOMINATION OR MORPHING POWERS.
I HAVE A COMPUTER IN MY QUARTERS. I USE IT FOR INTRA-LEAGUE COMMUNICATION, CASUAL STUFF, BUT THAT'S ABOUT IT.
TOO EASY TO HACK.

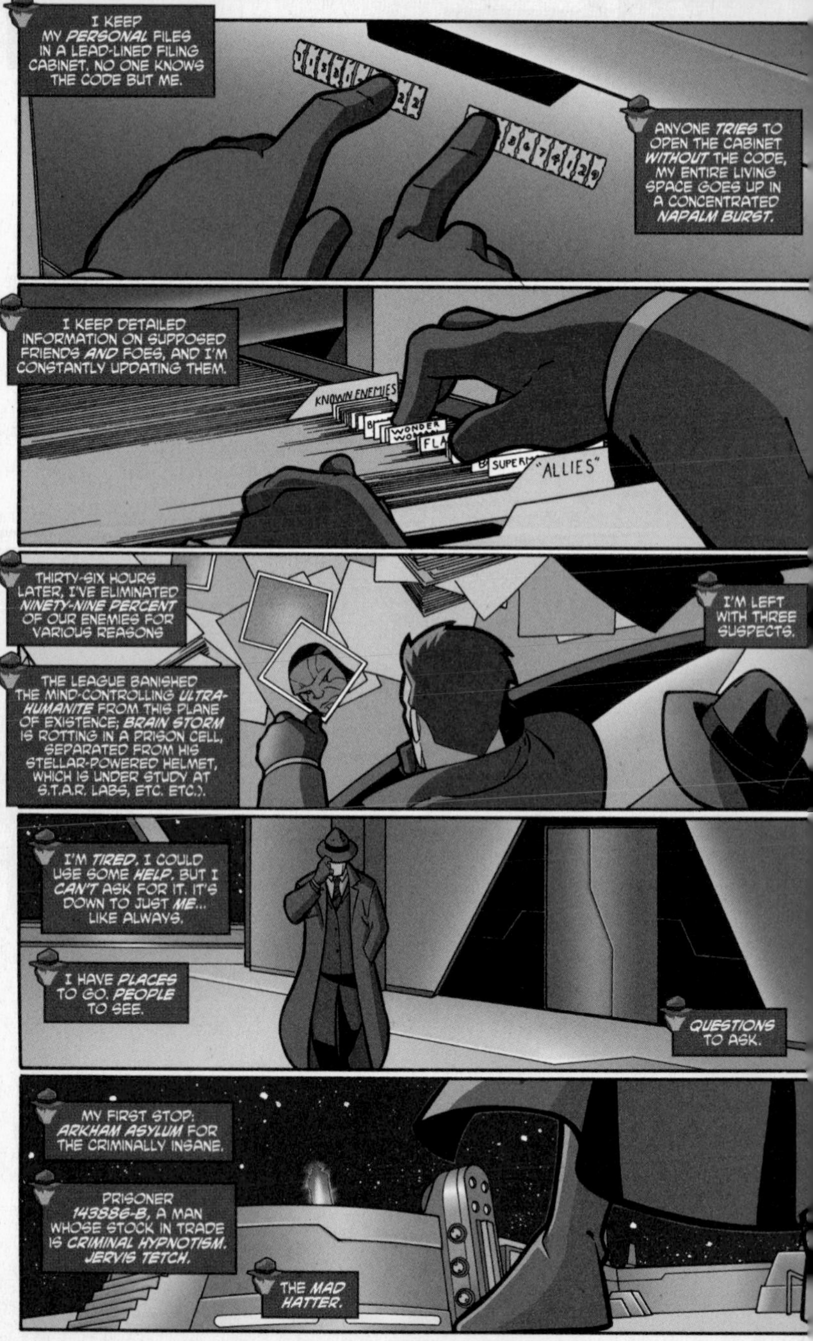
I KEEP MY PERSONAL FILES IN A LEAD-LINED FILING CABINET. NO ONE KNOWS THE CODE BUT ME.
ANYONE TRIES TO OPEN THE CABINET WITHOUT THE CODE, MY ENTIRE LIVING SPACE GOES UP IN A CONCENTRATED NAPALM BURST.
I KEEP DETAILED INFORMATION ON SUPPOSED FRIENDS AND FOES, AND I'M CONSTANTLY UPDATING THEM.
KNOWN ENEMIES
WONDER WO
FLA
SUPERM
"ALLIES"
THIRTY-SIX HOURS LATER, I'VE ELIMINATED NINETY-NINE PERCENT OF OUR ENEMIES FOR VARIOUS REASONS
THE LEAGUE BANISHED THE MIND-CONTROLLING ULTRA-HUMANITE FROM THIS PLANE OF EXISTENCE; BRAIN STORM IS ROTTING IN A PRISON CELL, SEPARATED FROM HIS STELLAR-POWERED HELMET, WHICH IS UNDER STUDY AT S.T.A.R. LABS, ETC. ETC.).
I'M LEFT WITH THREE SUSPECTS.
I'M TIRED. I COULD USE SOME HELP. BUT I CAN'T ASK FOR IT. IT'S DOWN TO JUST ME... LIKE ALWAYS.
I HAVE PLACES TO GO. PEOPLE TO SEE.
QUESTIONS TO ASK.
MY FIRST STOP: ARKHAM ASYLUM FOR THE CRIMINALLY INSANE.
PRISONER 143886-B, A MAN WHOSE STOCK IN TRADE IS CRIMINAL HYPNOTISM. JERVIS TETCH.
THE MAD HATTER.

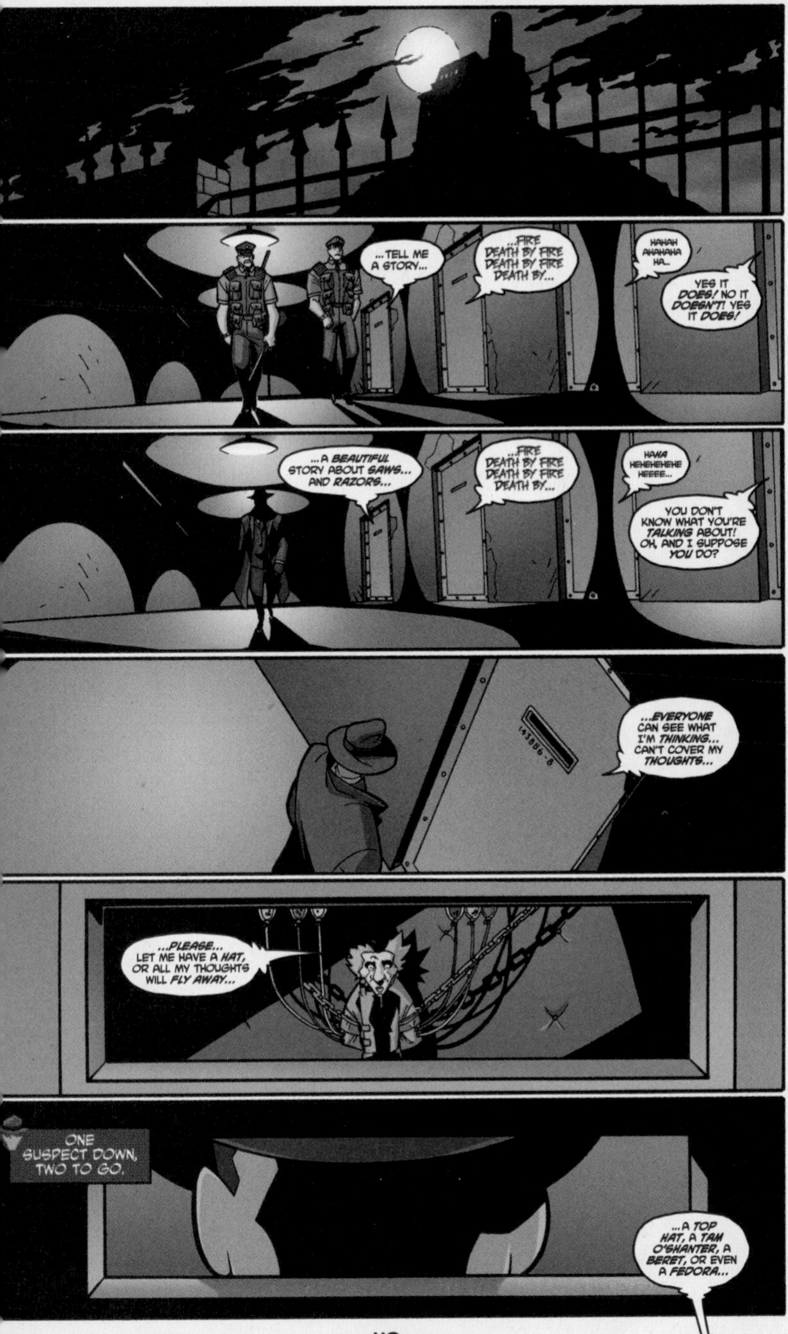
...TELL ME A STORY...
...FIRE DEATH BY FIRE DEATH BY FIRE DEATH BY...
HAHAH AHAHAHA HA...
YES IT DOES! NO IT DOESN'T! YES IT DOES!
...A BEAUTIFUL STORY ABOUT SAWS... AND RAZORS...
...FIRE DEATH BY FIRE DEATH BY FIRE DEATH BY...
HAHA HEHEHEHEHE HEEEE...
YOU DON'T KNOW WHAT YOU'RE TALKING ABOUT! OH, AND I SUPPOSE YOU DO?
...EVERYONE CAN SEE WHAT I'M THINKING... CAN'T COVER MY THOUGHTS...
...PLEASE... LET ME HAVE A HAT, OR ALL MY THOUGHTS WILL FLY AWAY...
ONE SUSPECT DOWN, TWO TO GO.
...A TOP HAT, A TAM O'SHANTER, A BERET, OR EVEN A FEDORA...

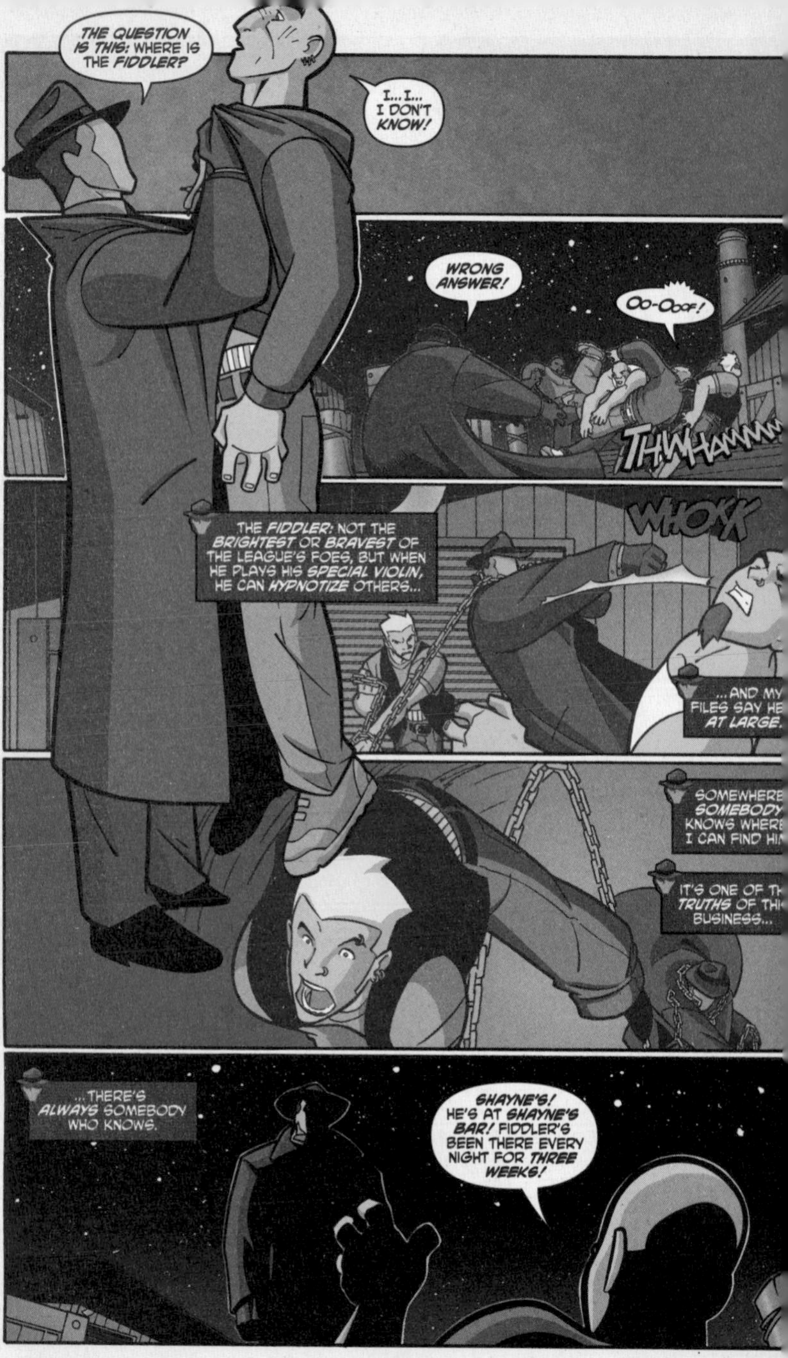
THE QUESTION IS THIS: WHERE IS THE FIDDLER?
I... I... I DON'T KNOW!
WRONG ANSWER!
OO-OOOF!
THWHAMMM
WHOKK
THE FIDDLER: NOT THE BRIGHTEST OR BRAVEST OF THE LEAGUE'S FOES, BUT WHEN HE PLAYS HIS SPECIAL VIOLIN, HE CAN HYPNOTIZE OTHERS...
...AND MY FILES SAY HE AT LARGE.
SOMEWHERE SOMEBODY KNOWS WHERE I CAN FIND HI
IT'S ONE OF TH TRUTHS OF THI BUSINESS...
...THERE'S ALWAYS SOMEBODY WHO KNOWS.
SHAYNE'S! HE'S AT SHAYNE'S BAR! FIDDLER'S BEEN THERE EVERY NIGHT FOR THREE WEEKS!

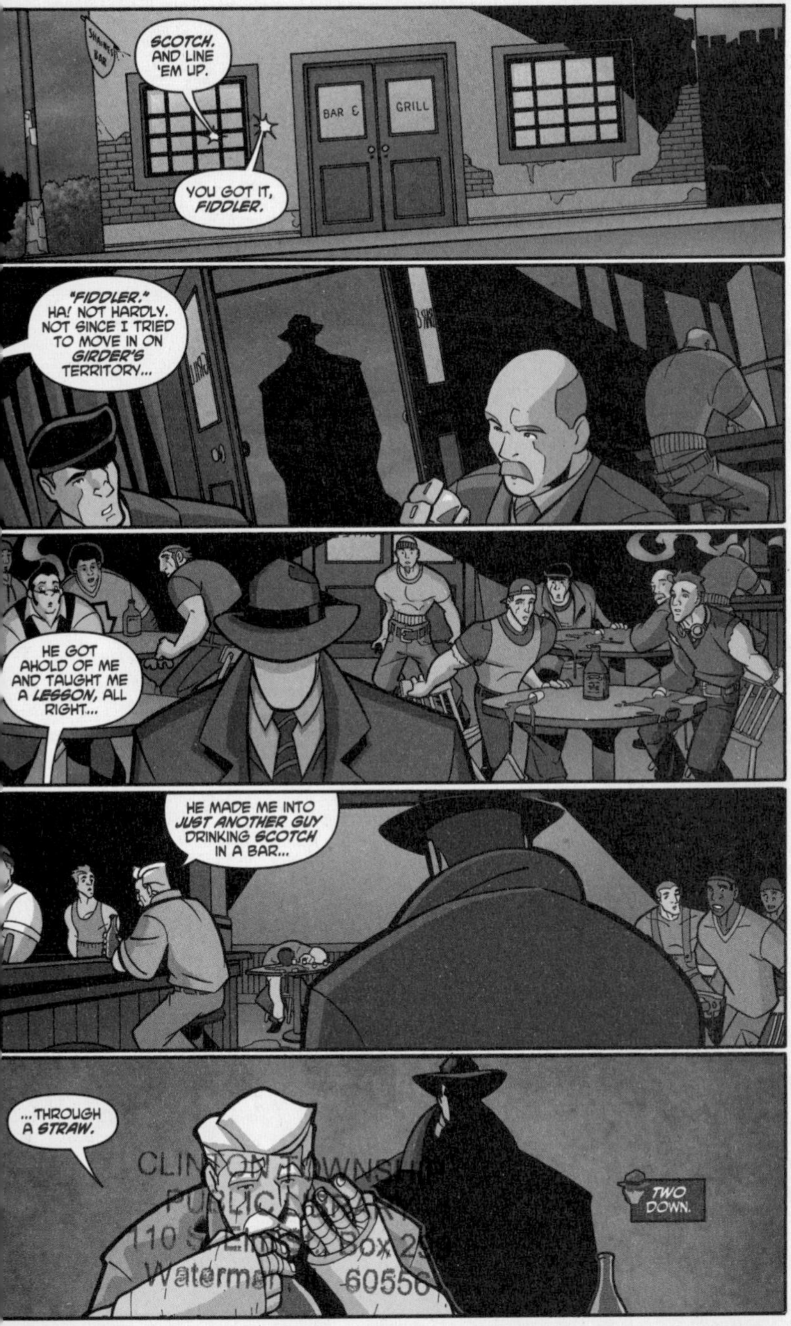
SCOTCH. AND LINE 'EM UP.
BAR & GRILL
YOU GOT IT, FIDDLER.
"FIDDLER." HA! NOT HARDLY. NOT SINCE I TRIED TO MOVE IN ON GIRDER'S TERRITORY...
HE GOT AHOLD OF ME AND TAUGHT ME A LESSON, ALL RIGHT...
HE MADE ME INTO JUST ANOTHER GUY DRINKING SCOTCH IN A BAR...
...THROUGH A STRAW.
TWO DOWN.

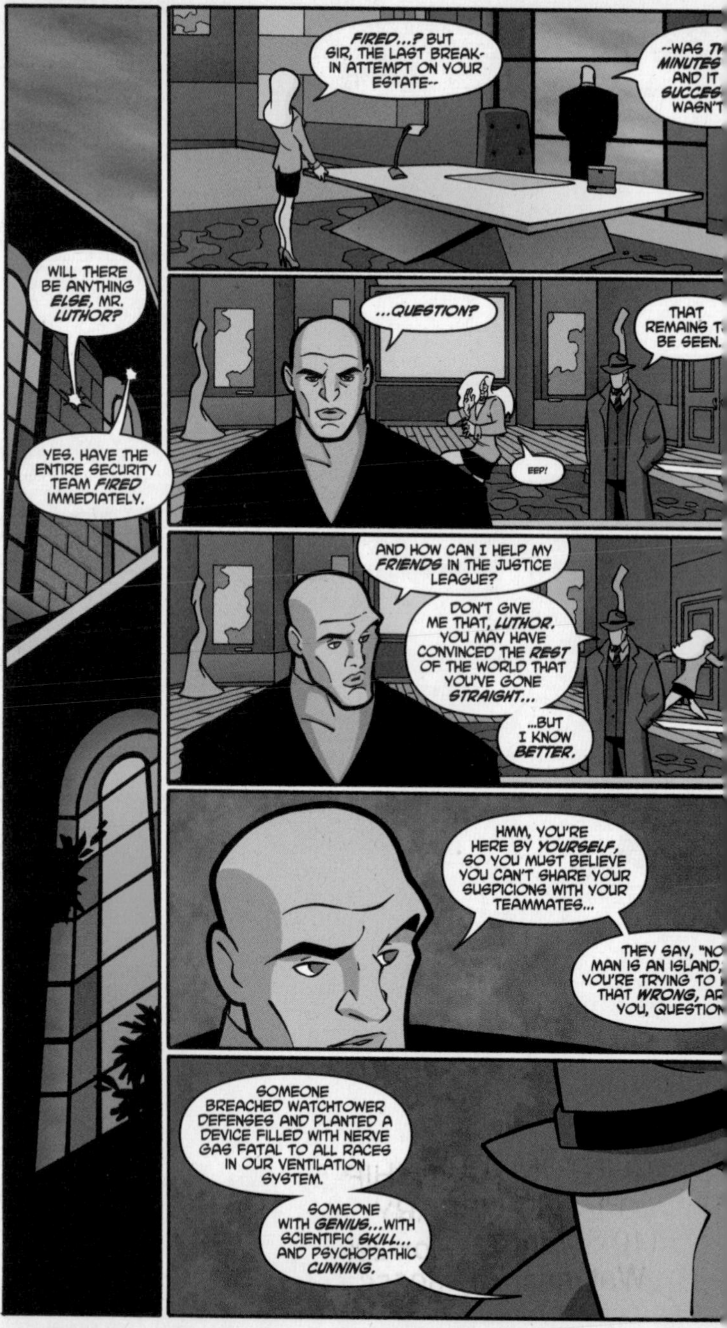

WILL THERE BE ANYTHING ELSE, MR. LUTHOR?
YES. HAVE THE ENTIRE SECURITY TEAM FIRED IMMEDIATELY.
FIRED...? BUT SIR, THE LAST BREAK-IN ATTEMPT ON YOUR ESTATE--
--WAS T MINUTES AND IT SUCCES WASN'T
...QUESTION?
THAT REMAINS T BE SEEN.
EEP!
AND HOW CAN I HELP MY FRIENDS IN THE JUSTICE LEAGUE?
DON'T GIVE ME THAT, LUTHOR. YOU MAY HAVE CONVINCED THE REST OF THE WORLD THAT YOU'VE GONE STRAIGHT...
...BUT I KNOW BETTER.
HMM, YOU'RE HERE BY YOURSELF, SO YOU MUST BELIEVE YOU CAN'T SHARE YOUR SUSPICIONS WITH YOUR TEAMMATES...
THEY SAY, "NO MAN IS AN ISLAND, YOU'RE TRYING TO THAT WRONG, AR YOU, QUESTION
SOMEONE BREACHED WATCHTOWER DEFENSES AND PLANTED A DEVICE FILLED WITH NERVE GAS FATAL TO ALL RACES IN OUR VENTILATION SYSTEM.
SOMEONE WITH GENIUS...WITH SCIENTIFIC SKILL... AND PSYCHOPATHIC CUNNING.

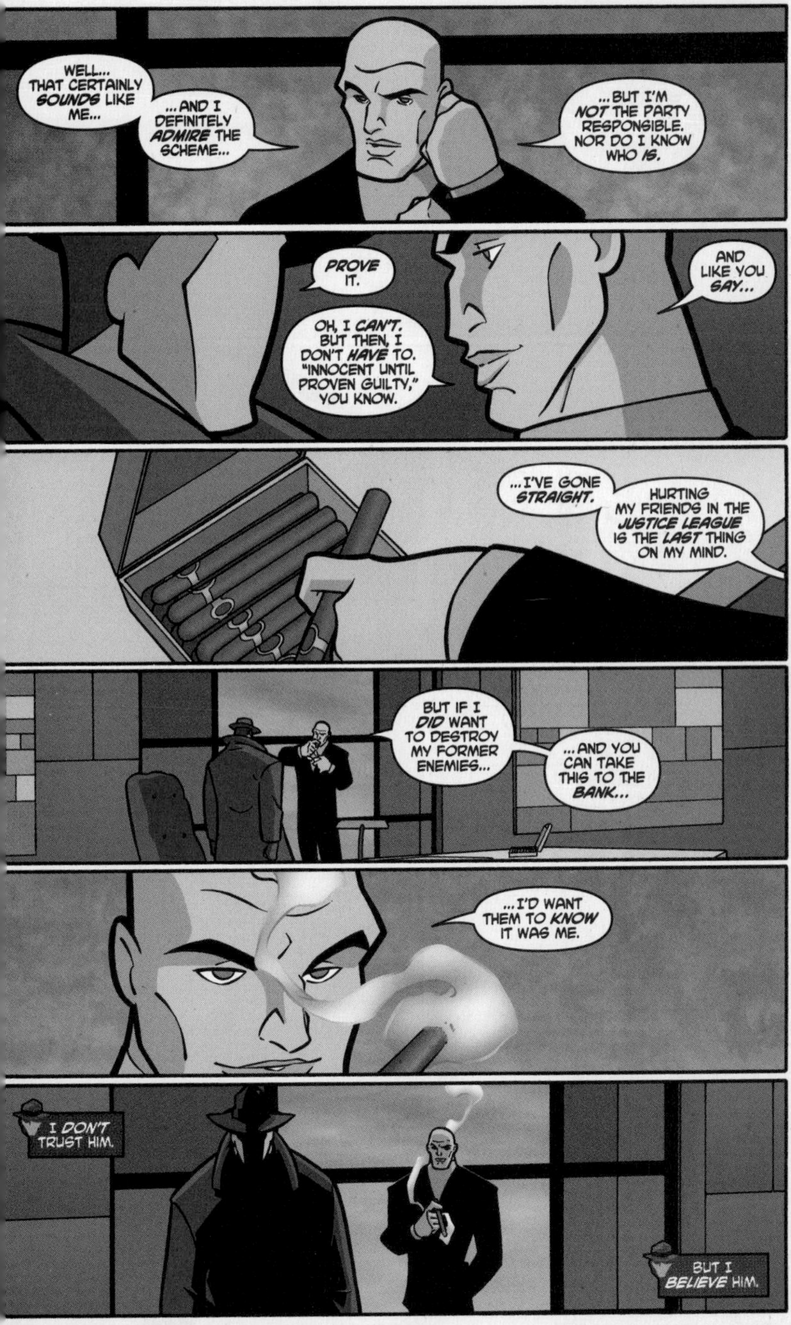
WELL... THAT CERTAINLY SOUNDS LIKE ME...
...AND I DEFINITELY ADMIRE THE SCHEME...
...BUT I'M NOT THE PARTY RESPONSIBLE. NOR DO I KNOW WHO IS.
PROVE IT.
OH, I CAN'T. BUT THEN, I DON'T HAVE TO. "INNOCENT UNTIL PROVEN GUILTY," YOU KNOW.
AND LIKE YOU SAY...
...I'VE GONE STRAIGHT.
HURTING MY FRIENDS IN THE JUSTICE LEAGUE IS THE LAST THING ON MY MIND.
BUT IF I DID WANT TO DESTROY MY FORMER ENEMIES...
...AND YOU CAN TAKE THIS TO THE BANK...
...I'D WANT THEM TO KNOW IT WAS ME.
I DON'T TRUST HIM.
BUT I BELIEVE HIM.

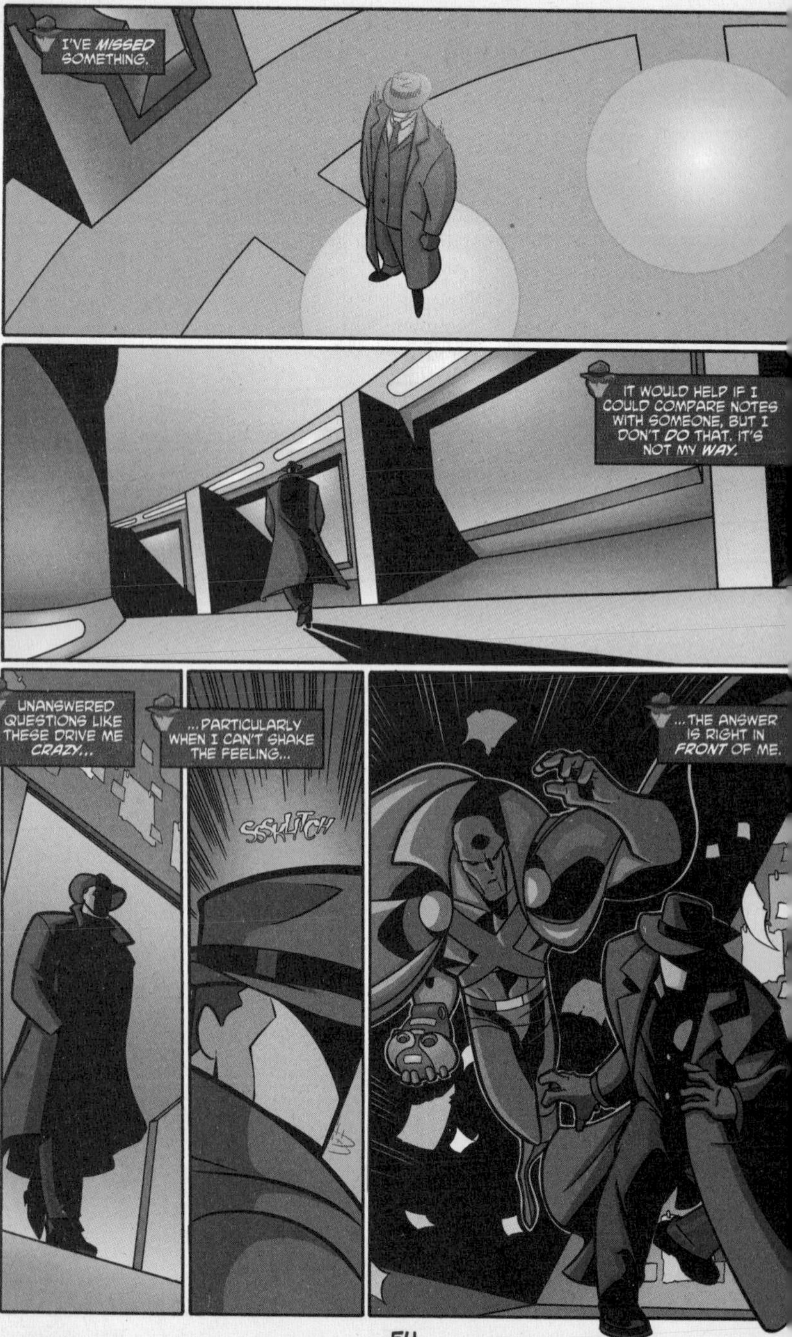
I'VE MISSED SOMETHING.
IT WOULD HELP IF I COULD COMPARE NOTES WITH SOMEONE, BUT I DON'T DO THAT. IT'S NOT MY WAY.
UNANSWERED QUESTIONS LIKE THESE DRIVE ME CRAZY...
...PARTICULARLY WHEN I CAN'T SHAKE THE FEELING...
SSKLITCH
...THE ANSWER IS RIGHT IN FRONT OF ME.

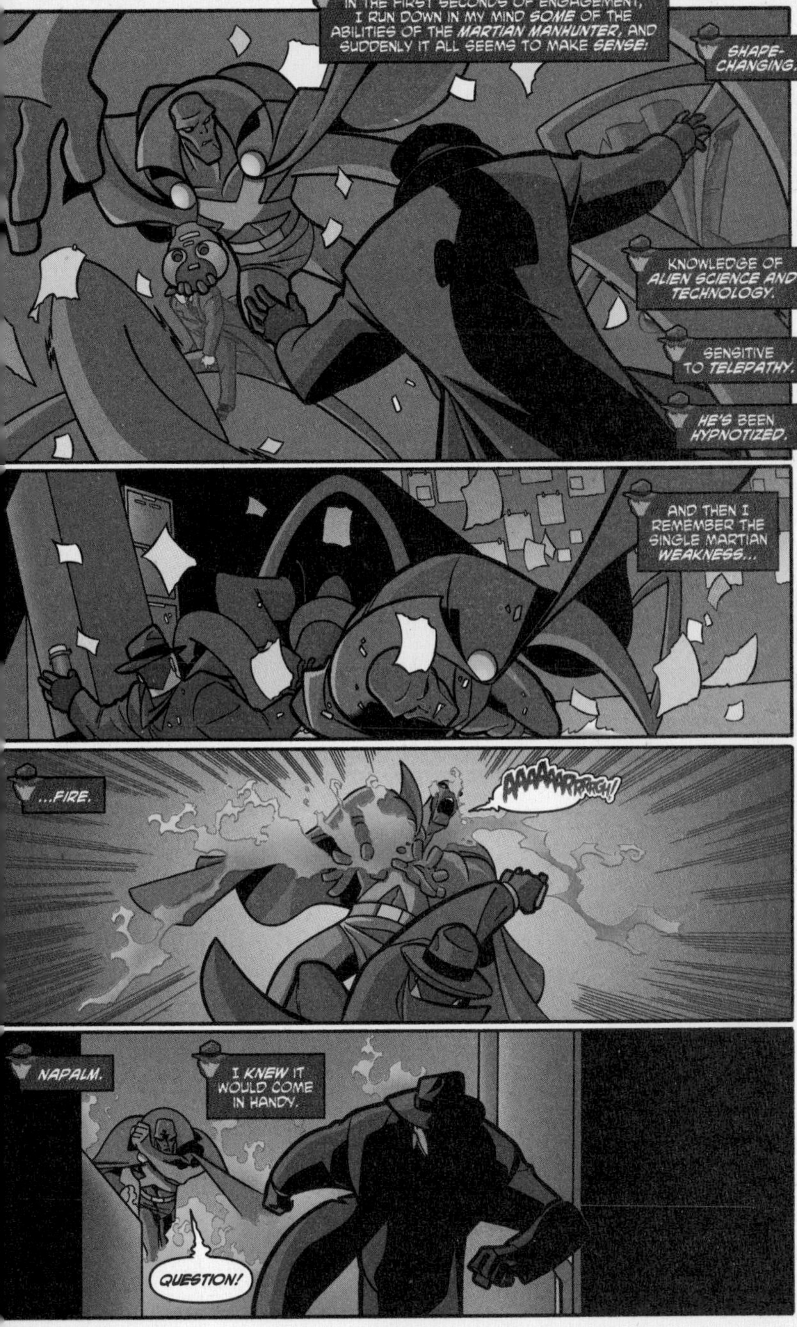
IN THE FIRST SECONDS OF ENGAGEMENT, I RUN DOWN IN MY MIND SOME OF THE ABILITIES OF THE MARTIAN MANHUNTER, AND SUDDENLY IT ALL SEEMS TO MAKE SENSE:
SHAPE-CHANGING.
KNOWLEDGE OF ALIEN SCIENCE AND TECHNOLOGY.
SENSITIVE TO TELEPATHY.
HE'S BEEN HYPNOTIZED.
AND THEN I REMEMBER THE SINGLE MARTIAN WEAKNESS...
...FIRE.
AAAAAARRRRGH!
NAPALM.
I KNEW IT WOULD COME IN HANDY.
QUESTION!

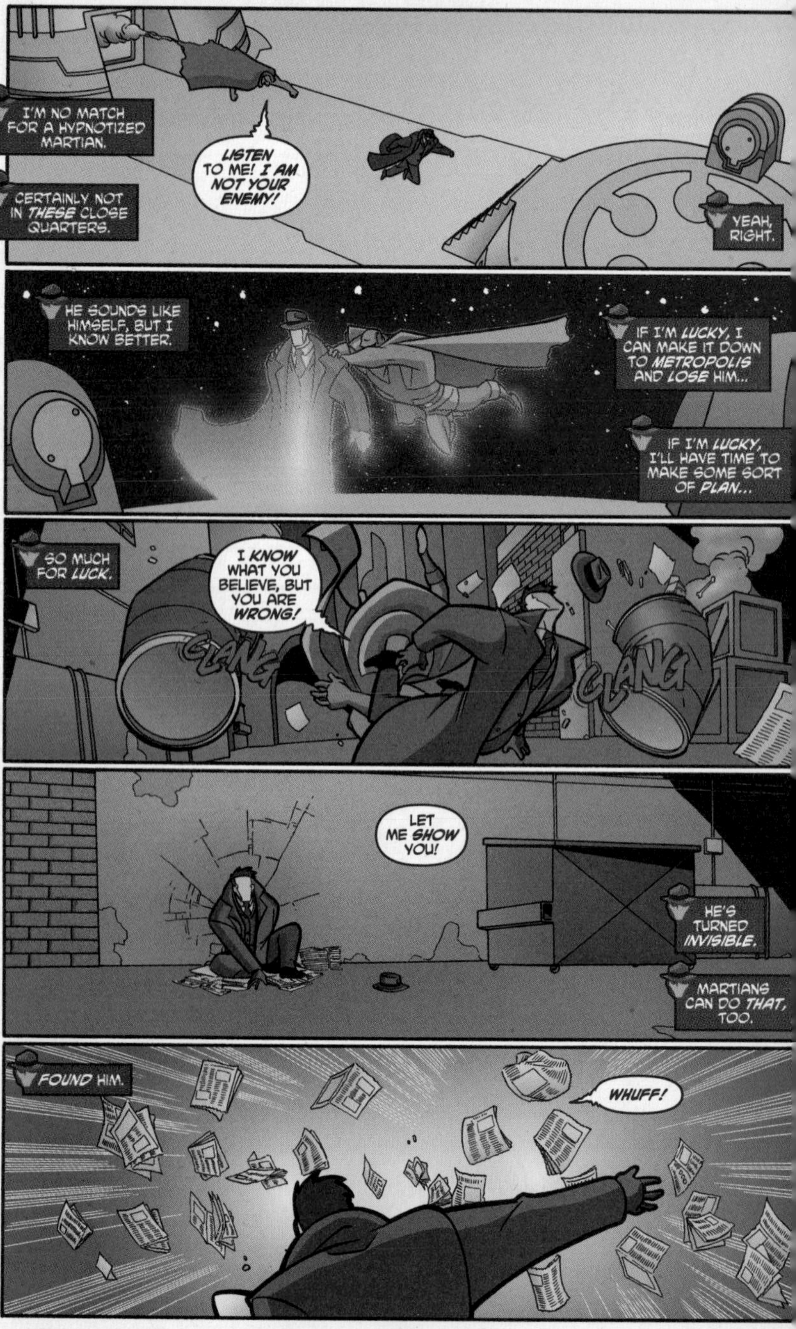
I'M NO MATCH FOR A HYPNOTIZED MARTIAN.
CERTAINLY NOT IN THESE CLOSE QUARTERS.
LISTEN TO ME! I AM NOT YOUR ENEMY!
YEAH, RIGHT.
HE SOUNDS LIKE HIMSELF, BUT I KNOW BETTER.
IF I'M LUCKY, I CAN MAKE IT DOWN TO METROPOLIS AND LOSE HIM...
IF I'M LUCKY, I'LL HAVE TIME TO MAKE SOME SORT OF PLAN...
SO MUCH FOR LUCK.
I KNOW WHAT YOU BELIEVE, BUT YOU ARE WRONG!
CLANG
CLANG
LET ME SHOW YOU!
HE'S TURNED INVISIBLE.
MARTIANS CAN DO THAT, TOO.
FOUND HIM.
WHUFF!

I'M GOING TO HAVE TO STAY IN CLOSE, TRY TO KEEP HIM FROM DISAPPEARING, TRY TO KEEP HIM OFF-BALANCE...

UNGH!

THWACK

...KEEP HIM FROM PULVERIZING ME.

THA BOOOM

QUESTION, STOP FIGHTING!

LET ME INTO YOUR MIND SO I CAN SHOW YOU THE TRUTH!

TRUST M-- HWUH?

NEVER! THE QUESTION TRUSTS NO ONE!

I'LL GO BACK TO THE WATCHTOWER, FIND WEAPONS STRONG ENOUGH TO DEFEAT HIM. THEN I'LL FIND THE ONES DOING THIS, AND--

NO!

SHWHAM

IT'S THE ONLY WAY I CAN MAKE YOU BELIEVE THE TRUTH, QUESTION, BUT I WON'T ENTER YOUR MIND UNLESS YOU LET ME!

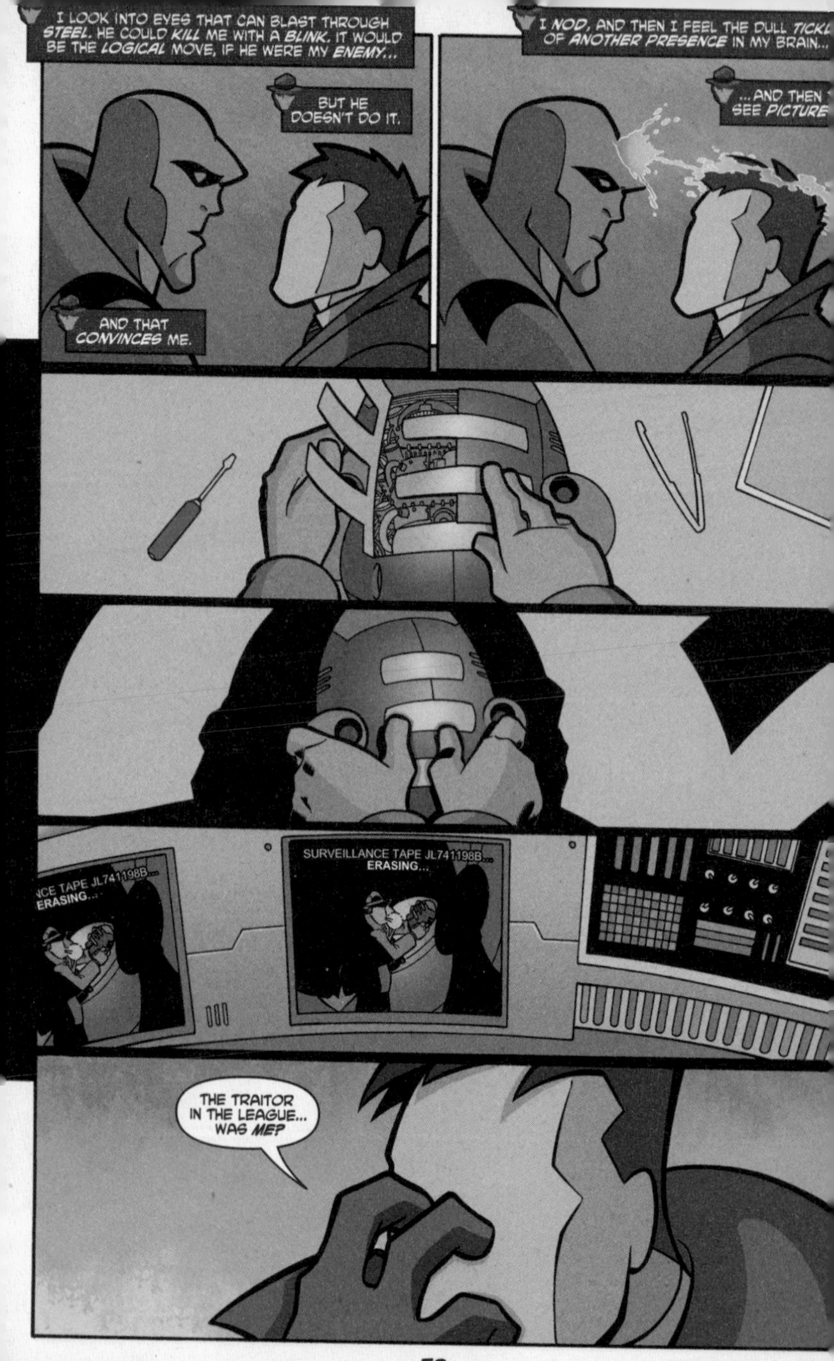
I LOOK INTO EYES THAT CAN BLAST THROUGH STEEL. HE COULD KILL ME WITH A BLINK. IT WOULD BE THE LOGICAL MOVE, IF HE WERE MY ENEMY...
BUT HE DOESN'T DO IT.
AND THAT CONVINCES ME.
I NOD, AND THEN I FEEL THE DULL TICKL
OF ANOTHER PRESENCE IN MY BRAIN...
...AND THEN
SEE PICTURE
SURVEILLANCE TAPE JL741198B... ERASING...
THE TRAITOR IN THE LEAGUE... WAS ME?

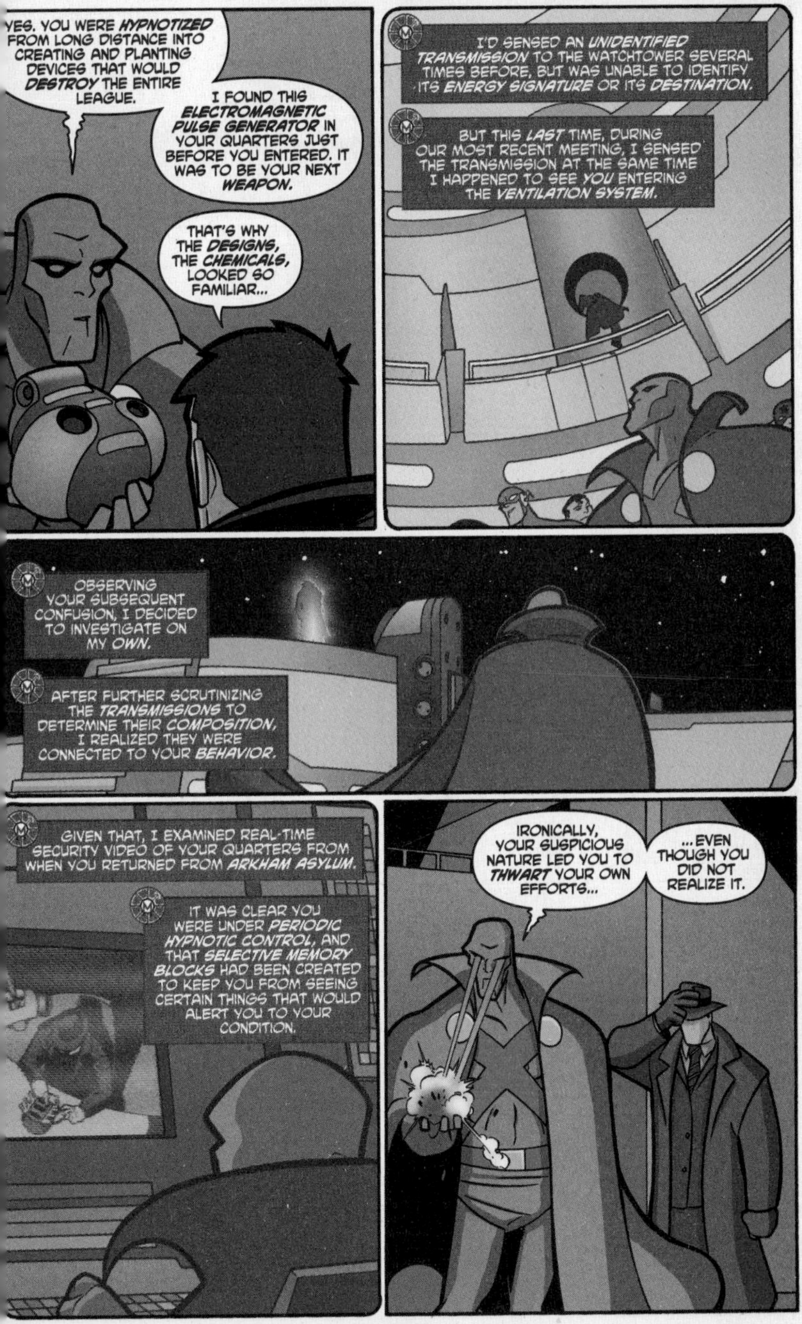
YES. YOU WERE HYPNOTIZED FROM LONG DISTANCE INTO CREATING AND PLANTING DEVICES THAT WOULD DESTROY THE ENTIRE LEAGUE.
I FOUND THIS ELECTROMAGNETIC PULSE GENERATOR IN YOUR QUARTERS JUST BEFORE YOU ENTERED. IT WAS TO BE YOUR NEXT WEAPON.
THAT'S WHY THE DESIGNS, THE CHEMICALS, LOOKED SO FAMILIAR...
I'D SENSED AN UNIDENTIFIED TRANSMISSION TO THE WATCHTOWER SEVERAL TIMES BEFORE, BUT WAS UNABLE TO IDENTIFY ITS ENERGY SIGNATURE OR ITS DESTINATION.
BUT THIS LAST TIME, DURING OUR MOST RECENT MEETING, I SENSED THE TRANSMISSION AT THE SAME TIME I HAPPENED TO SEE YOU ENTERING THE VENTILATION SYSTEM.
OBSERVING YOUR SUBSEQUENT CONFUSION, I DECIDED TO INVESTIGATE ON MY OWN.
AFTER FURTHER SCRUTINIZING THE TRANSMISSIONS TO DETERMINE THEIR COMPOSITION, I REALIZED THEY WERE CONNECTED TO YOUR BEHAVIOR.
GIVEN THAT, I EXAMINED REAL-TIME SECURITY VIDEO OF YOUR QUARTERS FROM WHEN YOU RETURNED FROM ARKHAM ASYLUM.
IT WAS CLEAR YOU WERE UNDER PERIODIC HYPNOTIC CONTROL, AND THAT SELECTIVE MEMORY BLOCKS HAD BEEN CREATED TO KEEP YOU FROM SEEING CERTAIN THINGS THAT WOULD ALERT YOU TO YOUR CONDITION.
IRONICALLY, YOUR SUSPICIOUS NATURE LED YOU TO THWART YOUR OWN EFFORTS...
...EVEN THOUGH YOU DID NOT REALIZE IT.

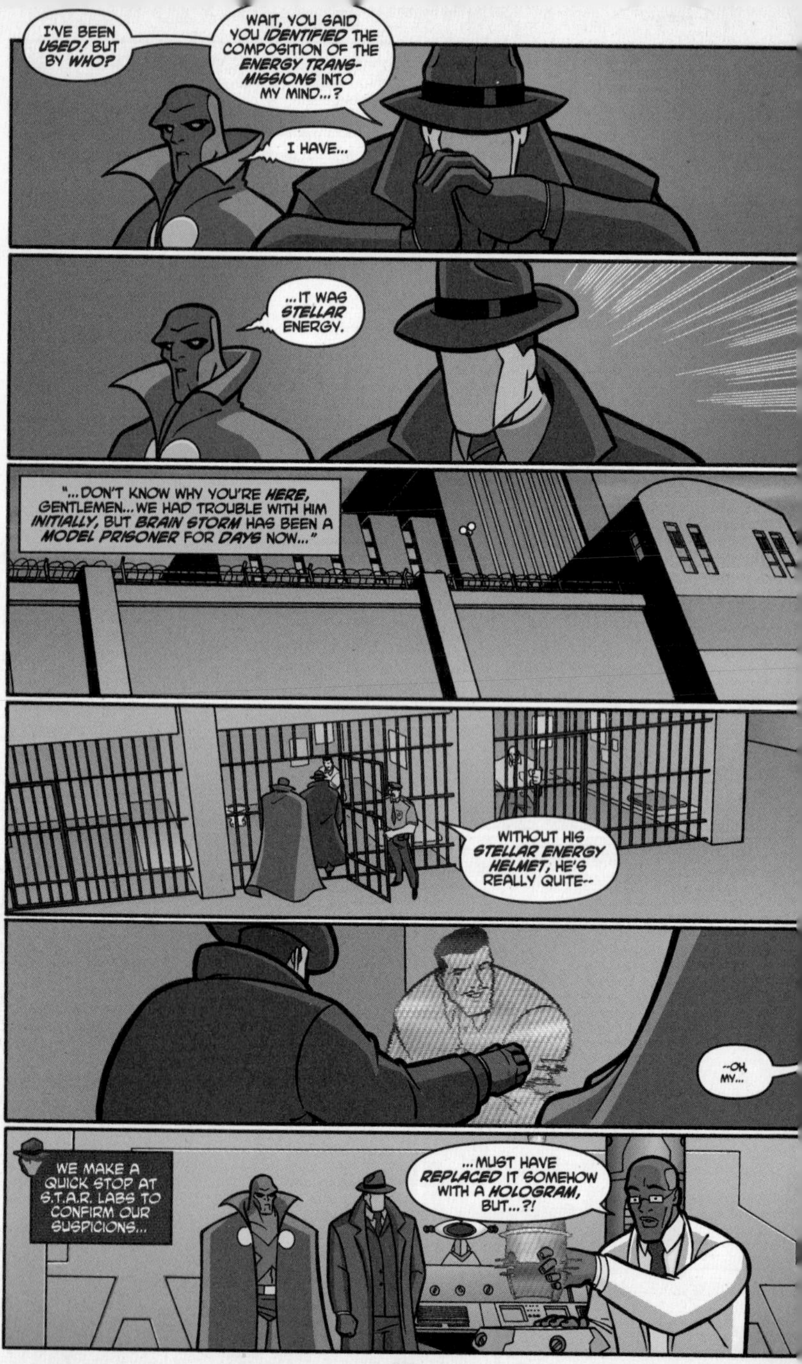
I'VE BEEN USED! BUT BY WHO?
WAIT, YOU SAID YOU IDENTIFIED THE COMPOSITION OF THE ENERGY TRANSMISSIONS INTO MY MIND...?
I HAVE...
...IT WAS STELLAR ENERGY.
"...DON'T KNOW WHY YOU'RE HERE, GENTLEMEN...WE HAD TROUBLE WITH HIM INITIALLY, BUT BRAIN STORM HAS BEEN A MODEL PRISONER FOR DAYS NOW..."
WITHOUT HIS STELLAR ENERGY HELMET, HE'S REALLY QUITE--
--OH, MY...
WE MAKE A QUICK STOP AT S.T.A.R. LABS TO CONFIRM OUR SUSPICIONS...
...MUST HAVE REPLACED IT SOMEHOW WITH A HOLOGRAM, BUT...?!

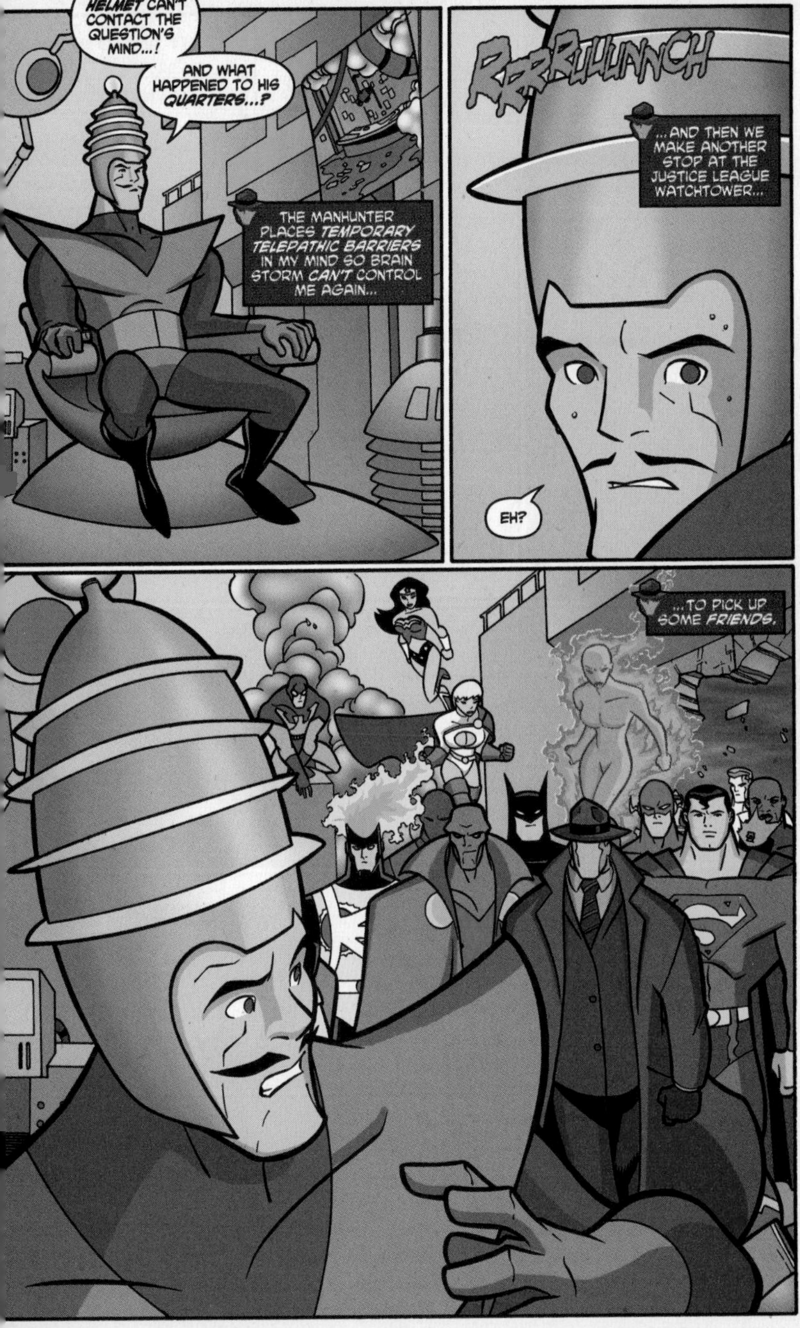
EH? MY HELMET CAN'T CONTACT THE QUESTION'S MIND...!
AND WHAT HAPPENED TO HIS QUARTERS...?
THE MANHUNTER PLACES TEMPORARY TELEPATHIC BARRIERS IN MY MIND SO BRAIN STORM CAN'T CONTROL ME AGAIN...
RRRRUUUNCH
...AND THEN WE MAKE ANOTHER STOP AT THE JUSTICE LEAGUE WATCHTOWER...
EH?
...TO PICK UP SOME FRIENDS.

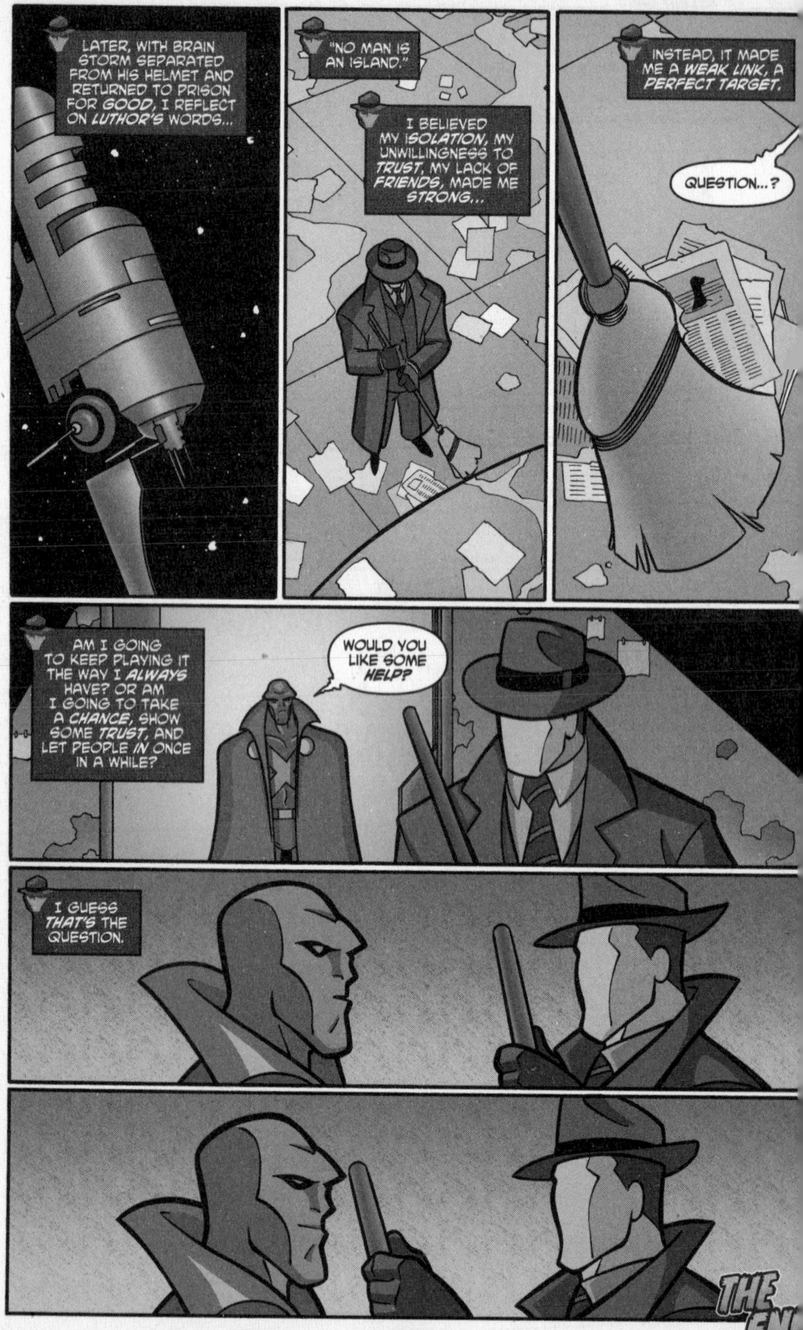
LATER, WITH BRAIN STORM SEPARATED FROM HIS HELMET AND RETURNED TO PRISON FOR GOOD, I REFLECT ON LUTHOR'S WORDS...
"NO MAN IS AN ISLAND."
I BELIEVED MY ISOLATION, MY UNWILLINGNESS TO TRUST, MY LACK OF FRIENDS, MADE ME STRONG...
INSTEAD, IT MADE ME A WEAK LINK, A PERFECT TARGET.
QUESTION...?
AM I GOING TO KEEP PLAYING IT THE WAY I ALWAYS HAVE? OR AM I GOING TO TAKE A CHANCE, SHOW SOME TRUST, AND LET PEOPLE IN ONCE IN A WHILE?
WOULD YOU LIKE SOME HELP?
I GUESS THAT'S THE QUESTION.

THOSE GRAY CLOUDS? THEY'RE NOT *REALLY* CLOUDS.

THEY'RE PARTICLES OF THE *TIME STREAM*.

I STILL CAN'T QUITE WRAP MY HEAD AROUND THAT.

THIS IS MY FIRST TRIP BACK IN TIME.

I FIGURED, AS A MEMBER OF THE *JUSTICE LEAGUE*, I'D PROBABLY HAVE TO GO THROUGH TIME TRAVEL SOONER OR LATER...

I HOPED, OF COURSE, THAT MY FIRST TIME WOULD BE SOMETHING *SIMPLE*, SOMETHING *EASY*, SOMETHING THAT'D GIVE ME A CHANCE TO *ADJUST*...

I SHOULD'VE KNOWN BETTER.

I'M A MEMBER OF THE *JUSTICE LEAGUE*.

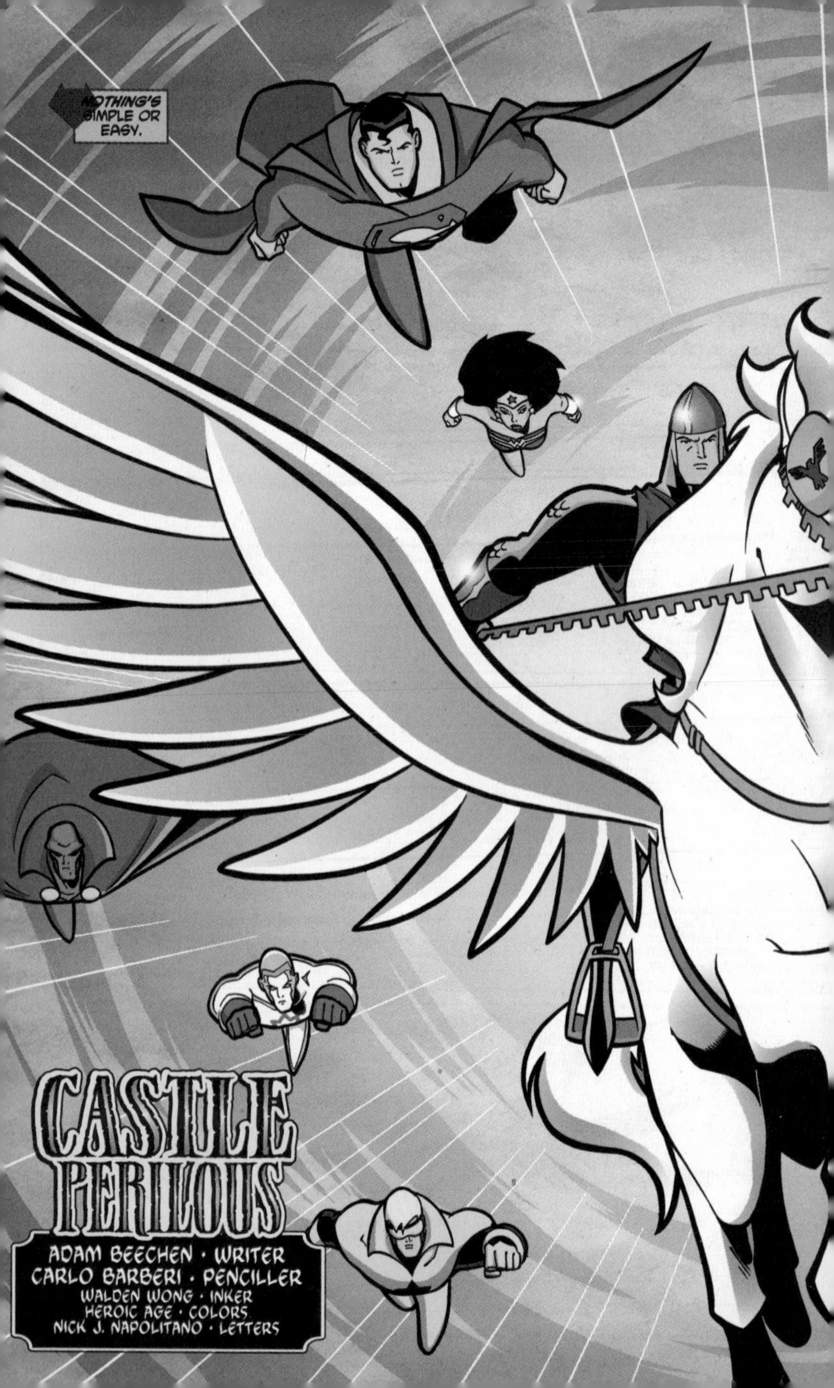

NOTHING'S SIMPLE OR EASY.
CASTLE PERILOUS
ADAM BEECHEN · WRITER
CARLO BARBERI · PENCILLER
WALDEN WONG · INKER
HEROIC AGE · COLORS
NICK J. NAPOLITANO · LETTERS

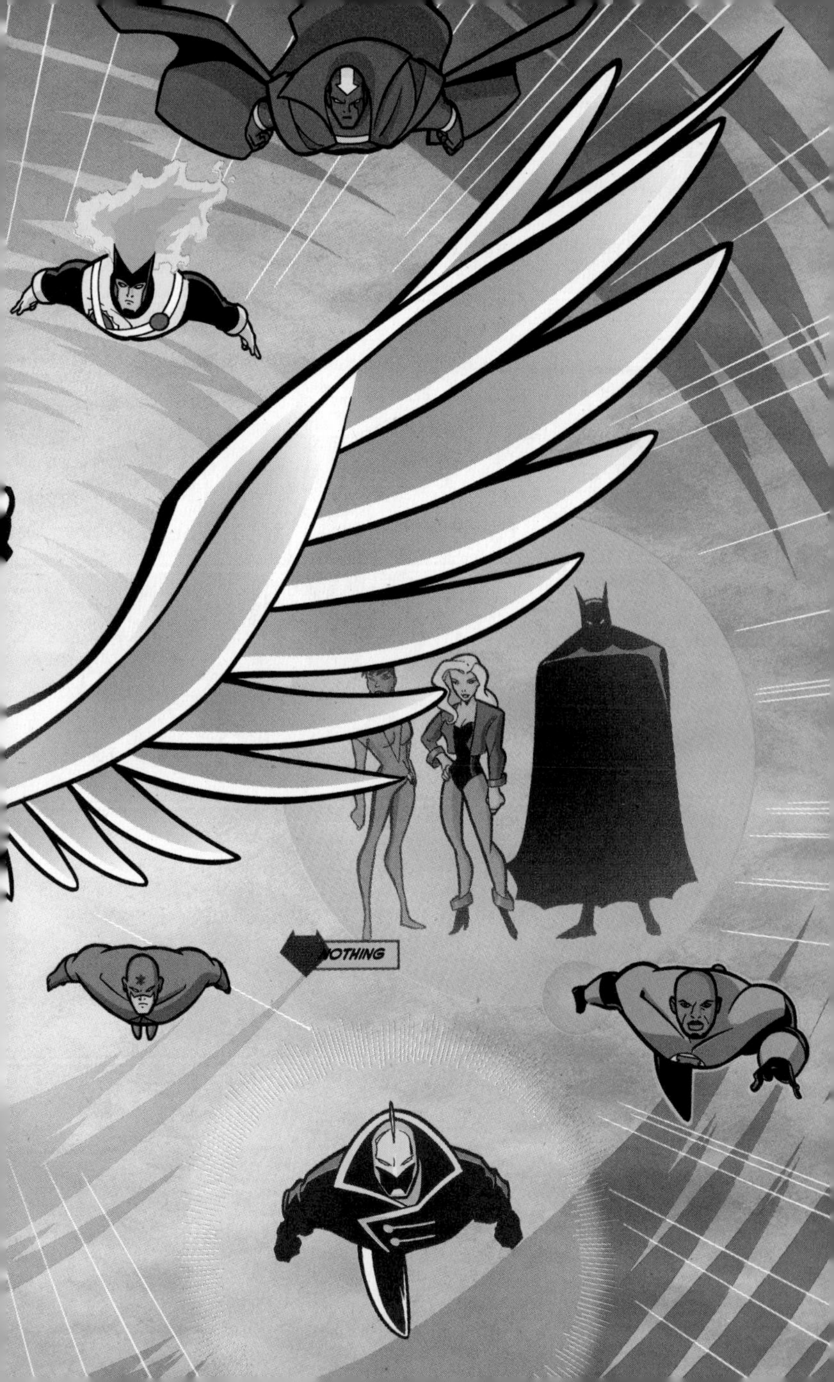
NOTHING

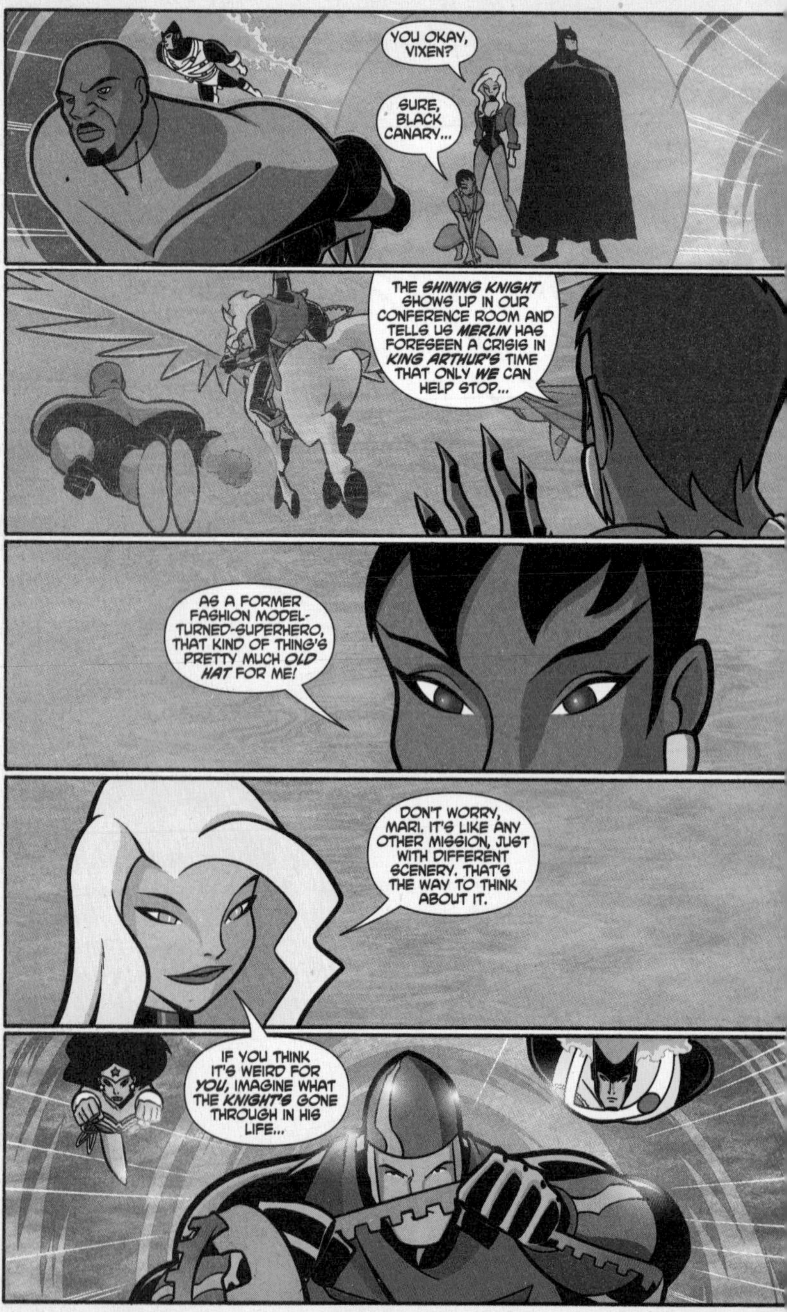
YOU OKAY, VIXEN?
SURE, BLACK CANARY...
THE SHINING KNIGHT SHOWS UP IN OUR CONFERENCE ROOM AND TELLS US MERLIN HAS FORESEEN A CRISIS IN KING ARTHUR'S TIME THAT ONLY WE CAN HELP STOP...
AS A FORMER FASHION MODEL-TURNED-SUPERHERO, THAT KIND OF THING'S PRETTY MUCH OLD HAT FOR ME!
DON'T WORRY, MARI. IT'S LIKE ANY OTHER MISSION, JUST WITH DIFFERENT SCENERY. THAT'S THE WAY TO THINK ABOUT IT.
IF YOU THINK IT'S WEIRD FOR YOU, IMAGINE WHAT THE KNIGHT'S GONE THROUGH IN HIS LIFE...

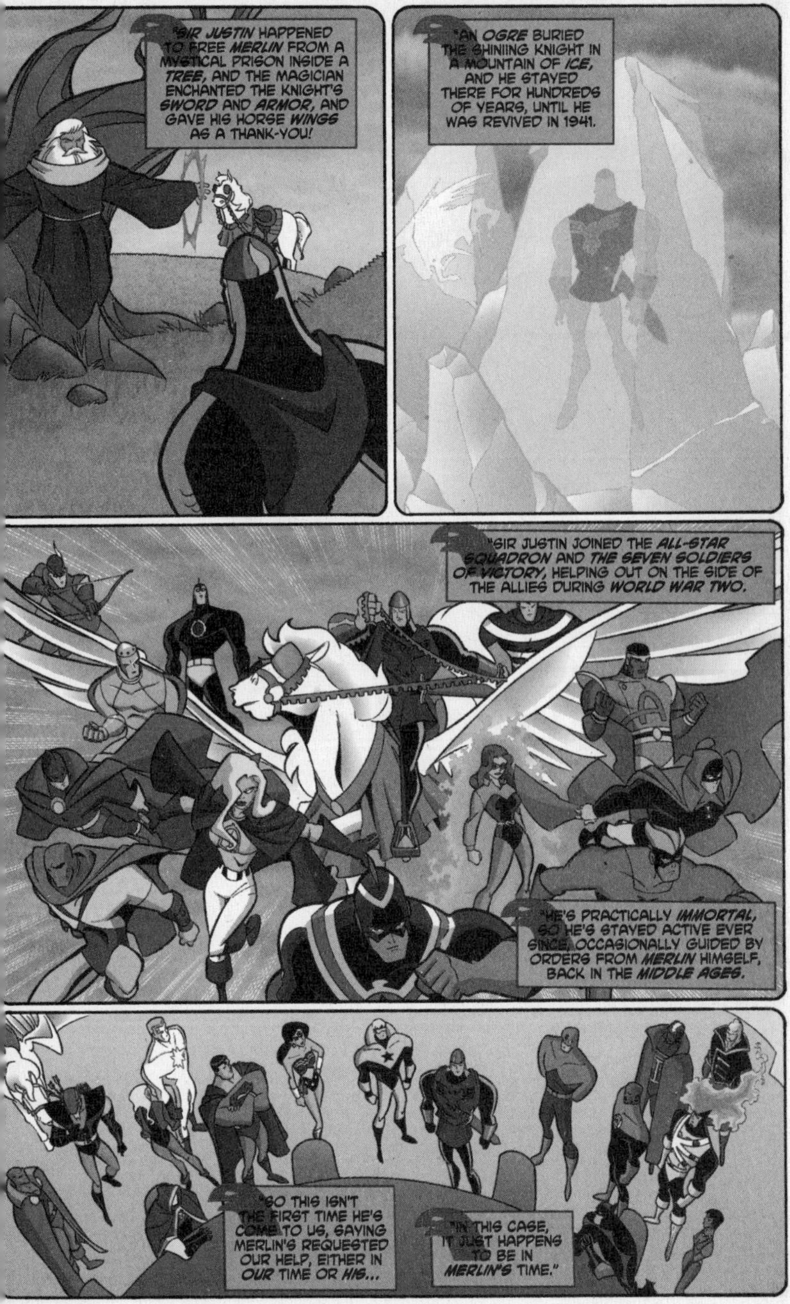
"SIR JUSTIN HAPPENED TO FREE MERLIN FROM A MYSTICAL PRISON INSIDE A TREE, AND THE MAGICIAN ENCHANTED THE KNIGHT'S SWORD AND ARMOR, AND GAVE HIS HORSE WINGS AS A THANK-YOU!
"AN OGRE BURIED THE SHINIING KNIGHT IN A MOUNTAIN OF ICE, AND HE STAYED THERE FOR HUNDREDS OF YEARS, UNTIL HE WAS REVIVED IN 1941.
"SIR JUSTIN JOINED THE ALL-STAR SQUADRON AND THE SEVEN SOLDIERS OF VICTORY, HELPING OUT ON THE SIDE OF THE ALLIES DURING WORLD WAR TWO.
"HE'S PRACTICALLY IMMORTAL, SO HE'S STAYED ACTIVE EVER SINCE, OCCASIONALLY GUIDED BY ORDERS FROM MERLIN HIMSELF, BACK IN THE MIDDLE AGES.
"SO THIS ISN'T THE FIRST TIME HE'S COME TO US, SAYING MERLIN'S REQUESTED OUR HELP, EITHER IN OUR TIME OR HIS...
"IN THIS CASE, IT JUST HAPPENS TO BE IN MERLIN'S TIME."

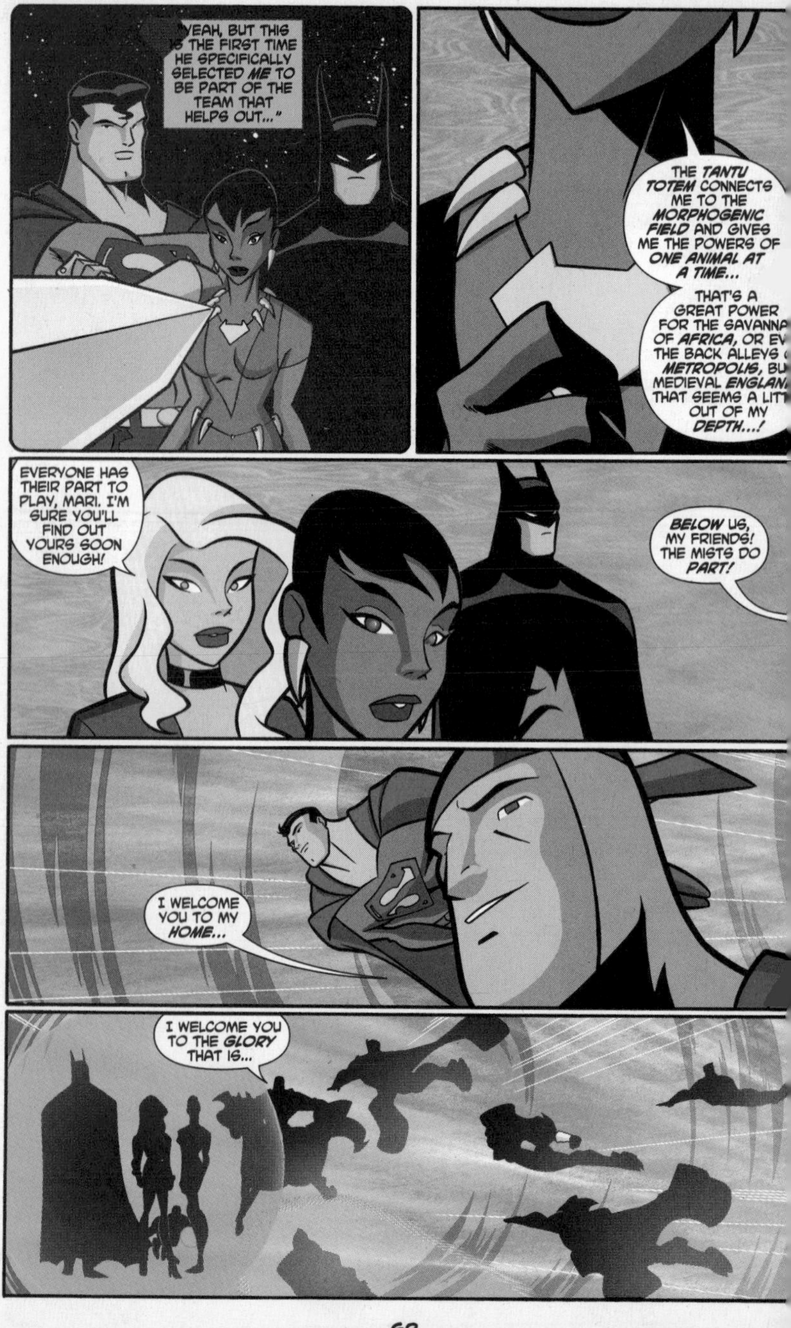
"YEAH, BUT THIS IS THE FIRST TIME HE SPECIFICALLY SELECTED ME TO BE PART OF THE TEAM THAT HELPS OUT..."
THE TANTU TOTEM CONNECTS ME TO THE MORPHOGENIC FIELD AND GIVES ME THE POWERS OF ONE ANIMAL AT A TIME...
THAT'S A GREAT POWER FOR THE SAVANNA OF AFRICA, OR EV THE BACK ALLEYS METROPOLIS, BU MEDIEVAL ENGLAN THAT SEEMS A LIT OUT OF MY DEPTH...!
EVERYONE HAS THEIR PART TO PLAY, MARI. I'M SURE YOU'LL FIND OUT YOURS SOON ENOUGH!
BELOW US, MY FRIENDS! THE MISTS DO PART!
I WELCOME YOU TO MY HOME...
I WELCOME YOU TO THE GLORY THAT IS...

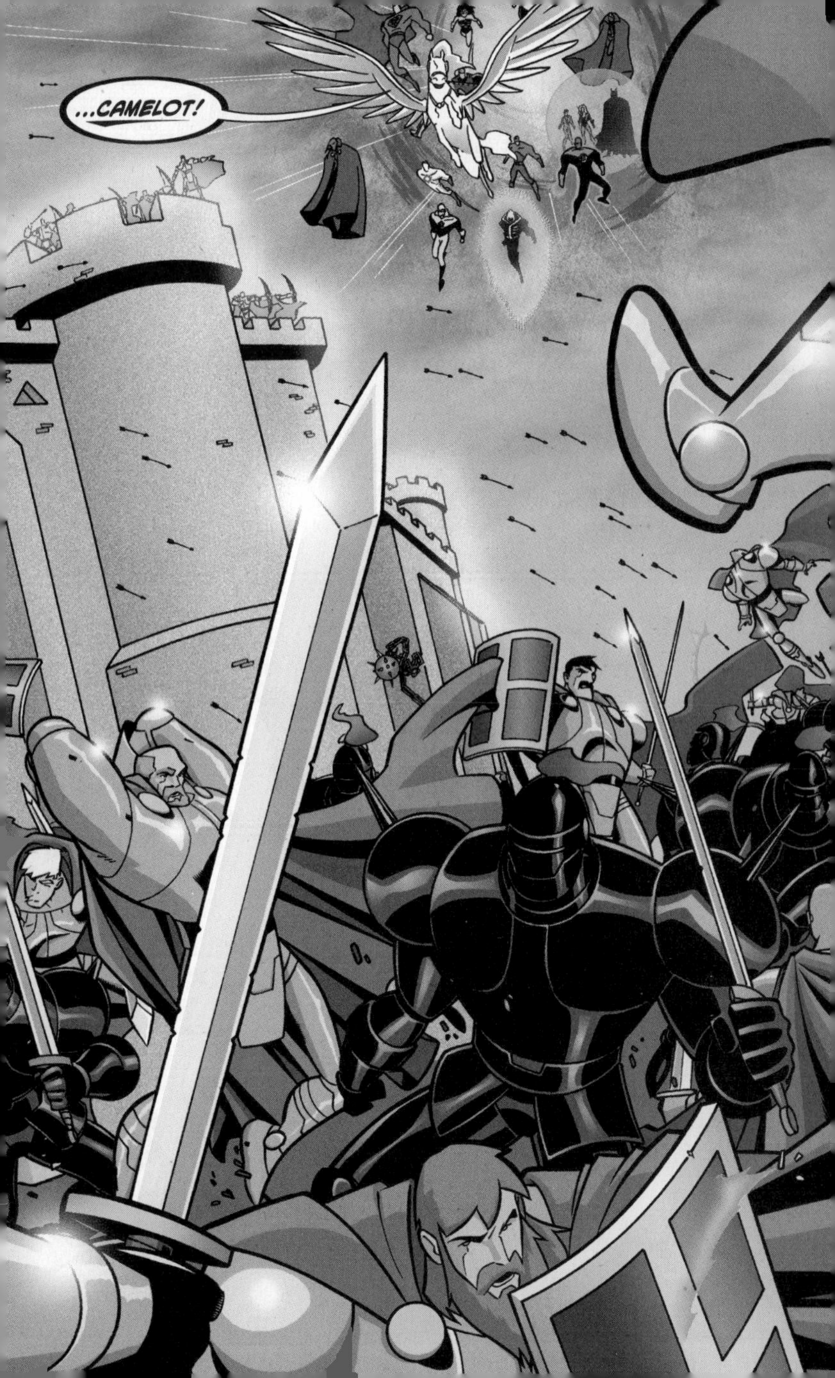
...CAMELOT!

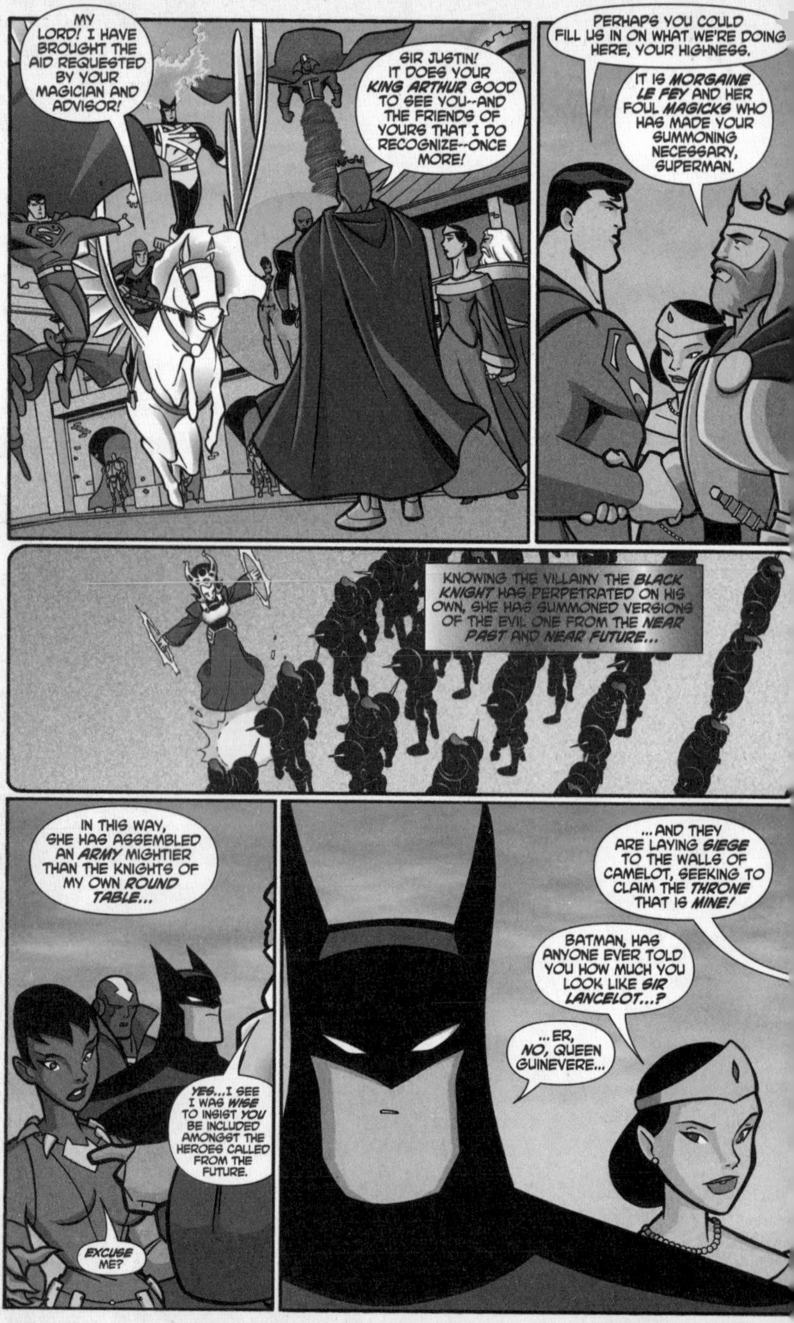
MY LORD! I HAVE BROUGHT THE AID REQUESTED BY YOUR MAGICIAN AND ADVISOR!
SIR JUSTIN! IT DOES YOUR KING ARTHUR GOOD TO SEE YOU--AND THE FRIENDS OF YOURS THAT I DO RECOGNIZE--ONCE MORE!
PERHAPS YOU COULD FILL US IN ON WHAT WE'RE DOING HERE, YOUR HIGHNESS.
IT IS MORGAINE LE FEY AND HER FOUL MAGICKS WHO HAS MADE YOUR SUMMONING NECESSARY, SUPERMAN.
KNOWING THE VILLAINY THE BLACK KNIGHT HAS PERPETRATED ON HIS OWN, SHE HAS SUMMONED VERSIONS OF THE EVIL ONE FROM THE NEAR PAST AND NEAR FUTURE...
IN THIS WAY, SHE HAS ASSEMBLED AN ARMY MIGHTIER THAN THE KNIGHTS OF MY OWN ROUND TABLE...
...AND THEY ARE LAYING SIEGE TO THE WALLS OF CAMELOT, SEEKING TO CLAIM THE THRONE THAT IS MINE!
YES...I SEE I WAS WISE TO INSIST YOU BE INCLUDED AMONGST THE HEROES CALLED FROM THE FUTURE.
EXCUSE ME?
BATMAN, HAS ANYONE EVER TOLD YOU HOW MUCH YOU LOOK LIKE SIR LANCELOT...?
...ER, NO, QUEEN GUINEVERE...

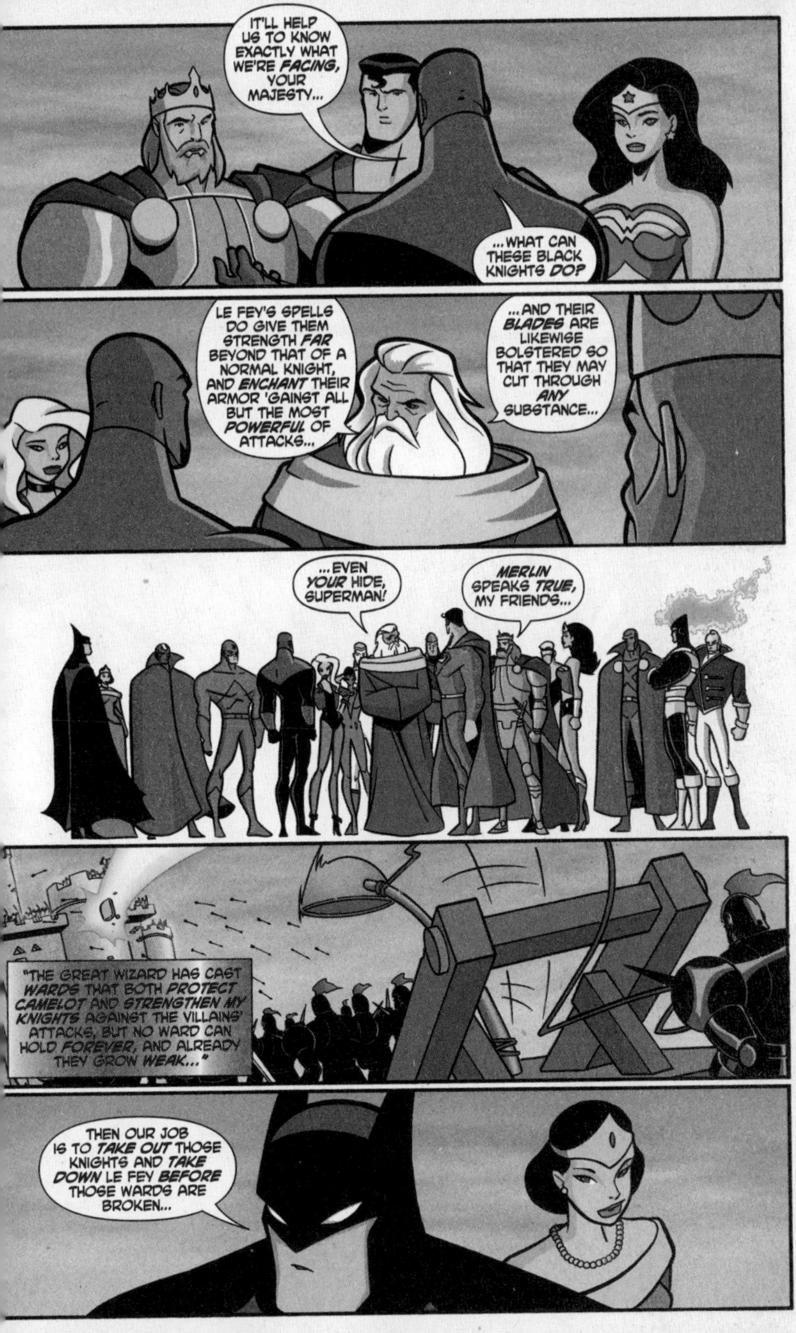

IT'LL HELP US TO KNOW EXACTLY WHAT WE'RE FACING, YOUR MAJESTY...
...WHAT CAN THESE BLACK KNIGHTS DO?
LE FEY'S SPELLS DO GIVE THEM STRENGTH FAR BEYOND THAT OF A NORMAL KNIGHT, AND ENCHANT THEIR ARMOR 'GAINST ALL BUT THE MOST POWERFUL OF ATTACKS...
...AND THEIR BLADES ARE LIKEWISE BOLSTERED SO THAT THEY MAY CUT THROUGH ANY SUBSTANCE...
...EVEN YOUR HIDE, SUPERMAN!
MERLIN SPEAKS TRUE, MY FRIENDS...
"THE GREAT WIZARD HAS CAST WARDS THAT BOTH PROTECT CAMELOT AND STRENGTHEN MY KNIGHTS AGAINST THE VILLAINS' ATTACKS, BUT NO WARD CAN HOLD FOREVER, AND ALREADY THEY GROW WEAK..."
THEN OUR JOB IS TO TAKE OUT THOSE KNIGHTS AND TAKE DOWN LE FEY BEFORE THOSE WARDS ARE BROKEN...

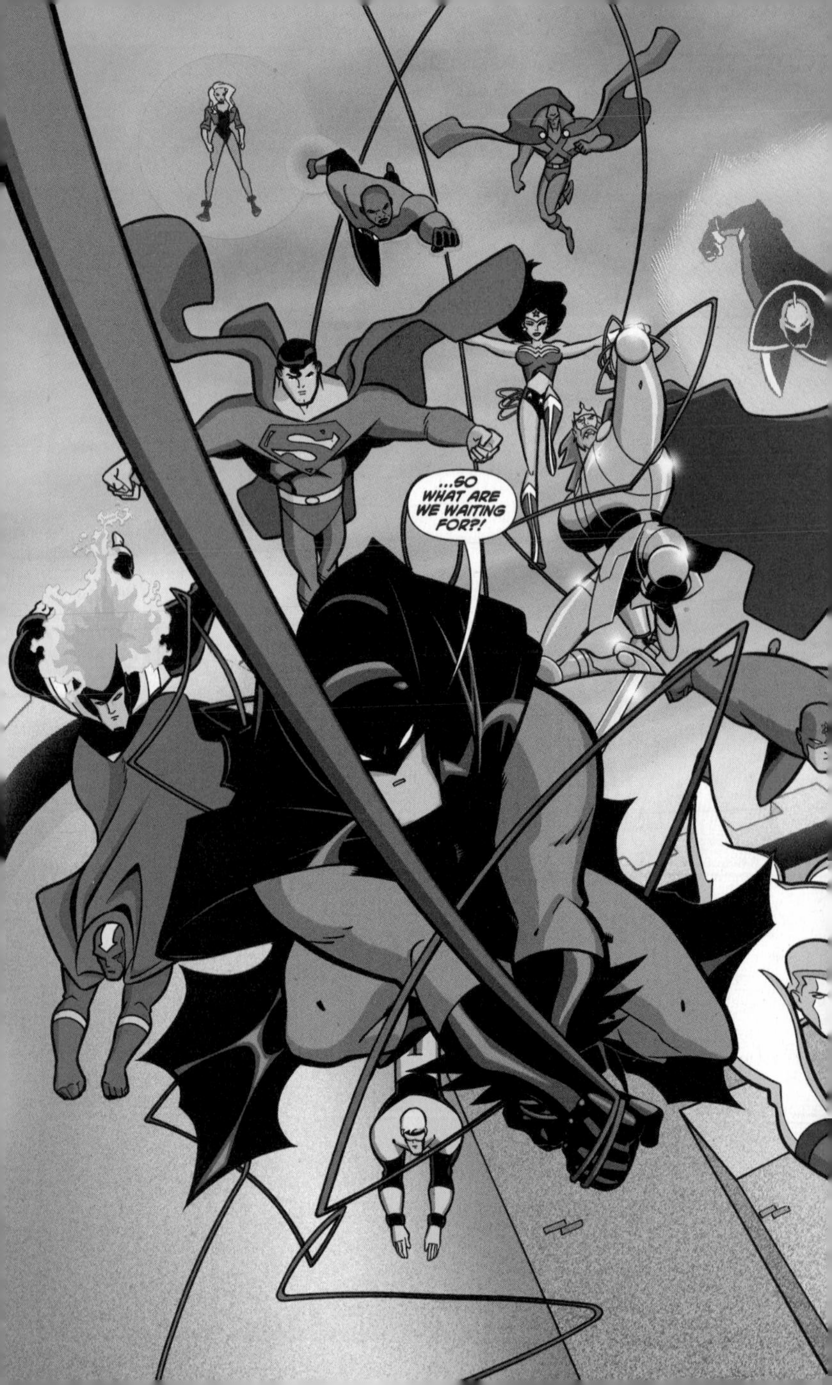
...SO WHAT ARE WE WAITING FOR?!

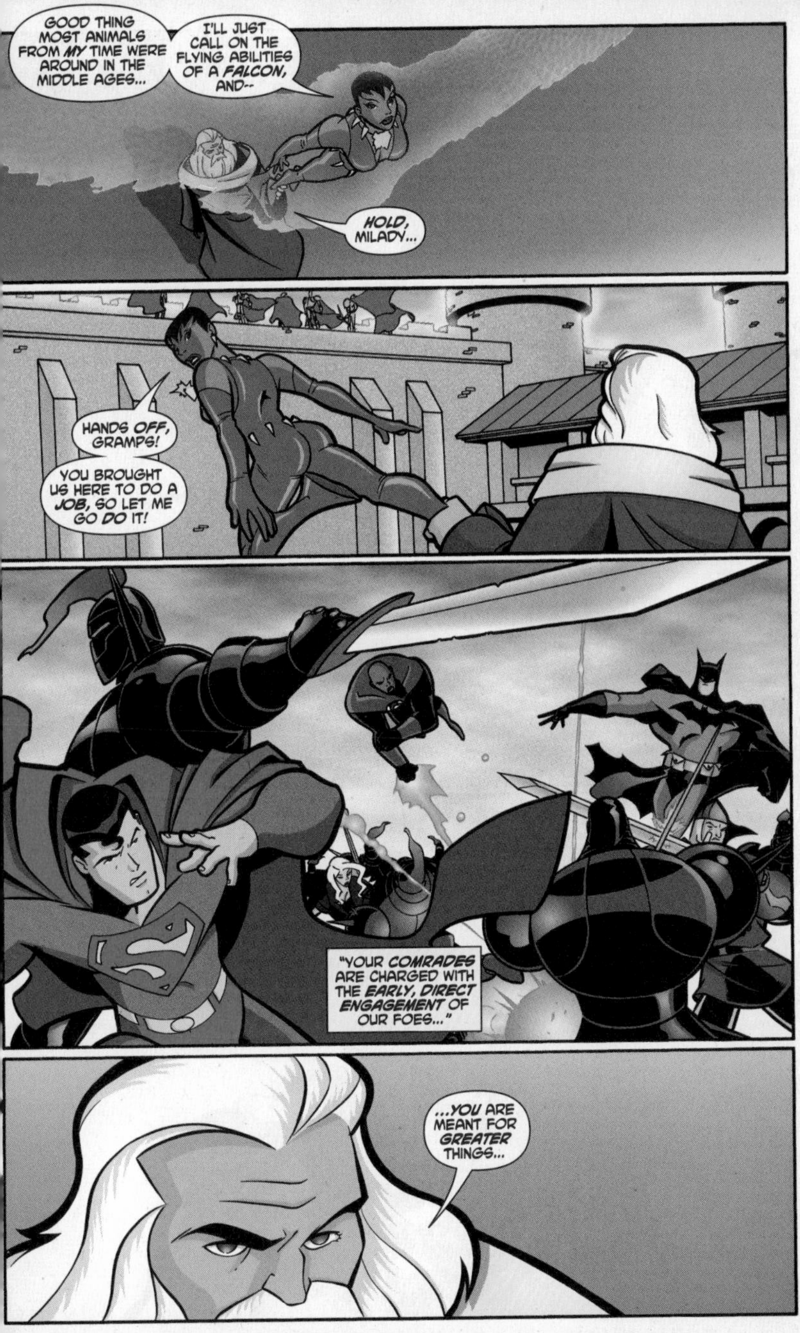
GOOD THING MOST ANIMALS FROM MY TIME WERE AROUND IN THE MIDDLE AGES...
I'LL JUST CALL ON THE FLYING ABILITIES OF A FALCON, AND--
HOLD, MILADY...
HANDS OFF, GRAMPS!
YOU BROUGHT US HERE TO DO A JOB, SO LET ME GO DO IT!
"YOUR COMRADES ARE CHARGED WITH THE EARLY, DIRECT ENGAGEMENT OF OUR FOES..."
...YOU ARE MEANT FOR GREATER THINGS...

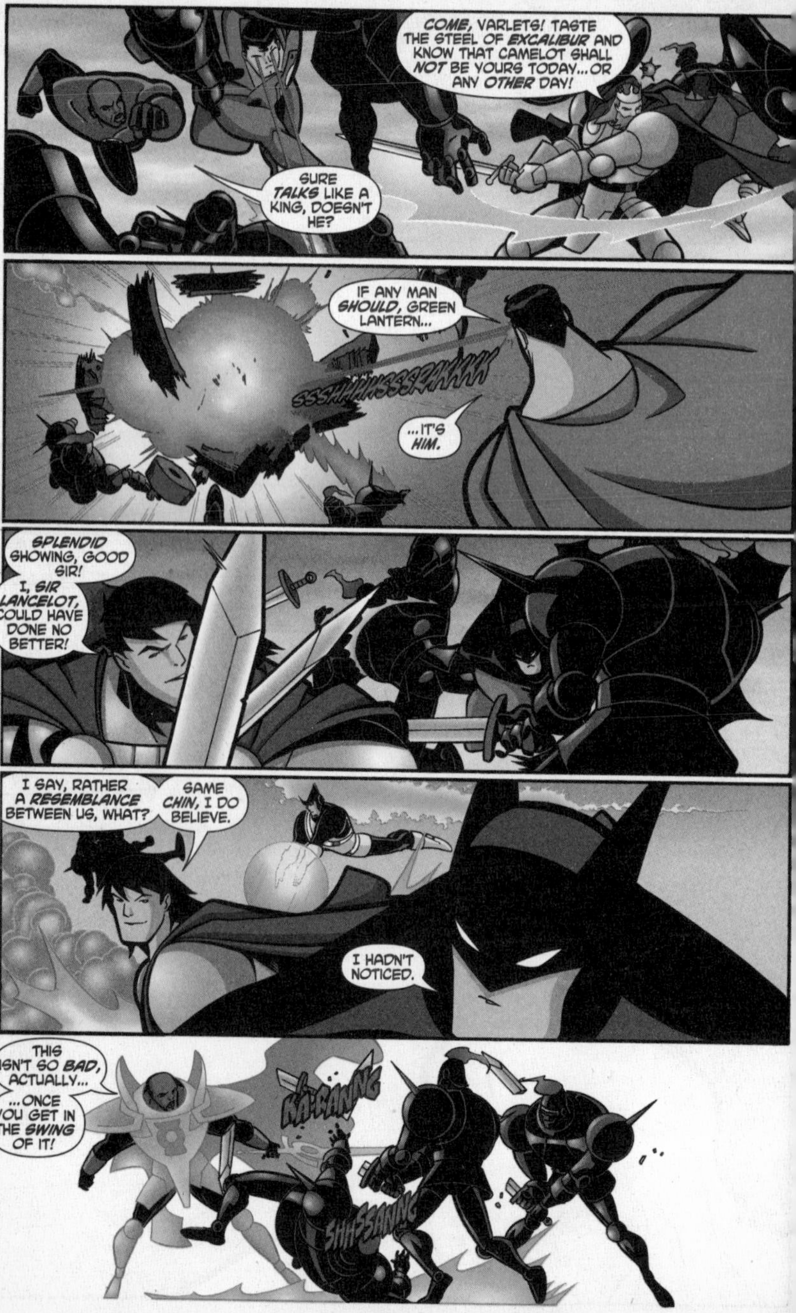
COME, VARLETS! TASTE THE STEEL OF EXCALIBUR AND KNOW THAT CAMELOT SHALL NOT BE YOURS TODAY...OR ANY OTHER DAY!
SURE TALKS LIKE A KING, DOESN'T HE?
IF ANY MAN SHOULD, GREEN LANTERN...
SSSHHHHSSSPAKKKK
...IT'S HIM.
SPLENDID SHOWING, GOOD SIR!
I, SIR LANCELOT, COULD HAVE DONE NO BETTER!
I SAY, RATHER A RESEMBLANCE BETWEEN US, WHAT?
SAME CHIN, I DO BELIEVE.
I HADN'T NOTICED.
THIS ISN'T SO BAD, ACTUALLY...
...ONCE YOU GET IN THE SWING OF IT!
KA-RANNG
SHHSSANNG

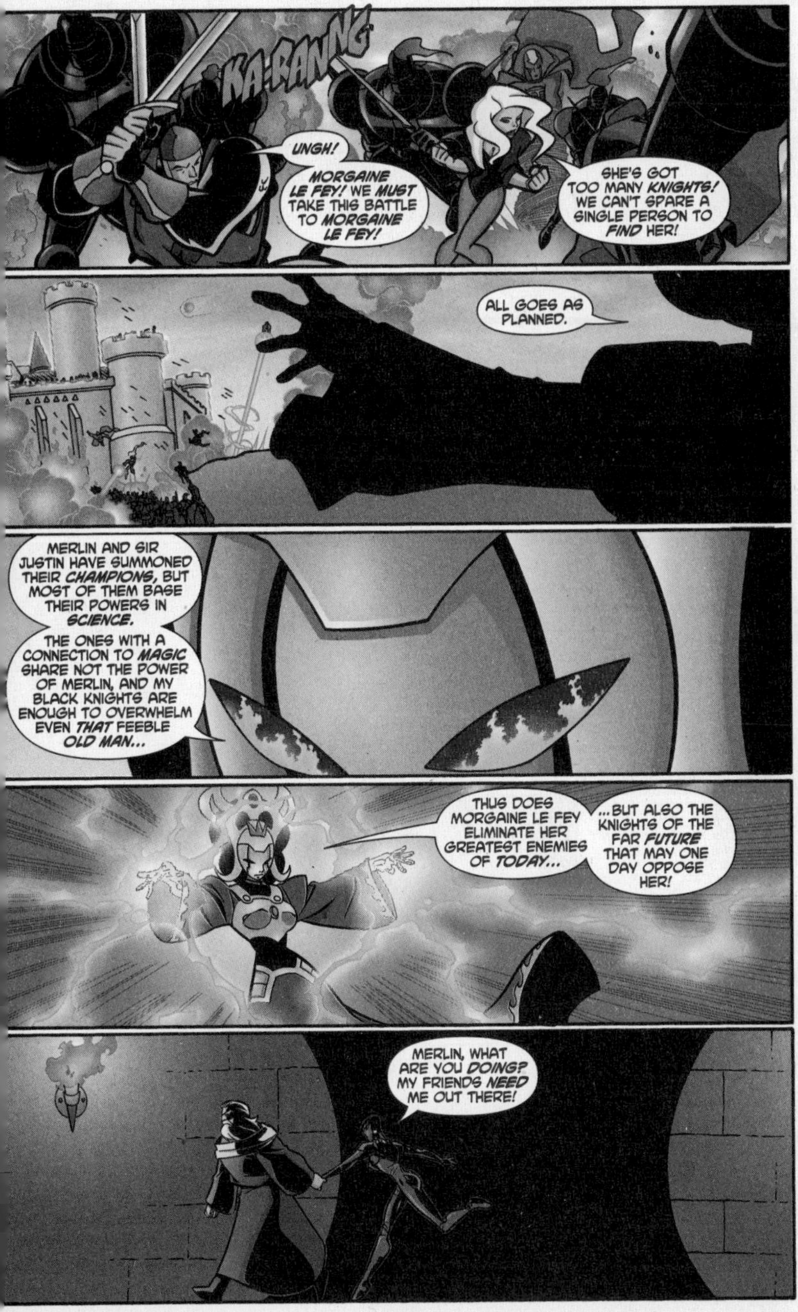
KA-RANNG
UNGH!
MORGAINE LE FEY! WE MUST TAKE THIS BATTLE TO MORGAINE LE FEY!
SHE'S GOT TOO MANY KNIGHTS! WE CAN'T SPARE A SINGLE PERSON TO FIND HER!
ALL GOES AS PLANNED.
MERLIN AND SIR JUSTIN HAVE SUMMONED THEIR CHAMPIONS, BUT MOST OF THEM BASE THEIR POWERS IN SCIENCE.
THE ONES WITH A CONNECTION TO MAGIC SHARE NOT THE POWER OF MERLIN, AND MY BLACK KNIGHTS ARE ENOUGH TO OVERWHELM EVEN THAT FEEBLE OLD MAN...
THUS DOES MORGAINE LE FEY ELIMINATE HER GREATEST ENEMIES OF TODAY...
...BUT ALSO THE KNIGHTS OF THE FAR FUTURE THAT MAY ONE DAY OPPOSE HER!
MERLIN, WHAT ARE YOU DOING? MY FRIENDS NEED ME OUT THERE!

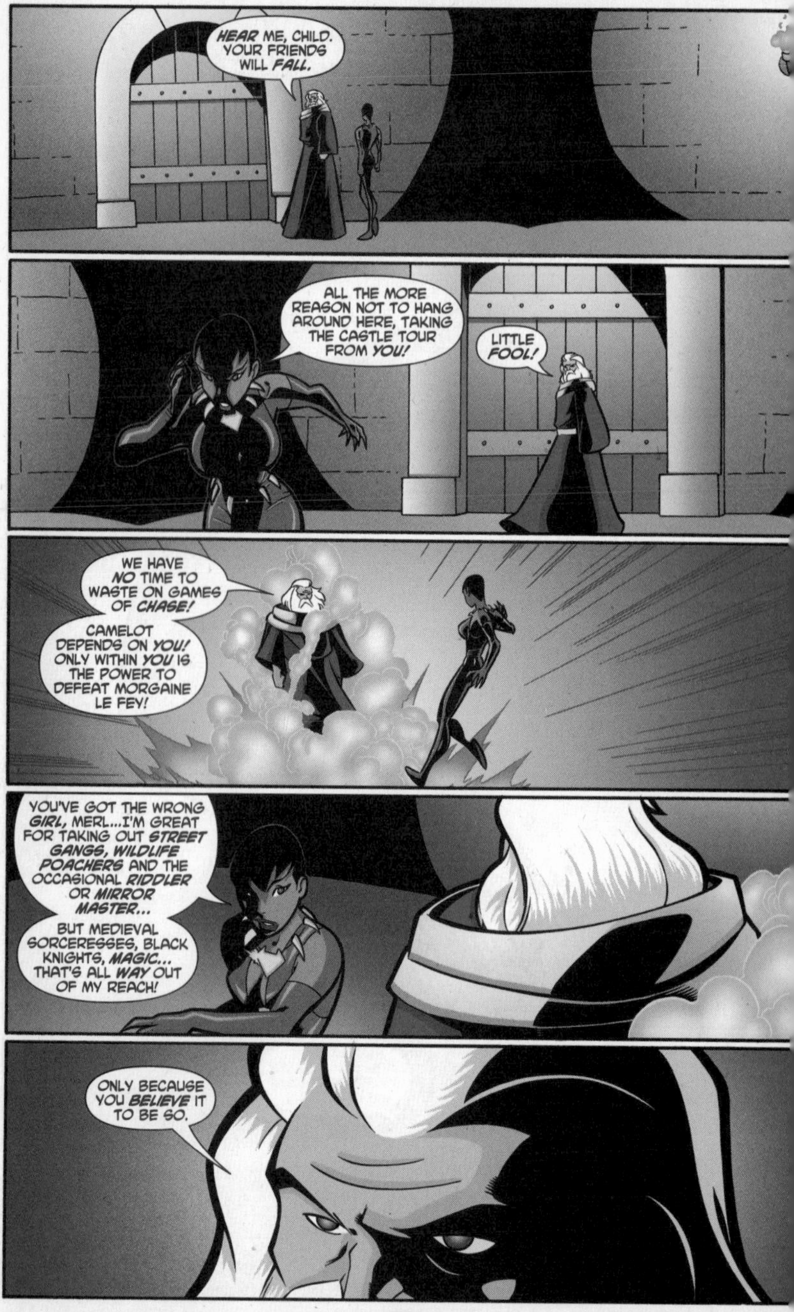
HEAR ME, CHILD. YOUR FRIENDS WILL FALL.
ALL THE MORE REASON NOT TO HANG AROUND HERE, TAKING THE CASTLE TOUR FROM YOU!
LITTLE FOOL!
WE HAVE NO TIME TO WASTE ON GAMES OF CHASE!
CAMELOT DEPENDS ON YOU! ONLY WITHIN YOU IS THE POWER TO DEFEAT MORGAINE LE FEY!
YOU'VE GOT THE WRONG GIRL, MERL...I'M GREAT FOR TAKING OUT STREET GANGS, WILDLIFE POACHERS AND THE OCCASIONAL RIDDLER OR MIRROR MASTER...
BUT MEDIEVAL SORCERESSES, BLACK KNIGHTS, MAGIC... THAT'S ALL WAY OUT OF MY REACH!
ONLY BECAUSE YOU BELIEVE IT TO BE SO.

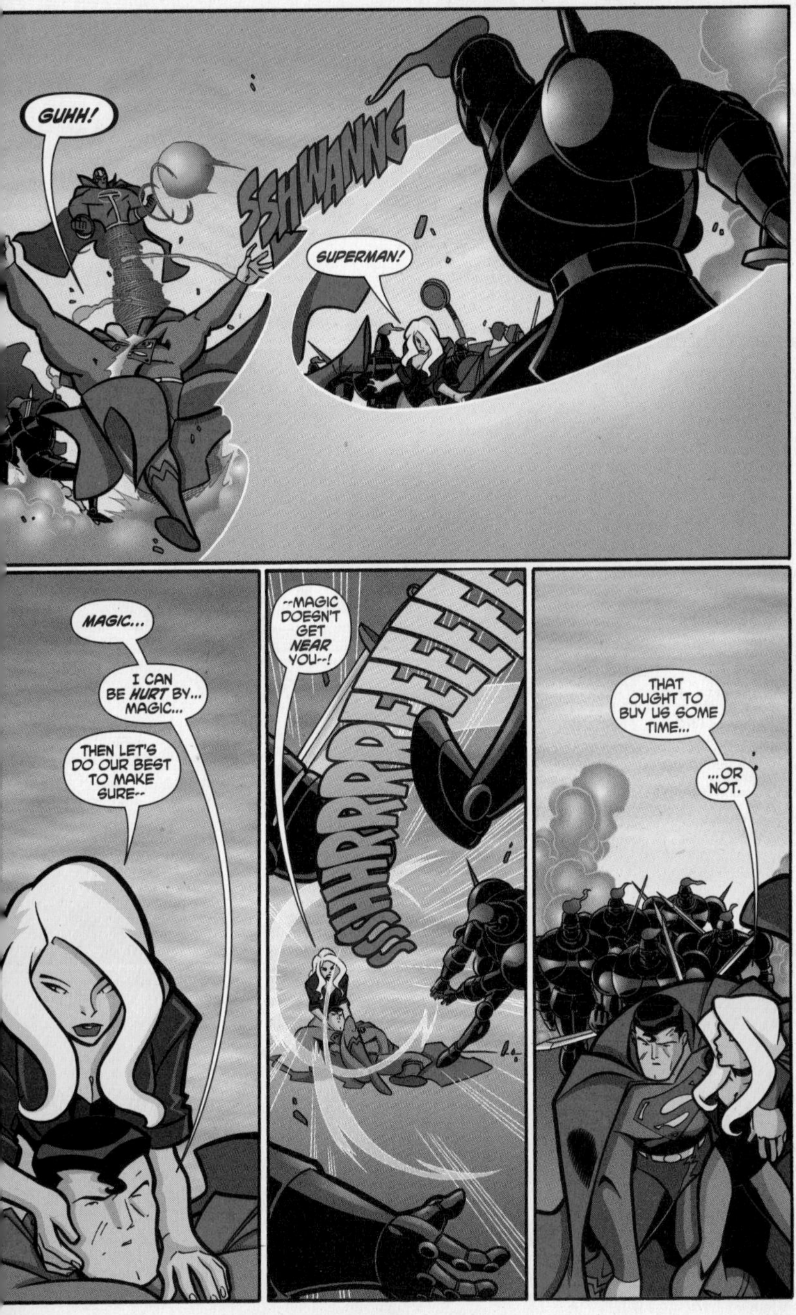
GUHH!
SSHWANNG
SUPERMAN!
MAGIC...
I CAN BE HURT BY... MAGIC...
THEN LET'S DO OUR BEST TO MAKE SURE--
--MAGIC DOESN'T GET NEAR YOU--!
SSHRRRREEEEE
THAT OUGHT TO BUY US SOME TIME...
...OR NOT.

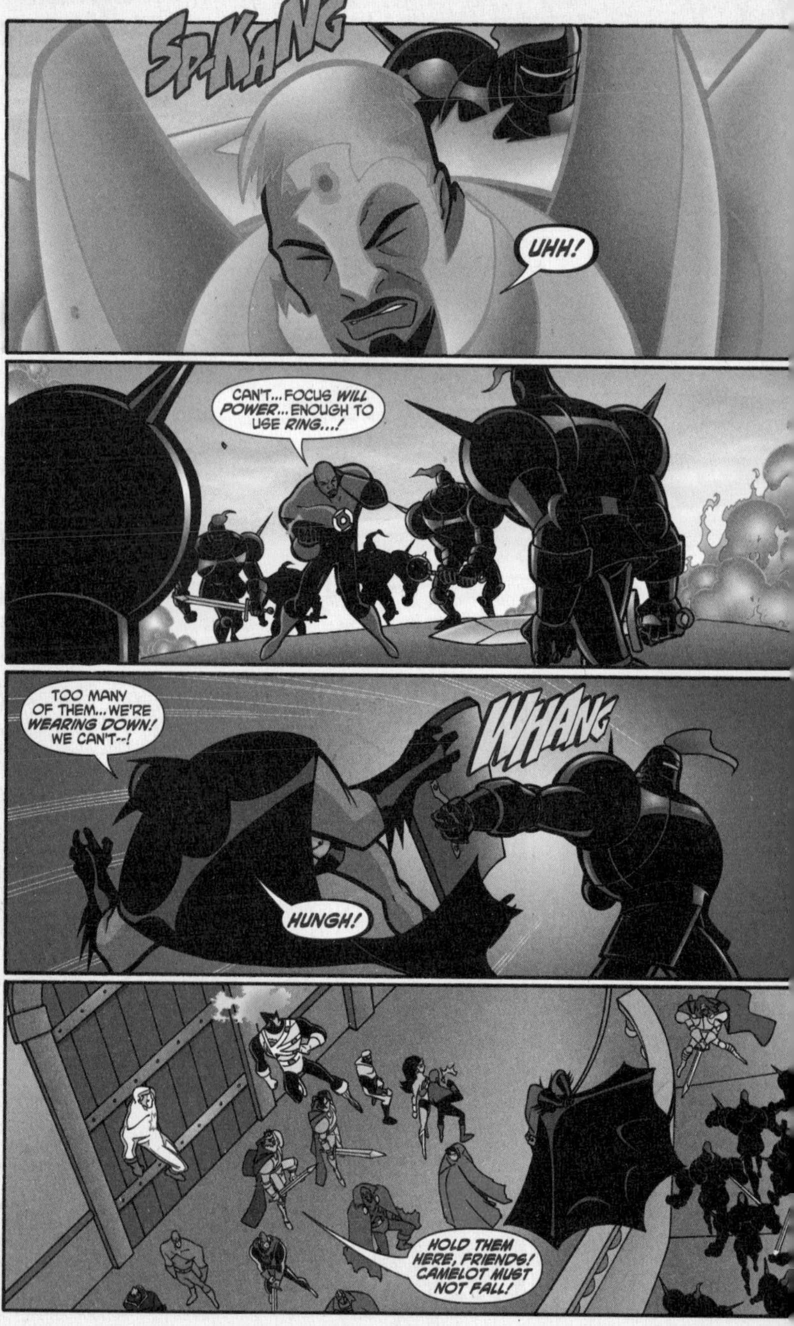
SP-KANG
UHH!
CAN'T...FOCUS WILL POWER...ENOUGH TO USE RING...!
TOO MANY OF THEM...WE'RE WEARING DOWN! WE CAN'T--!
WHANG
HUNGH!
HOLD THEM HERE, FRIENDS! CAMELOT MUST NOT FALL!

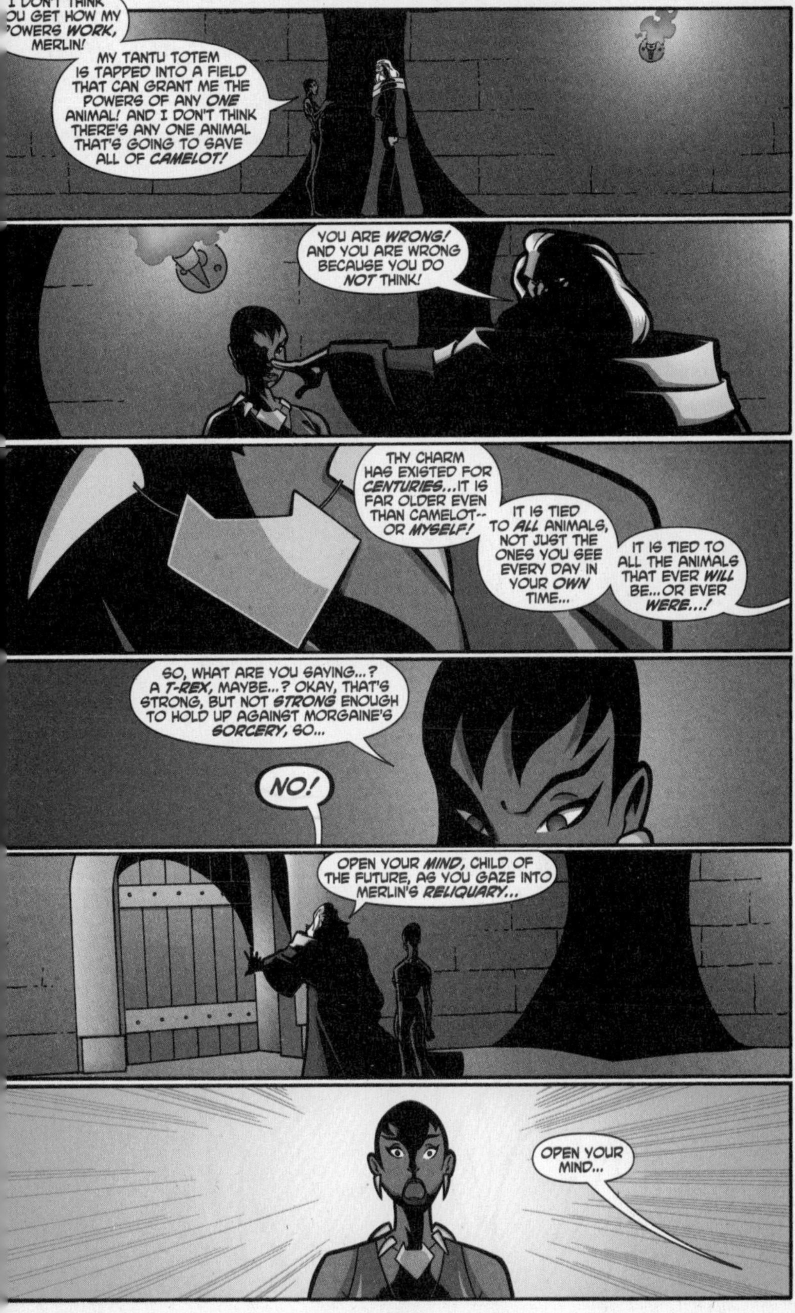
I DON'T THINK YOU GET HOW MY POWERS WORK, MERLIN!
MY TANTU TOTEM IS TAPPED INTO A FIELD THAT CAN GRANT ME THE POWERS OF ANY ONE ANIMAL! AND I DON'T THINK THERE'S ANY ONE ANIMAL THAT'S GOING TO SAVE ALL OF CAMELOT!
YOU ARE WRONG! AND YOU ARE WRONG BECAUSE YOU DO NOT THINK!
THY CHARM HAS EXISTED FOR CENTURIES...IT IS FAR OLDER EVEN THAN CAMELOT-- OR MYSELF!
IT IS TIED TO ALL ANIMALS, NOT JUST THE ONES YOU SEE EVERY DAY IN YOUR OWN TIME...
IT IS TIED TO ALL THE ANIMALS THAT EVER WILL BE...OR EVER WERE...!
SO, WHAT ARE YOU SAYING...? A T-REX, MAYBE...? OKAY, THAT'S STRONG, BUT NOT STRONG ENOUGH TO HOLD UP AGAINST MORGAINE'S SORCERY, SO...
NO!
OPEN YOUR MIND, CHILD OF THE FUTURE, AS YOU GAZE INTO MERLIN'S RELIQUARY...
OPEN YOUR MIND...

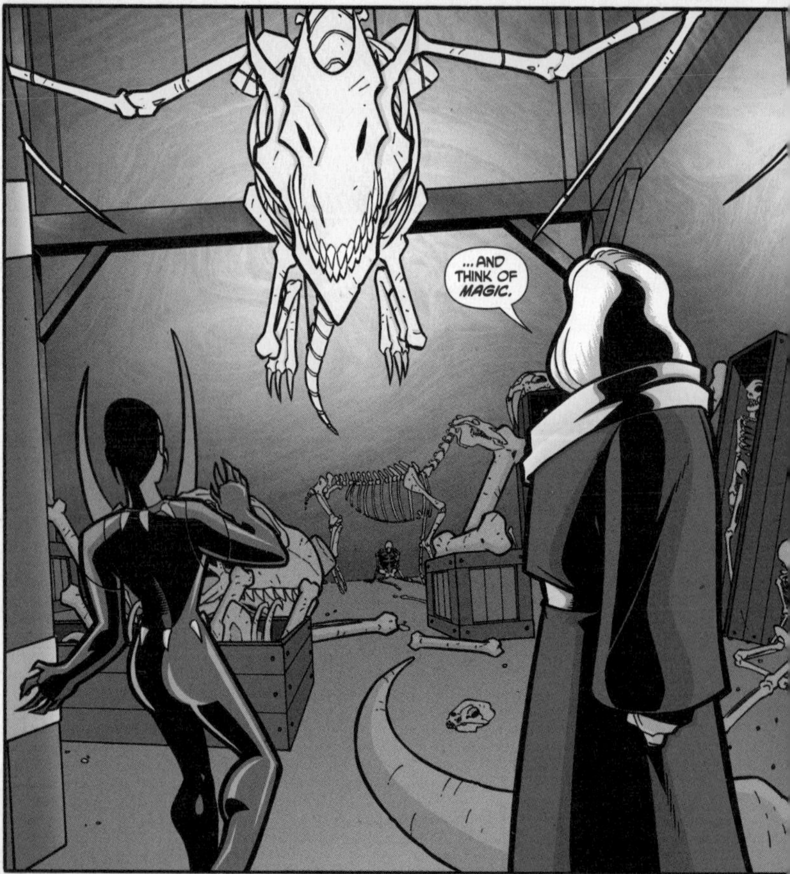
...AND THINK OF *MAGIC*.

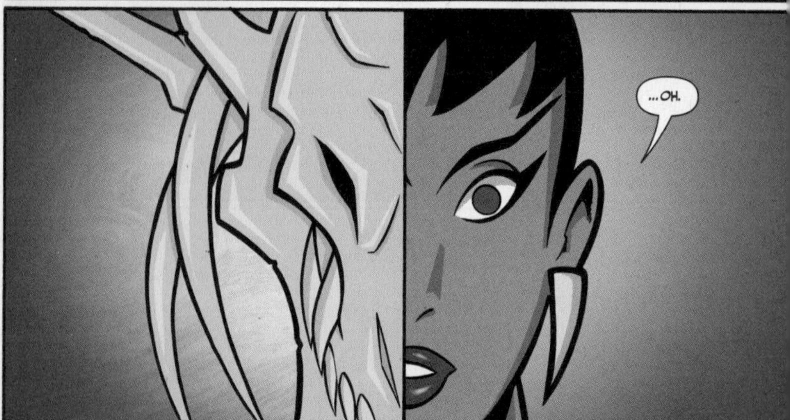
...OH.

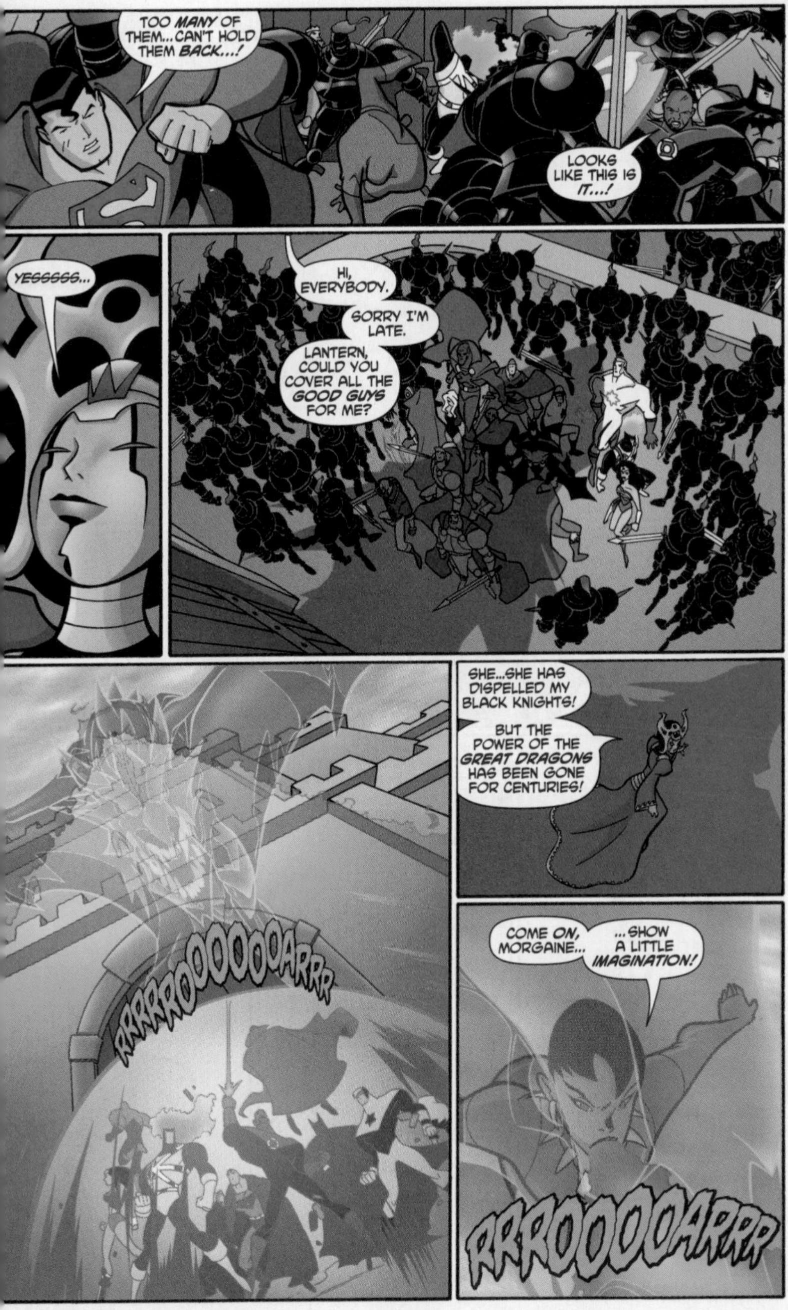
TOO MANY OF THEM...CAN'T HOLD THEM BACK...!
LOOKS LIKE THIS IS IT...!
YESSSSS...
HI, EVERYBODY.
SORRY I'M LATE.
LANTERN, COULD YOU COVER ALL THE GOOD GUYS FOR ME?
RRRROOOOOOARRR
SHE...SHE HAS DISPELLED MY BLACK KNIGHTS!
BUT THE POWER OF THE GREAT DRAGONS HAS BEEN GONE FOR CENTURIES!
COME ON, MORGAINE...
...SHOW A LITTLE IMAGINATION!
RRROOOOOARRR

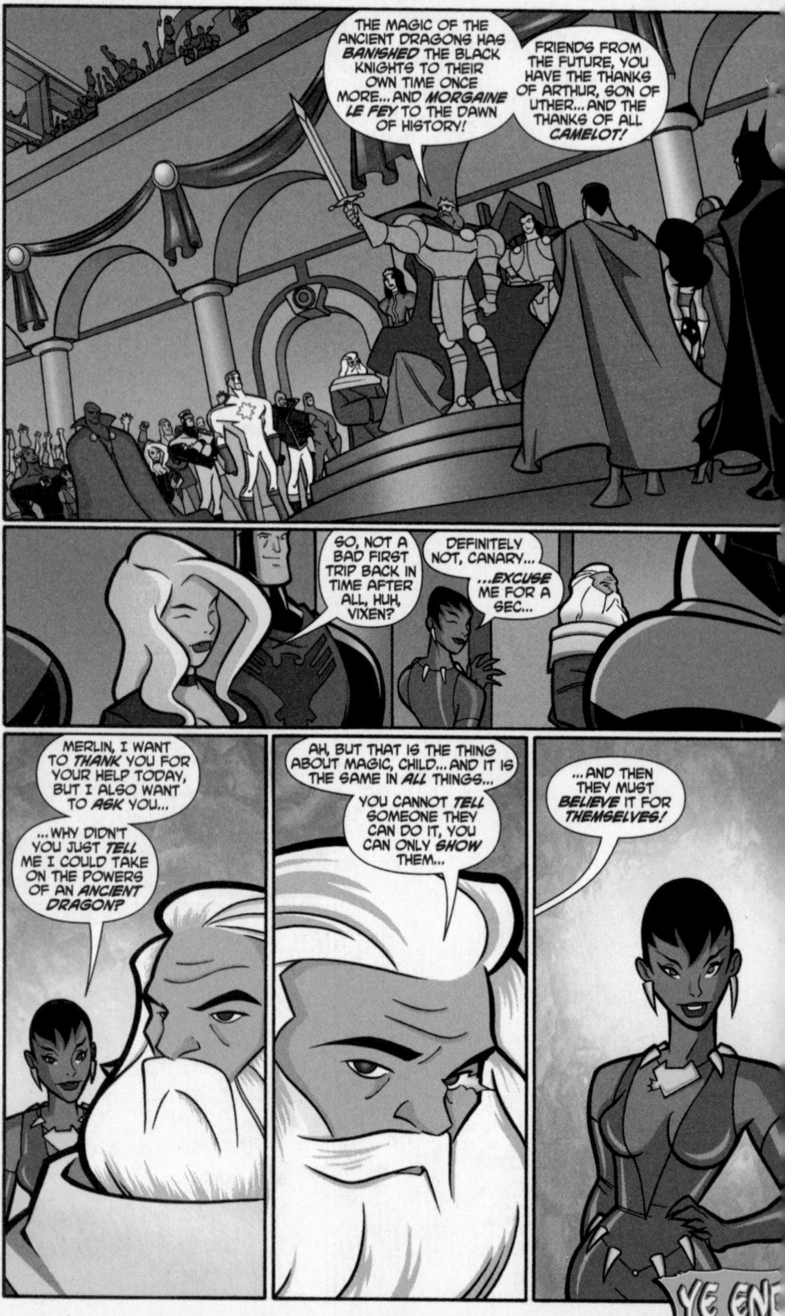
THE MAGIC OF THE ANCIENT DRAGONS HAS BANISHED THE BLACK KNIGHTS TO THEIR OWN TIME ONCE MORE... AND MORGAINE LE FEY TO THE DAWN OF HISTORY!
FRIENDS FROM THE FUTURE, YOU HAVE THE THANKS OF ARTHUR, SON OF UTHER... AND THE THANKS OF ALL CAMELOT!
SO, NOT A BAD FIRST TRIP BACK IN TIME AFTER ALL, HUH, VIXEN?
DEFINITELY NOT, CANARY...
...EXCUSE ME FOR A SEC...
MERLIN, I WANT TO THANK YOU FOR YOUR HELP TODAY, BUT I ALSO WANT TO ASK YOU...
...WHY DIDN'T YOU JUST TELL ME I COULD TAKE ON THE POWERS OF AN ANCIENT DRAGON?
AH, BUT THAT IS THE THING ABOUT MAGIC, CHILD... AND IT IS THE SAME IN ALL THINGS...
YOU CANNOT TELL SOMEONE THEY CAN DO IT, YOU CAN ONLY SHOW THEM...
...AND THEN THEY MUST BELIEVE IT FOR THEMSELVES!

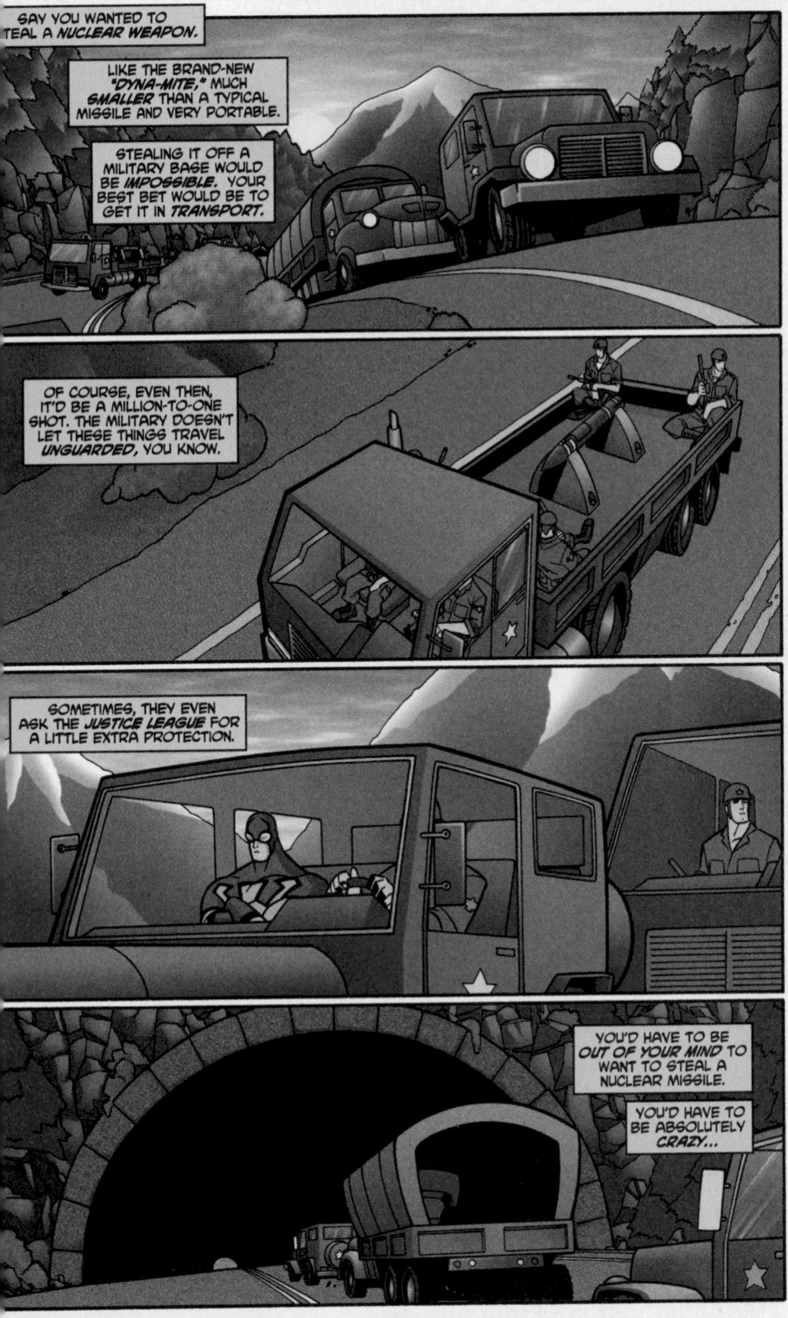

SAY YOU WANTED TO TEAL A NUCLEAR WEAPON.
LIKE THE BRAND-NEW "DYNA-MITE," MUCH SMALLER THAN A TYPICAL MISSILE AND VERY PORTABLE.
STEALING IT OFF A MILITARY BASE WOULD BE IMPOSSIBLE. YOUR BEST BET WOULD BE TO GET IT IN TRANSPORT.
OF COURSE, EVEN THEN, IT'D BE A MILLION-TO-ONE SHOT. THE MILITARY DOESN'T LET THESE THINGS TRAVEL UNGUARDED, YOU KNOW.
SOMETIMES, THEY EVEN ASK THE JUSTICE LEAGUE FOR A LITTLE EXTRA PROTECTION.
YOU'D HAVE TO BE OUT OF YOUR MIND TO WANT TO STEAL A NUCLEAR MISSILE.
YOU'D HAVE TO BE ABSOLUTELY CRAZY...

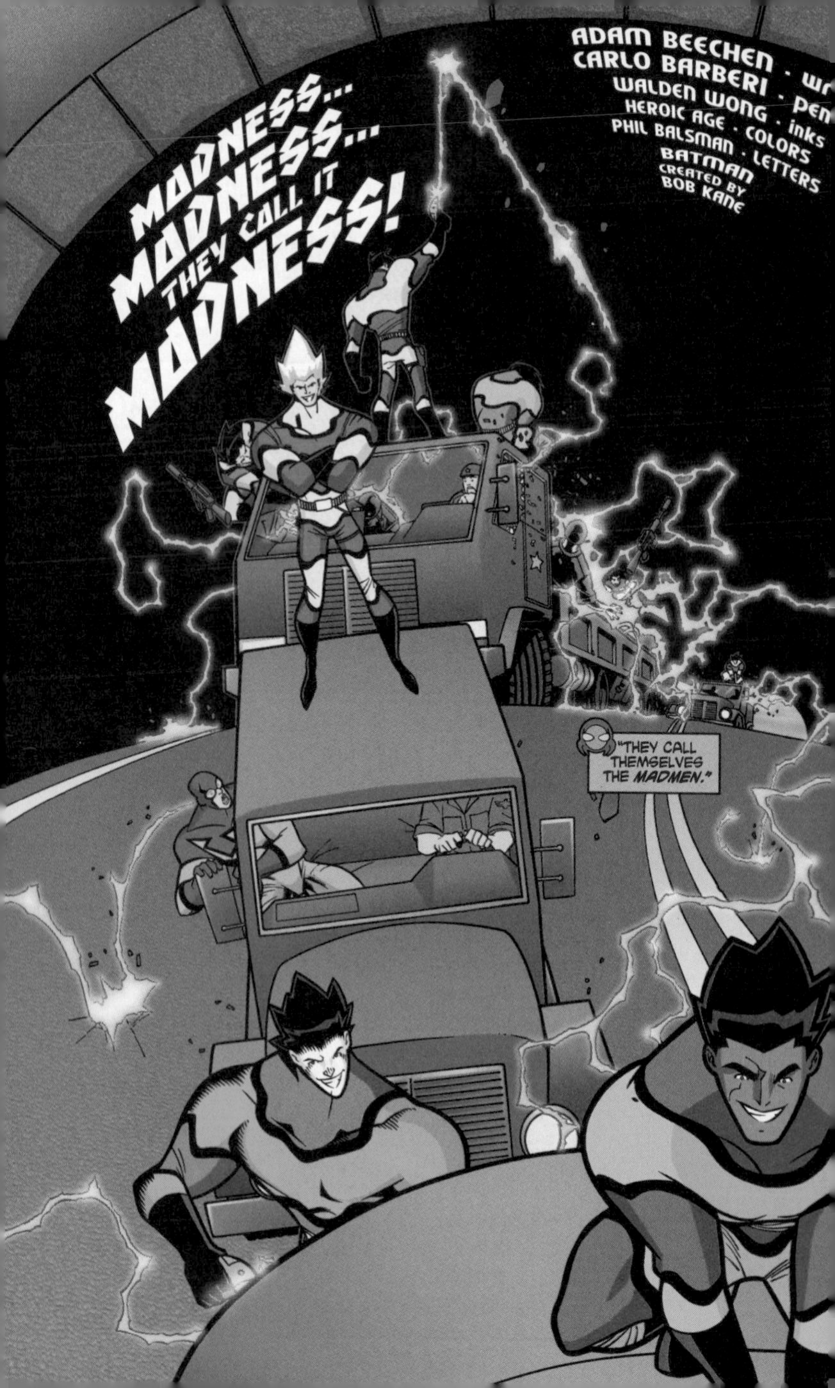

MADNESS... MADNESS... THEY CALL IT MADNESS!
ADAM BEECHEN - wr
CARLO BARBERI - pen
WALDEN WONG - inks
HEROIC AGE - COLORS
PHIL BALSMAN - LETTERS
BATMAN CREATED BY BOB KANE
"THEY CALL THEMSELVES THE MADMEN."

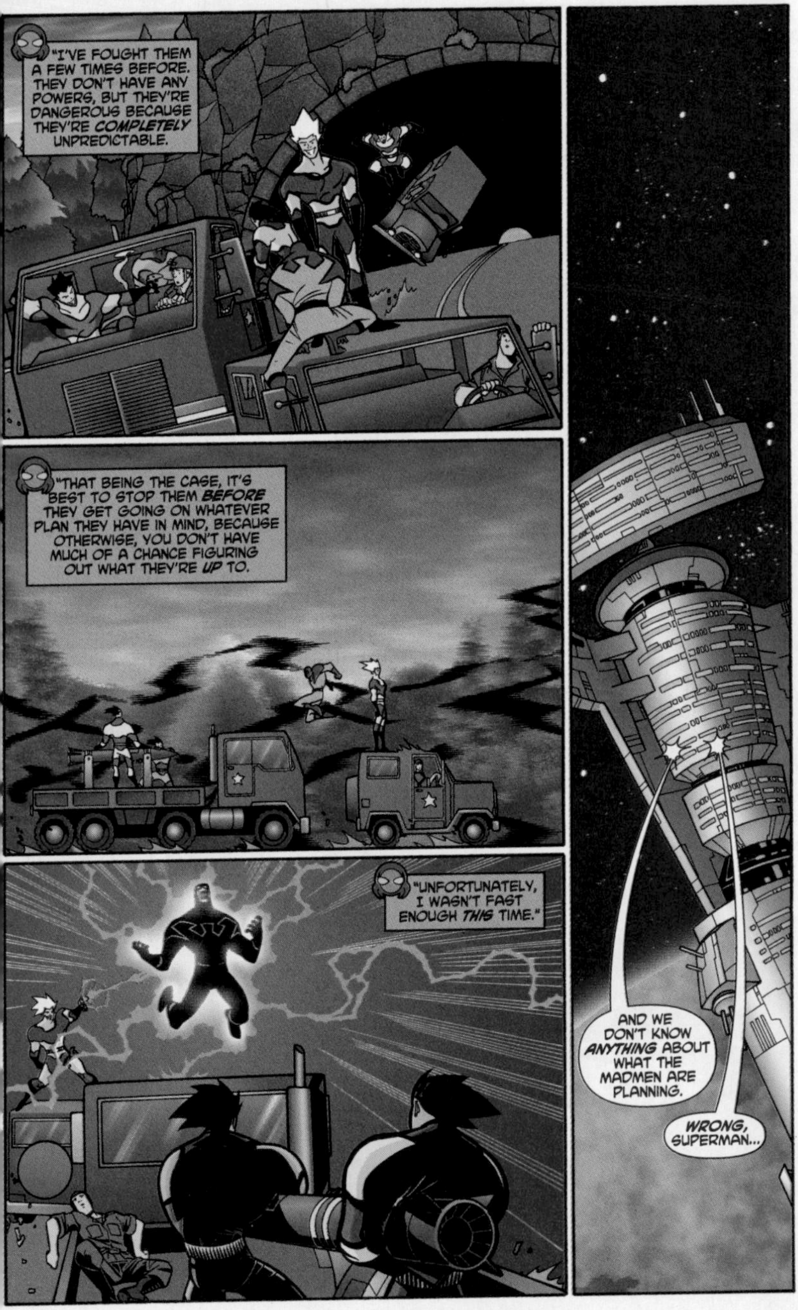
"I'VE FOUGHT THEM A FEW TIMES BEFORE. THEY DON'T HAVE ANY POWERS, BUT THEY'RE DANGEROUS BECAUSE THEY'RE COMPLETELY UNPREDICTABLE.
"THAT BEING THE CASE, IT'S BEST TO STOP THEM BEFORE THEY GET GOING ON WHATEVER PLAN THEY HAVE IN MIND, BECAUSE OTHERWISE, YOU DON'T HAVE MUCH OF A CHANCE FIGURING OUT WHAT THEY'RE UP TO.
"UNFORTUNATELY, I WASN'T FAST ENOUGH THIS TIME."
AND WE DON'T KNOW ANYTHING ABOUT WHAT THE MADMEN ARE PLANNING.
WRONG, SUPERMAN...

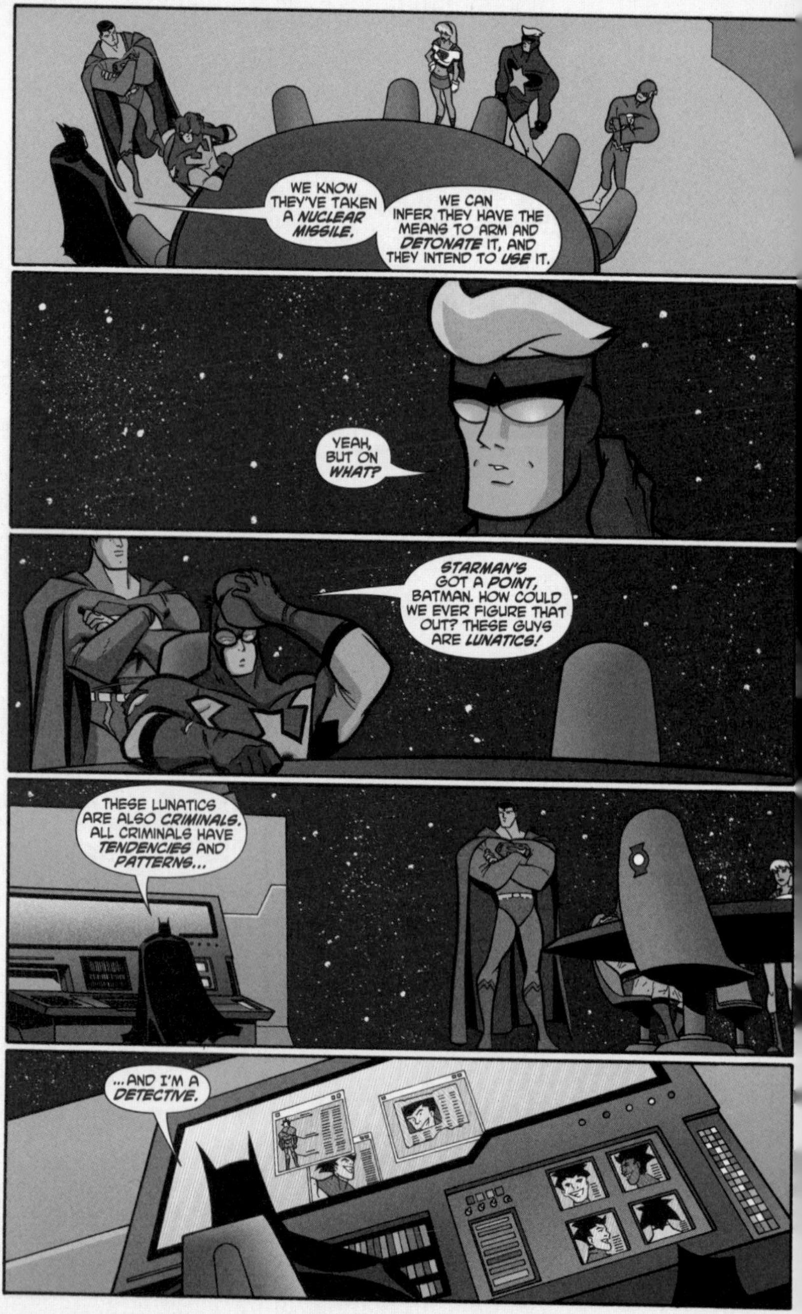
WE KNOW THEY'VE TAKEN A NUCLEAR MISSILE.
WE CAN INFER THEY HAVE THE MEANS TO ARM AND DETONATE IT, AND THEY INTEND TO USE IT.
YEAH, BUT ON WHAT?
STARMAN'S GOT A POINT, BATMAN. HOW COULD WE EVER FIGURE THAT OUT? THESE GUYS ARE LUNATICS!
THESE LUNATICS ARE ALSO CRIMINALS. ALL CRIMINALS HAVE TENDENCIES AND PATTERNS...
...AND I'M A DETECTIVE.

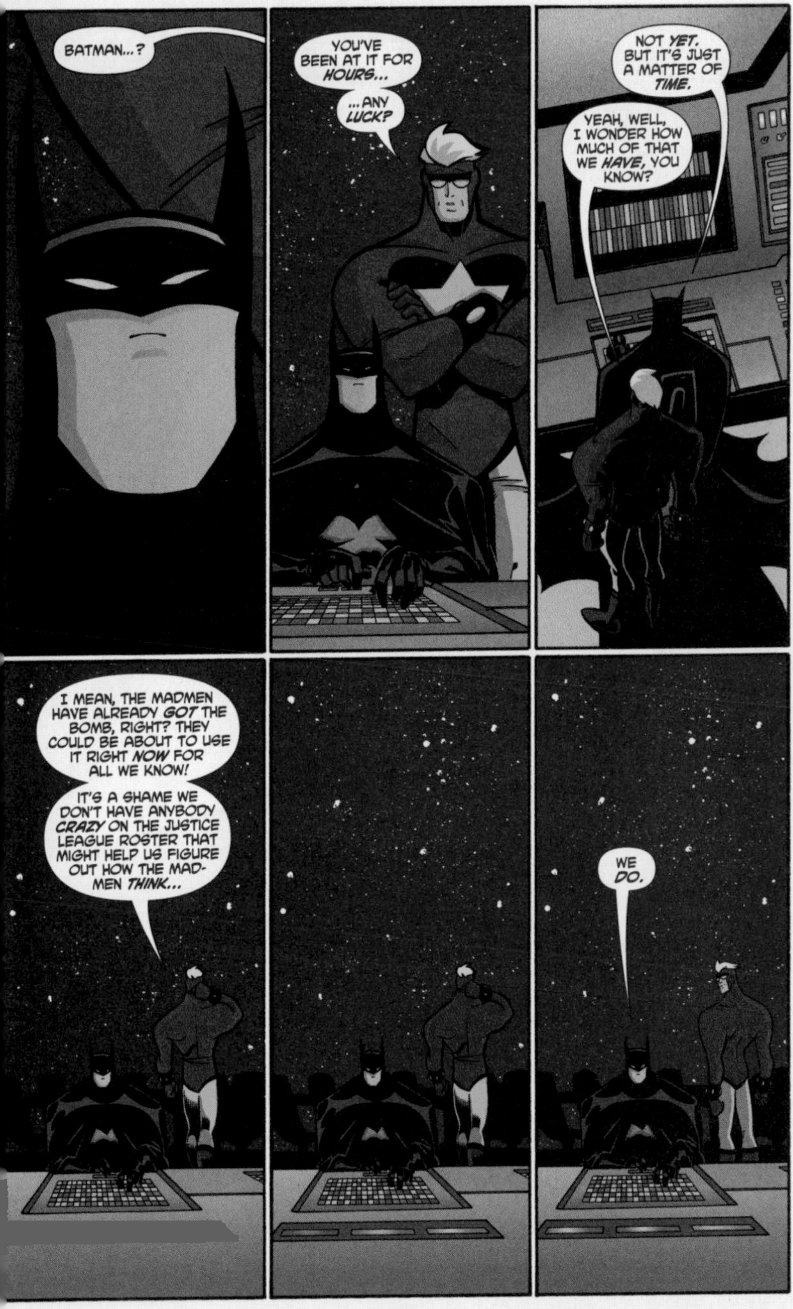
BATMAN...?
YOU'VE BEEN AT IT FOR HOURS...
...ANY LUCK?
NOT YET. BUT IT'S JUST A MATTER OF TIME.
YEAH, WELL, I WONDER HOW MUCH OF THAT WE HAVE, YOU KNOW?
I MEAN, THE MADMEN HAVE ALREADY GOT THE BOMB, RIGHT? THEY COULD BE ABOUT TO USE IT RIGHT NOW FOR ALL WE KNOW!
IT'S A SHAME WE DON'T HAVE ANYBODY CRAZY ON THE JUSTICE LEAGUE ROSTER THAT MIGHT HELP US FIGURE OUT HOW THE MAD-MEN THINK...
WE DO.

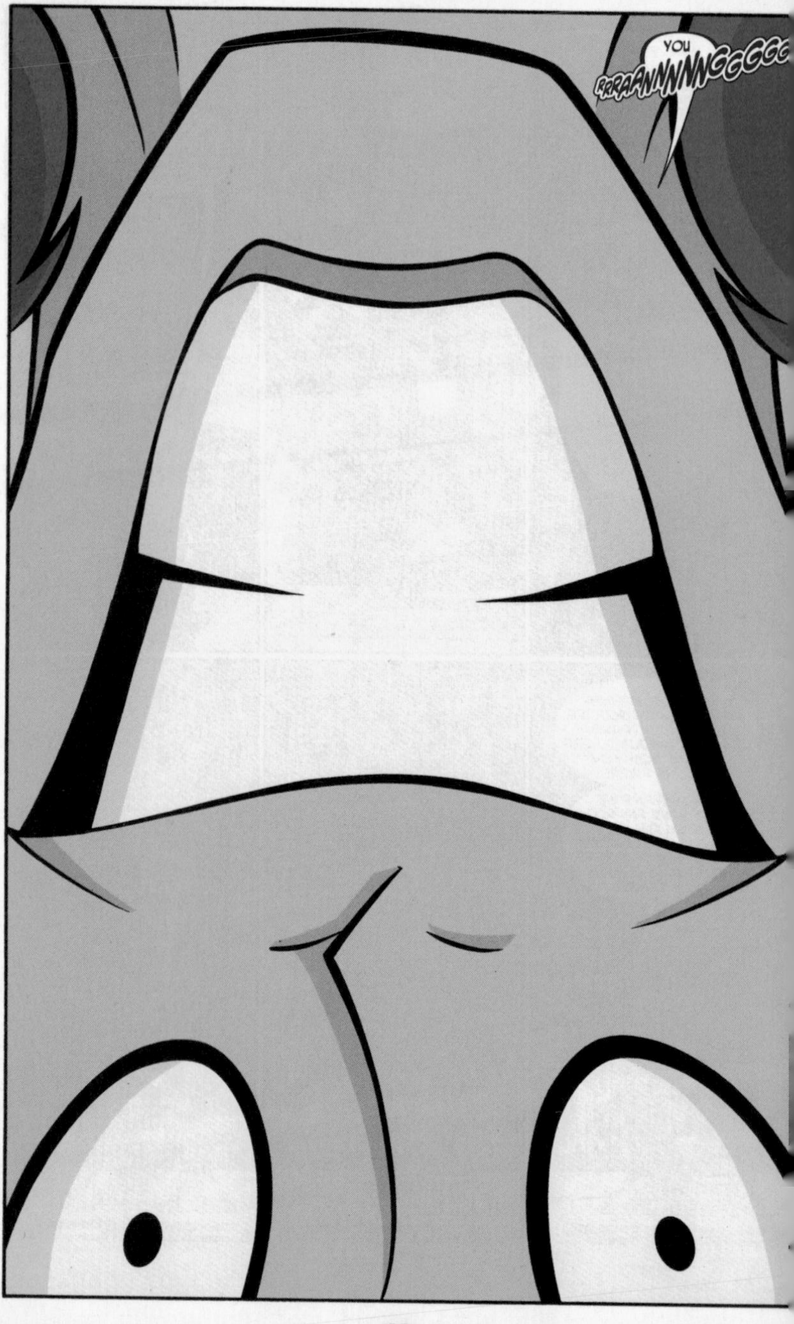
YOU
RRRAANNNNNGGGGG

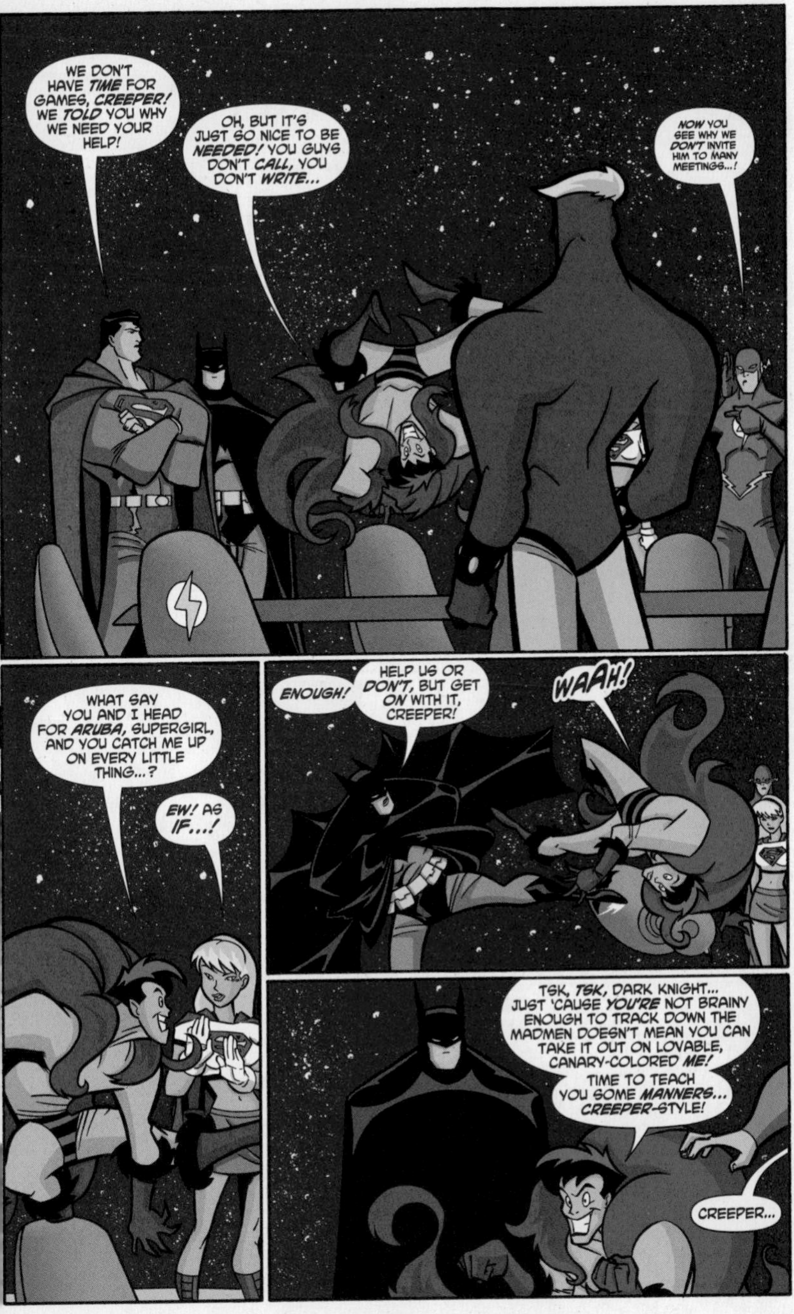
WE DON'T HAVE TIME FOR GAMES, CREEPER! WE TOLD YOU WHY WE NEED YOUR HELP!
OH, BUT IT'S JUST SO NICE TO BE NEEDED! YOU GUYS DON'T CALL, YOU DON'T WRITE...
NOW YOU SEE WHY WE DON'T INVITE HIM TO MANY MEETINGS...!
WHAT SAY YOU AND I HEAD FOR ARUBA, SUPERGIRL, AND YOU CATCH ME UP ON EVERY LITTLE THING...?
EW! AS IF...!
ENOUGH!
HELP US OR DON'T, BUT GET ON WITH IT, CREEPER!
WAAH!
TSK, TSK, DARK KNIGHT... JUST 'CAUSE YOU'RE NOT BRAINY ENOUGH TO TRACK DOWN THE MADMEN DOESN'T MEAN YOU CAN TAKE IT OUT ON LOVABLE, CANARY-COLORED ME!
TIME TO TEACH YOU SOME MANNERS... CREEPER-STYLE!
CREEPER...

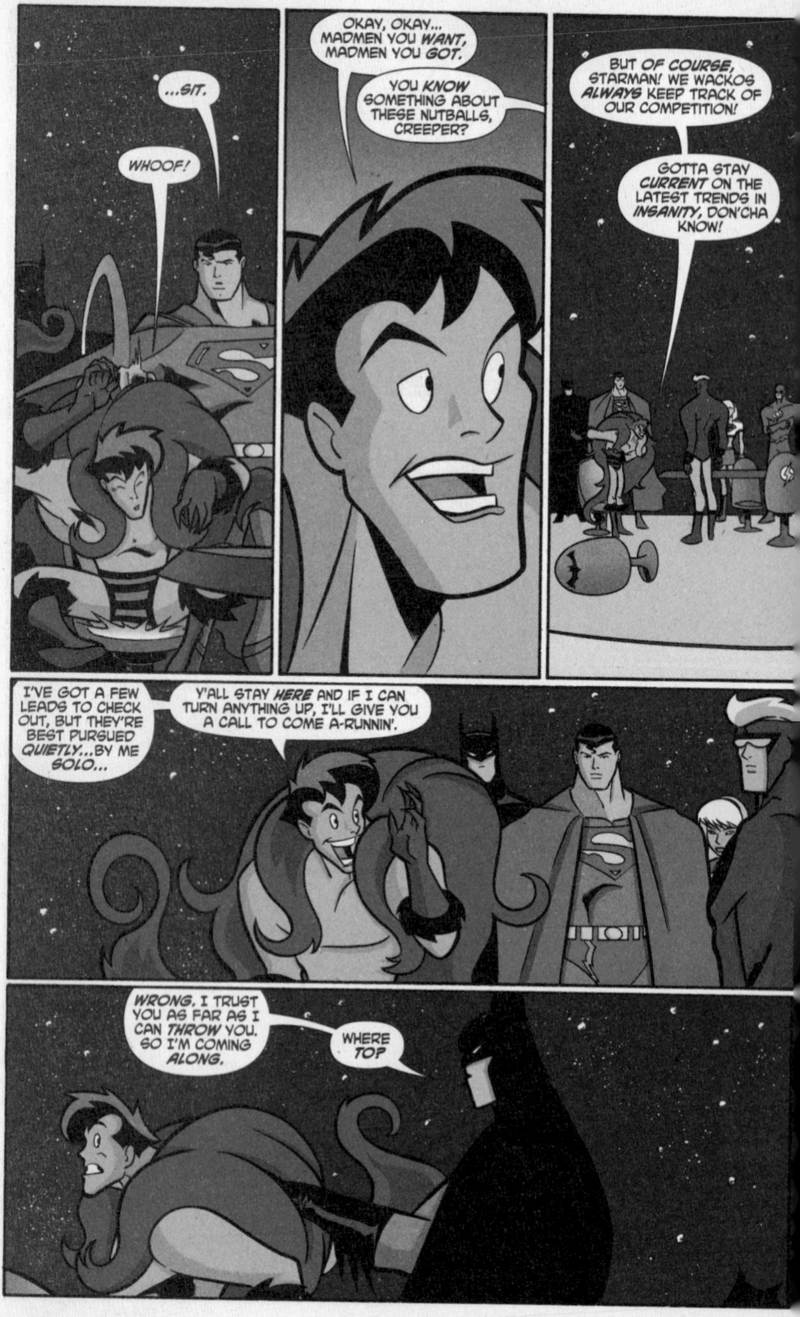
...SIT.
WHOOF!
OKAY, OKAY... MADMEN YOU WANT, MADMEN YOU GOT.
YOU KNOW SOMETHING ABOUT THESE NUTBALLS, CREEPER?
BUT OF COURSE, STARMAN! WE WACKOS ALWAYS KEEP TRACK OF OUR COMPETITION!
GOTTA STAY CURRENT ON THE LATEST TRENDS IN INSANITY, DON'CHA KNOW!
I'VE GOT A FEW LEADS TO CHECK OUT, BUT THEY'RE BEST PURSUED QUIETLY...BY ME SOLO...
Y'ALL STAY HERE AND IF I CAN TURN ANYTHING UP, I'LL GIVE YOU A CALL TO COME A-RUNNIN'.
WRONG. I TRUST YOU AS FAR AS I CAN THROW YOU. SO I'M COMING ALONG.
WHERE TO?

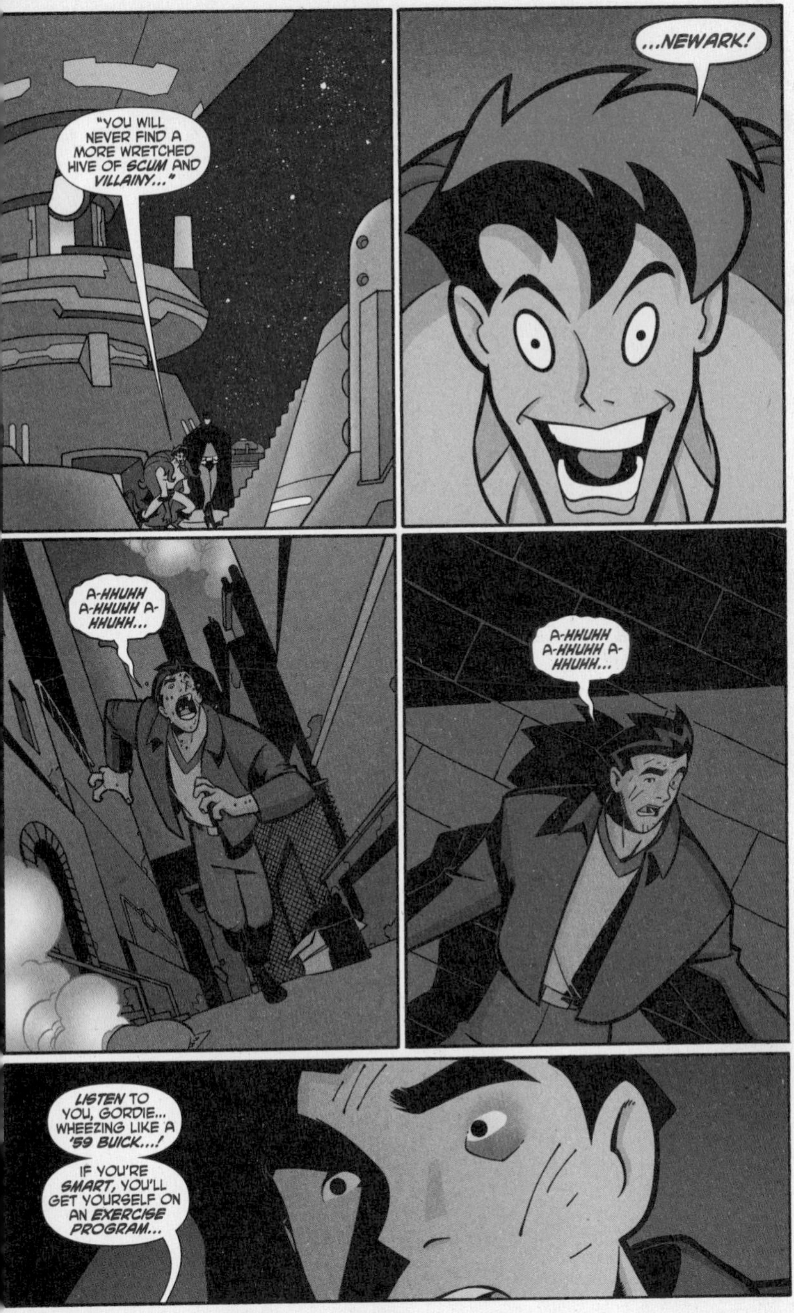
"YOU WILL NEVER FIND A MORE WRETCHED HIVE OF SCUM AND VILLAINY..."
...NEWARK!
A-HHUHH A-HHUHH A-HHUHH...
A-HHUHH A-HHUHH A-HHUHH...
LISTEN TO YOU, GORDIE... WHEEZING LIKE A '59 BUICK...!
IF YOU'RE SMART, YOU'LL GET YOURSELF ON AN EXERCISE PROGRAM...

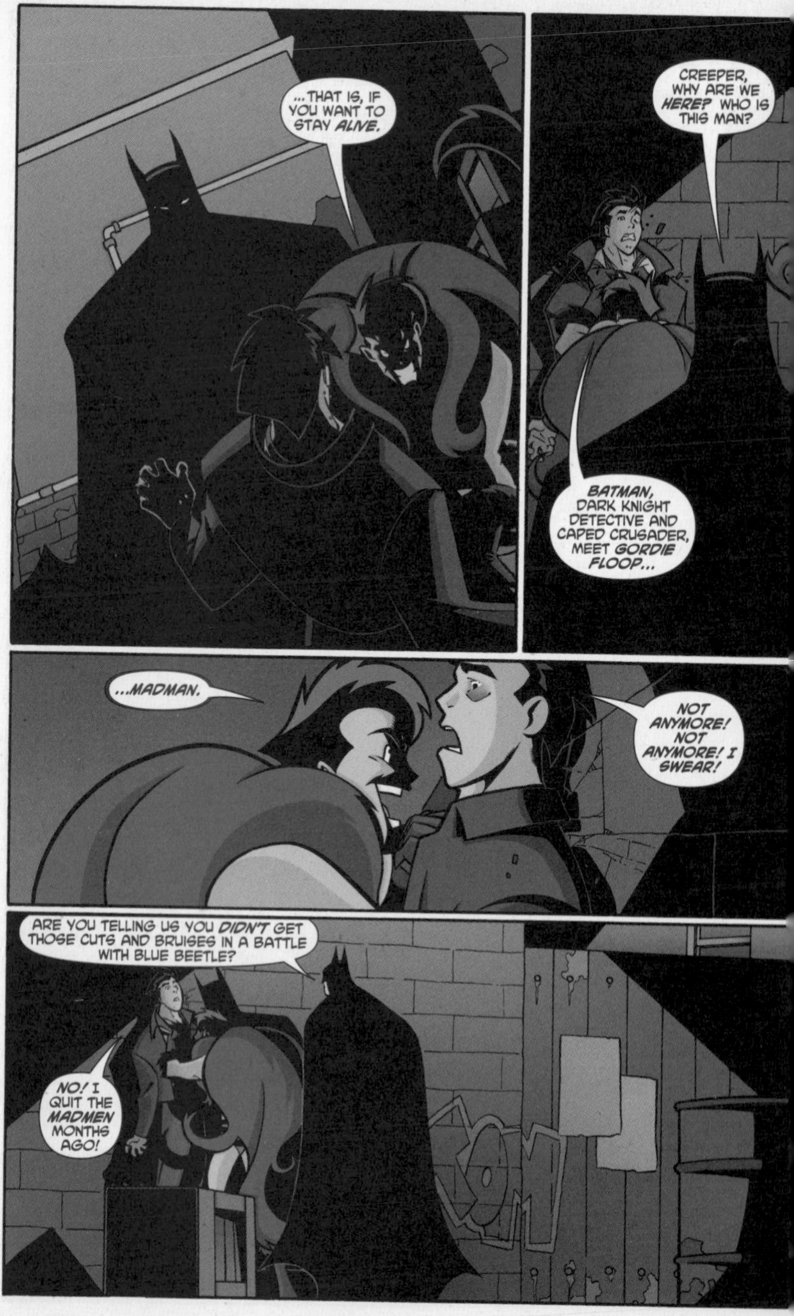

...THAT IS, IF YOU WANT TO STAY *ALIVE*.
CREEPER, WHY ARE WE *HERE?* WHO IS THIS MAN?
BATMAN, DARK KNIGHT DETECTIVE AND CAPED CRUSADER, MEET *GORDIE FLOOP...*
...MADMAN.
NOT ANYMORE! NOT ANYMORE! I SWEAR!
ARE YOU TELLING US YOU *DIDN'T* GET THOSE CUTS AND BRUISES IN A BATTLE WITH BLUE BEETLE?
NO! I QUIT THE *MADMEN* MONTHS AGO!

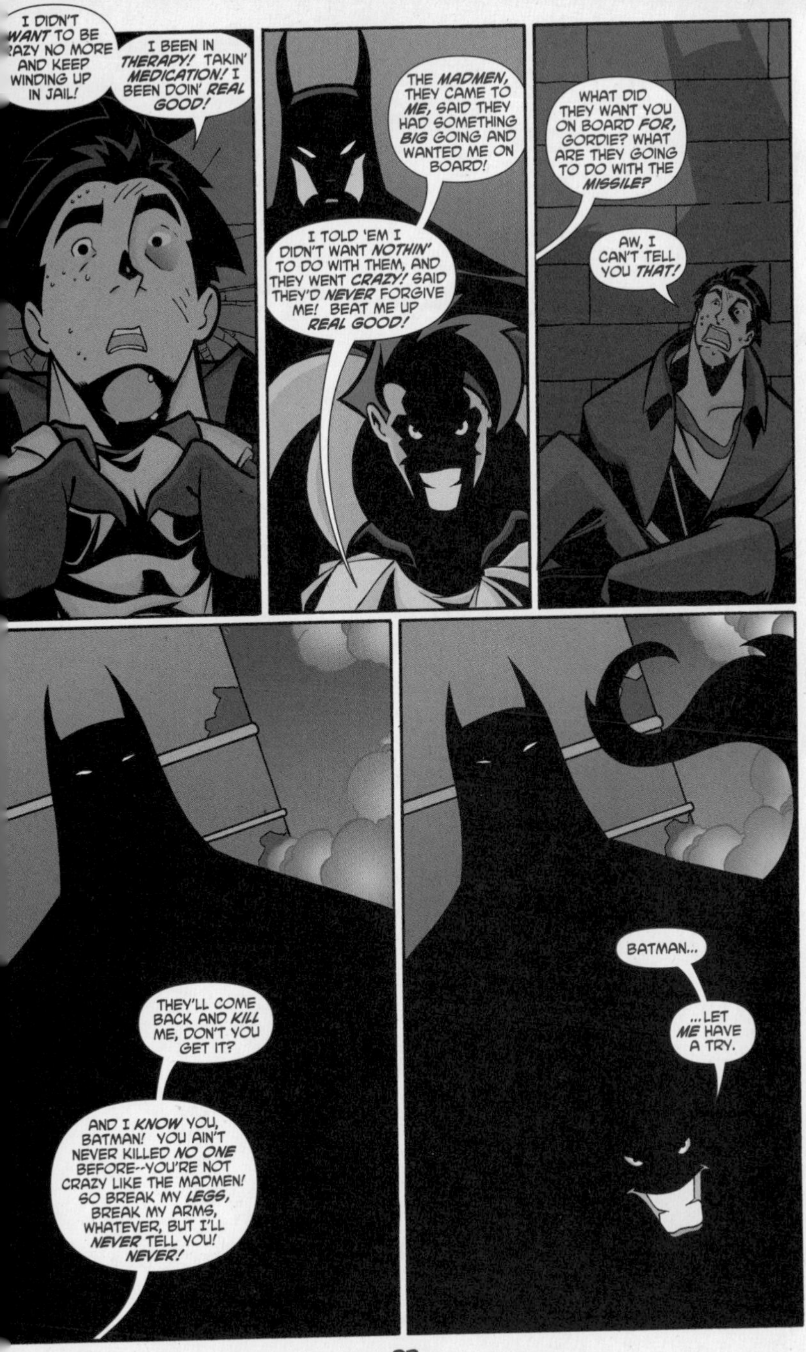

I DIDN'T WANT TO BE CRAZY NO MORE AND KEEP WINDING UP IN JAIL!
I BEEN IN THERAPY! TAKIN' MEDICATION! I BEEN DOIN' REAL GOOD!
THE MADMEN, THEY CAME TO ME, SAID THEY HAD SOMETHING BIG GOING AND WANTED ME ON BOARD!
I TOLD 'EM I DIDN'T WANT NOTHIN' TO DO WITH THEM, AND THEY WENT CRAZY! SAID THEY'D NEVER FORGIVE ME! BEAT ME UP REAL GOOD!
WHAT DID THEY WANT YOU ON BOARD FOR, GORDIE? WHAT ARE THEY GOING TO DO WITH THE MISSILE?
AW, I CAN'T TELL YOU THAT!
THEY'LL COME BACK AND KILL ME, DON'T YOU GET IT?
AND I KNOW YOU, BATMAN! YOU AIN'T NEVER KILLED NO ONE BEFORE--YOU'RE NOT CRAZY LIKE THE MADMEN! SO BREAK MY LEGS, BREAK MY ARMS, WHATEVER, BUT I'LL NEVER TELL YOU! NEVER!
BATMAN...
...LET ME HAVE A TRY.

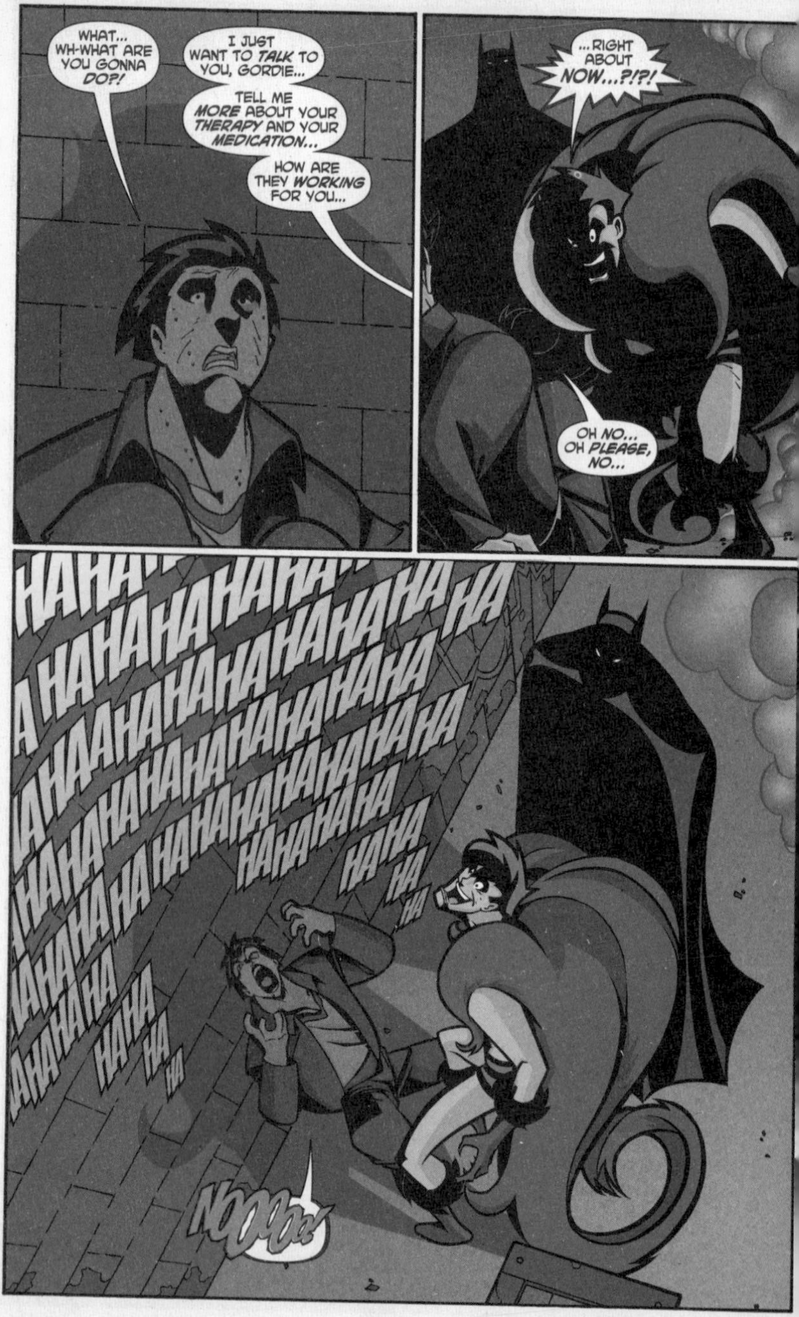
WHAT... WH-WHAT ARE YOU GONNA DO?!
I JUST WANT TO TALK TO YOU, GORDIE...
TELL ME MORE ABOUT YOUR THERAPY AND YOUR MEDICATION...
HOW ARE THEY WORKING FOR YOU...
...RIGHT ABOUT NOW...?!?!
OH NO... OH PLEASE, NO...
HAHAHAHAHAHAHAHAHAHAHA HAHAHAHA
NOOOOo!

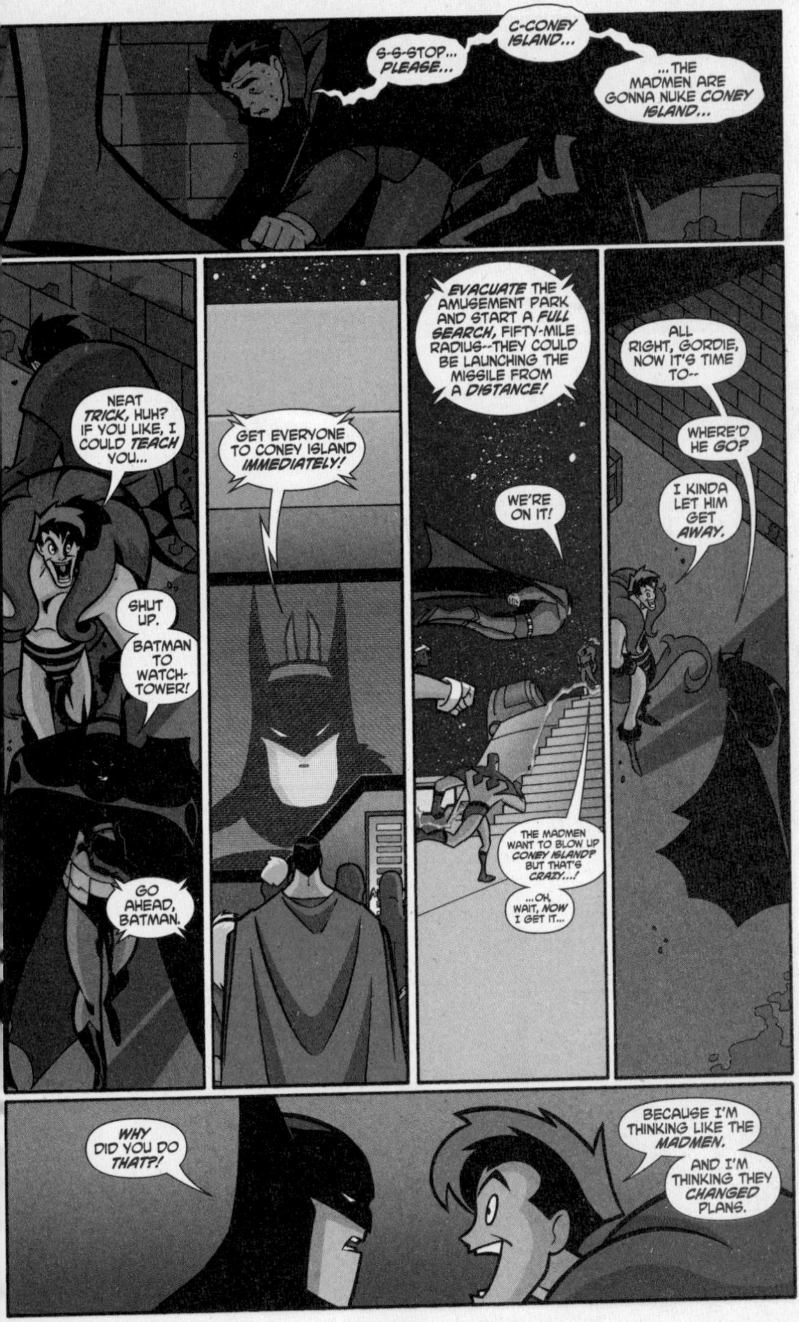
S-S-STOP... PLEASE...
C-CONEY ISLAND...
...THE MADMEN ARE GONNA NUKE CONEY ISLAND...
NEAT TRICK, HUH? IF YOU LIKE, I COULD TEACH YOU...
SHUT UP.
BATMAN TO WATCH-TOWER!
GO AHEAD, BATMAN.
GET EVERYONE TO CONEY ISLAND IMMEDIATELY!
EVACUATE THE AMUSEMENT PARK AND START A FULL SEARCH, FIFTY-MILE RADIUS--THEY COULD BE LAUNCHING THE MISSILE FROM A DISTANCE!
WE'RE ON IT!
THE MADMEN WANT TO BLOW UP CONEY ISLAND? BUT THAT'S CRAZY...!
...OH, WAIT, NOW I GET IT...
ALL RIGHT, GORDIE, NOW IT'S TIME TO--
WHERE'D HE GO?
I KINDA LET HIM GET AWAY.
WHY DID YOU DO THAT?!
BECAUSE I'M THINKING LIKE THE MADMEN.
AND I'M THINKING THEY CHANGED PLANS.

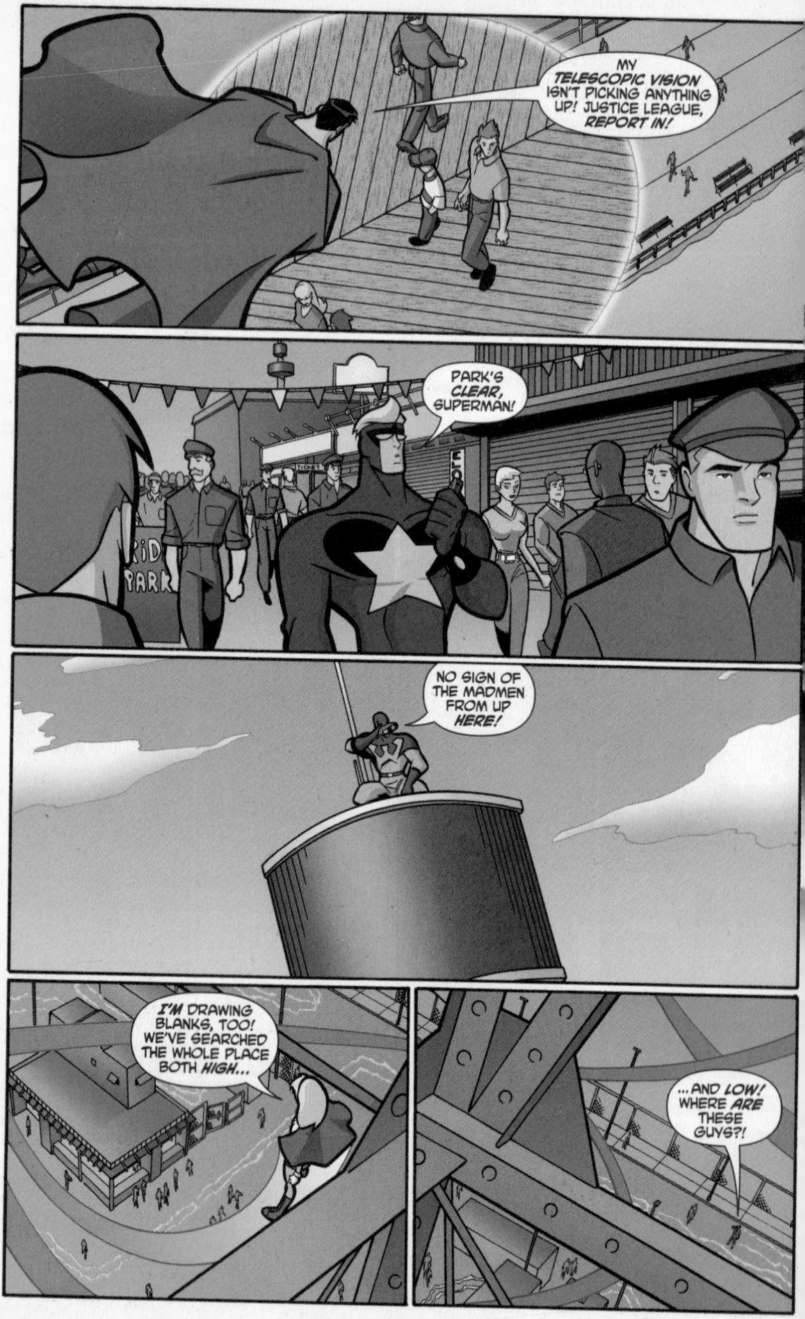
MY TELESCOPIC VISION ISN'T PICKING ANYTHING UP! JUSTICE LEAGUE, REPORT IN!
PARK'S CLEAR, SUPERMAN!
NO SIGN OF THE MADMEN FROM UP HERE!
I'M DRAWING BLANKS, TOO! WE'VE SEARCHED THE WHOLE PLACE BOTH HIGH...
...AND LOW! WHERE ARE THESE GUYS?!

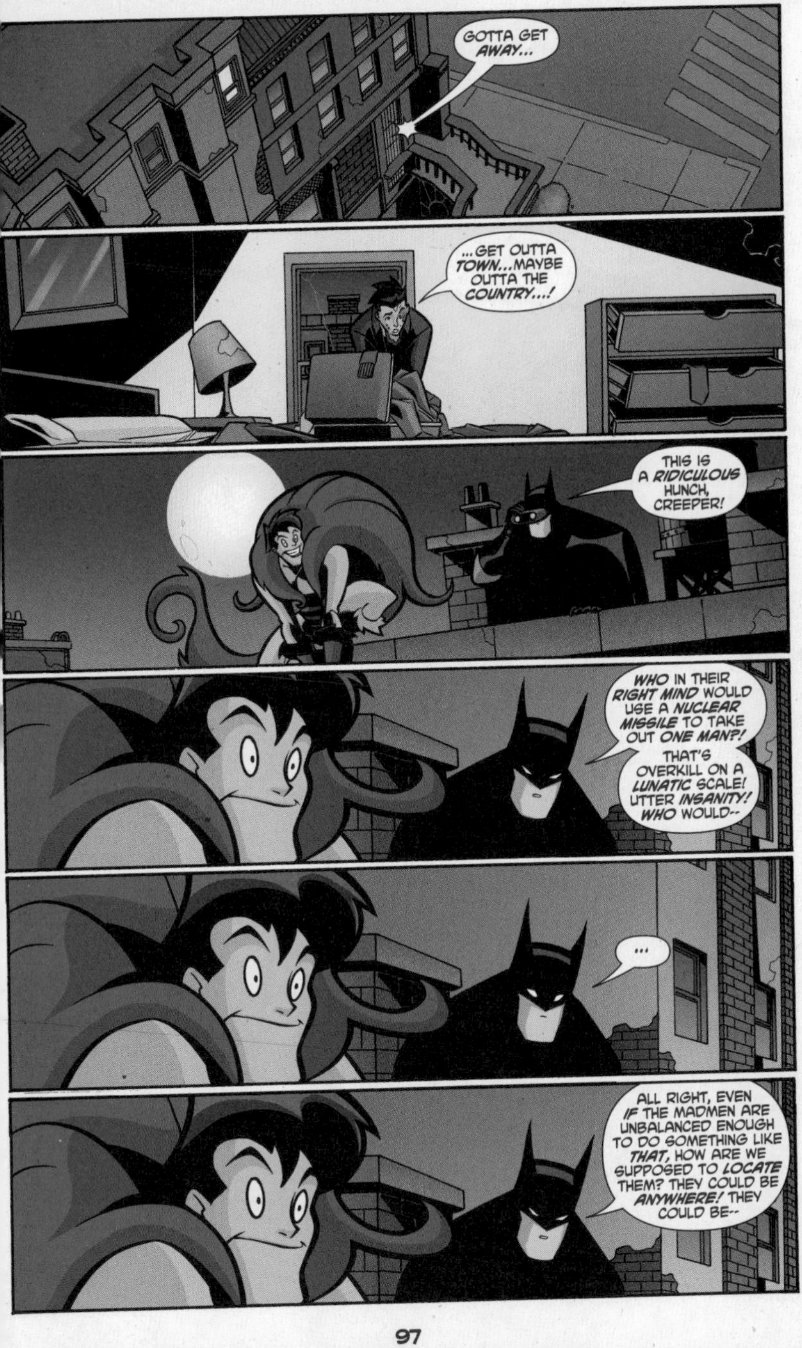
GOTTA GET AWAY...
...GET OUTTA TOWN...MAYBE OUTTA THE COUNTRY...!
THIS IS A RIDICULOUS HUNCH, CREEPER!
WHO IN THEIR RIGHT MIND WOULD USE A NUCLEAR MISSILE TO TAKE OUT ONE MAN?!
THAT'S OVERKILL ON A LUNATIC SCALE! UTTER INSANITY! WHO WOULD--
...
ALL RIGHT, EVEN IF THE MADMEN ARE UNBALANCED ENOUGH TO DO SOMETHING LIKE THAT, HOW ARE WE SUPPOSED TO LOCATE THEM? THEY COULD BE ANYWHERE! THEY COULD BE--

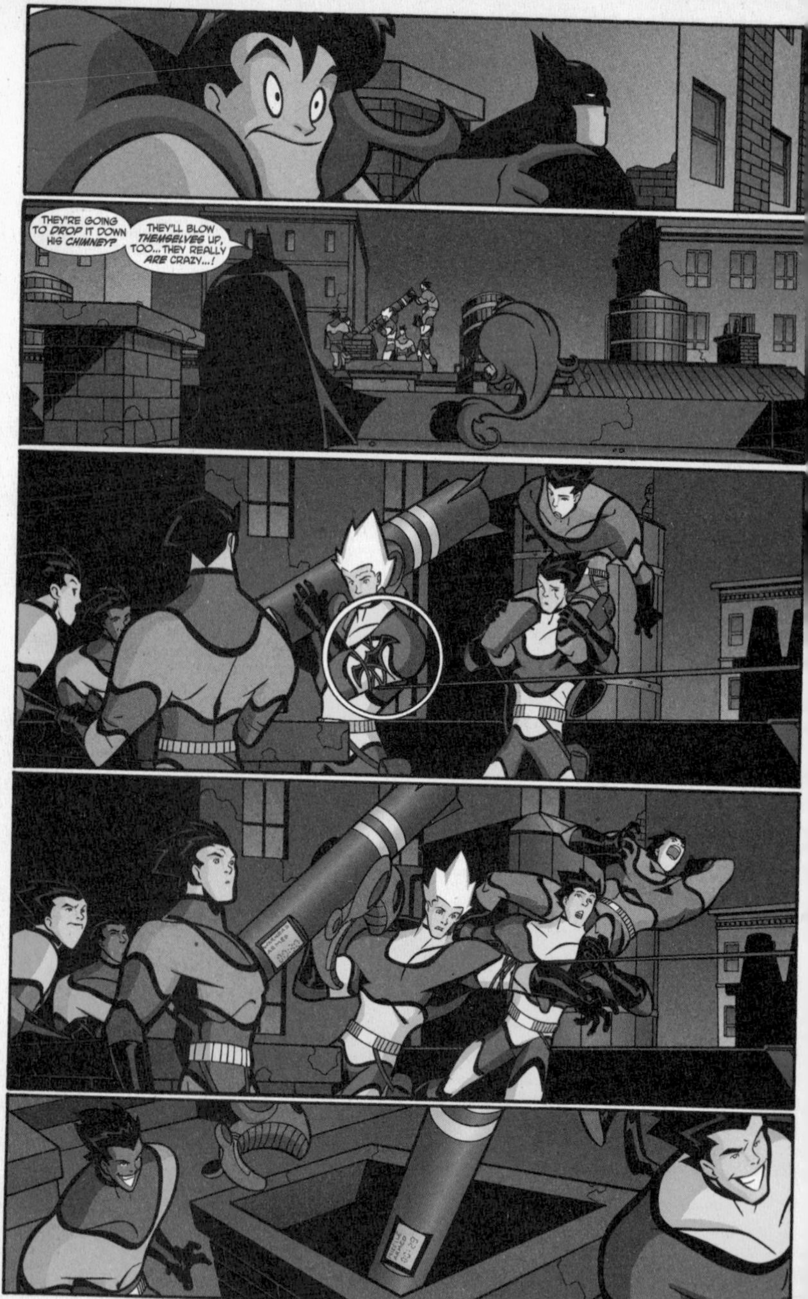
THEY'RE GOING TO *DROP* IT DOWN HIS *CHIMNEY*?
THEY'LL BLOW *THEMSELVES* UP, TOO... THEY REALLY *ARE* CRAZY...!

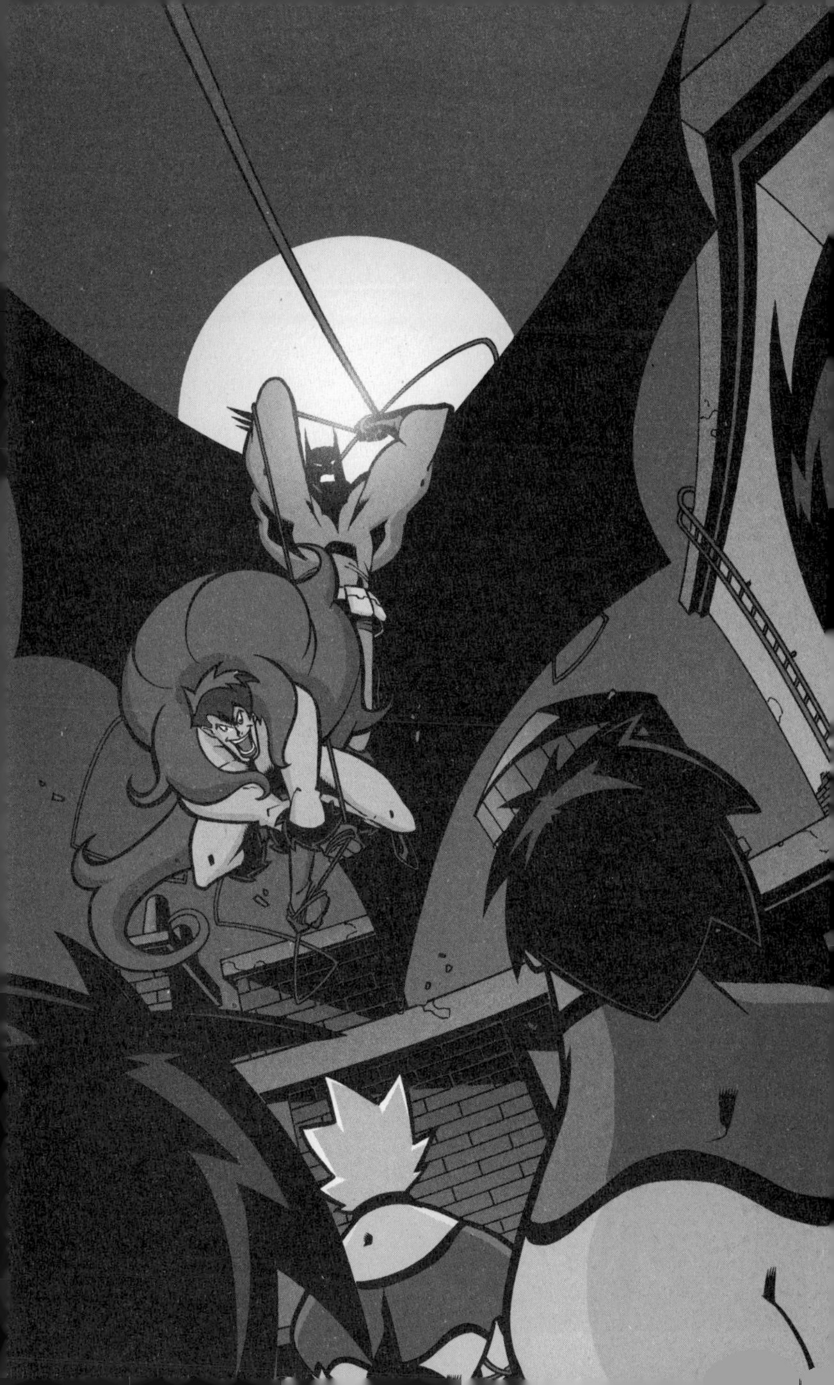

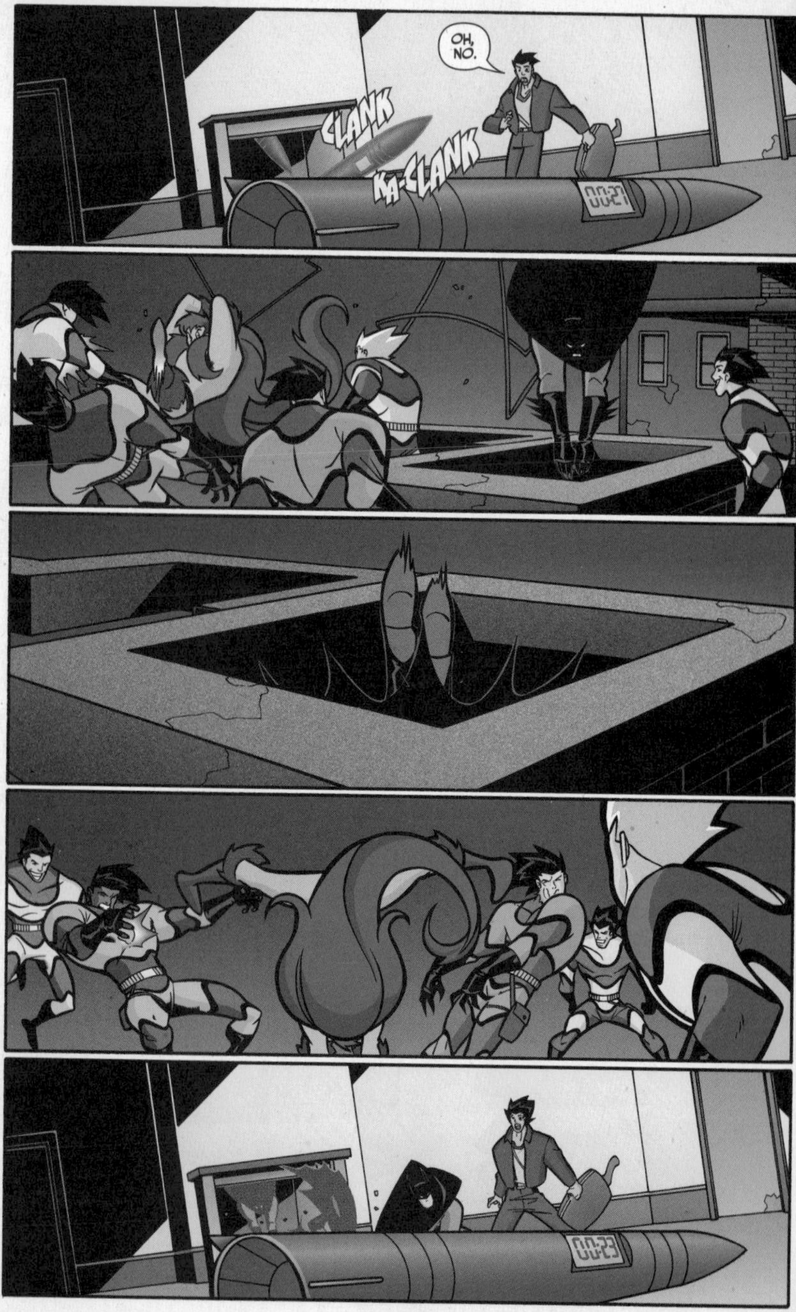

OH, NO.
CLANK
KA-CLANK
00:27
00:23

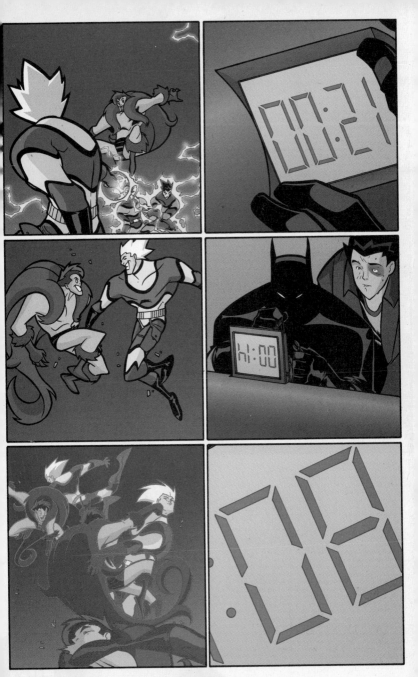

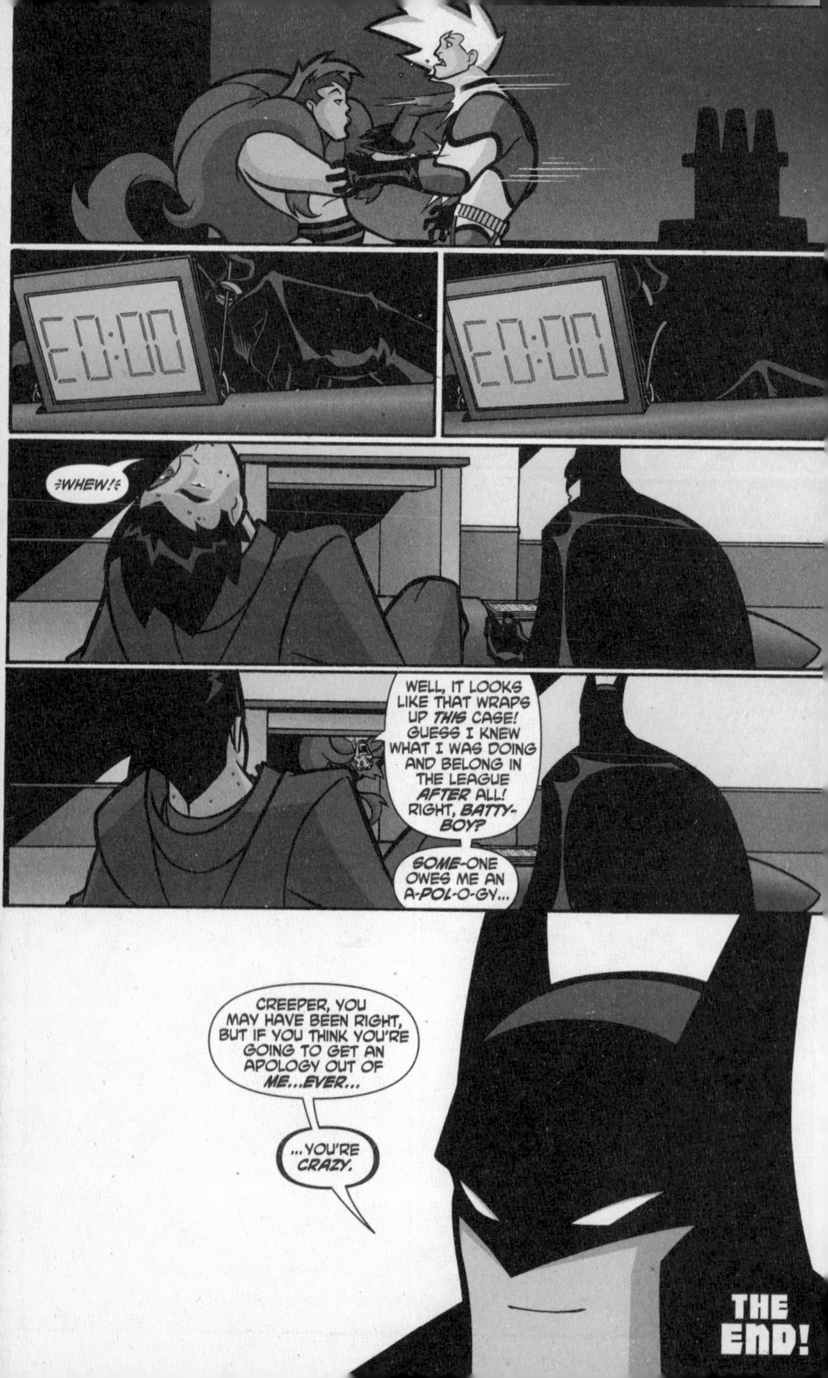

WHEW!
WELL, IT LOOKS LIKE THAT WRAPS UP *THIS* CASE! GUESS I KNEW WHAT I WAS DOING AND BELONG IN THE LEAGUE *AFTER* ALL! RIGHT, *BATTY-BOY*?
SOME-ONE OWES ME AN A-*POL*-O-GY...
CREEPER, YOU MAY HAVE BEEN RIGHT, BUT IF YOU THINK YOU'RE GOING TO GET AN APOLOGY OUT OF *ME...EVER...*
...YOU'RE *CRAZY.*
THE END!